Ted Harrison has been interested in the Elvis phenomenon for over twenty years. His 1992 book *Elvis People: the Cult of The King* is acknowledged as the first serious study to suggest that the devotion of some fans to Elvis has religious overtones. It is now on the booklist for many university students studying modern religious movements. Subsequently, he produced a television documentary for BBC Everyman, narrated by John Peel, entitled *Elvis and the Presleytarians* that looked at how the worship of The King was taking on a new dimension, with Elvis being seen as a Messianic figure.

This is Ted's 20th book but his first work of fiction and he takes the world of Elvis-fans into the realm of the absurdly possible. The story is entirely make-believe. The main characters and their names are the author's invention and not based on any living persons. However many of the events are set in real places and some well-known people are mentioned.

Ted Harrison was born in Kent, UK in 1948. He is a writer and artist, a former BBC Correspondent and reporter. He has a PhD in Theology. He divides his time between his two homes, one in Kent, England and the other on the island of Unst, Shetland.

KING CLONE

by

TED HARRISON

Published by

Balta Books
1 Kelda
Baltasound
Unst
Shetland ZE2 9DS

First published in Great Britain in 2010

Copyright © Ted Harrison 2010

The right of Ted Harrison to be identified as the Author of the
Work has been asserted by him in accordance with the
Copyright, Designs and Patents Act 1988

Printed and bound by
CPI Antony Rowe
48-50 Birch Close
Eastbourne
East Sussex BN23 6PE

ISBN 978-0-9566077-0-6

All rights reserved. No part of this publication may be reproduced, stored in a retrieval system, or transmitted, in any form or by any means, electronic, mechanical, photocopying, recording or otherwise without the prior permission of the author.

CHAPTER ONE

Aaron became aware of the distant sound of a brass-fanfare, the familiar, dramatic, unmistakable sound of the tone-poem *Also Sprach Zarathustra*, although Aaron recognised the music not as the work of Richard Strauss but as the opening notes of the theme-tune to the film *2001 - A Space Odyssey*.

It was dark and the only light available was that filtering through the bedroom curtains. As he listened to the urgent thud-thud of the timpani which followed the fanfare, Aaron became increasingly aware of the light - a strange, blue light, not that of a full moon or a street lamp but something ethereal and alien.

He swung his legs out of bed, stood up and pulled back the curtains to look outside. A curious, blue star was shining in the sky, larger and brighter than Venus, like a sparkling sapphire in the night sky. The music became louder. The timpani and brass were joined by a celestial orchestra and a heavenly pipe-organ. The light grew in size. It seemed to be coming nearer and nearer.

By the time the music had reached its climax and resolution the sapphire star had grown massively and was hovering over Aaron's garden at *Tupelo*, Number 28 Mulberry Avenue on The Woodland estate of new, executive homes where he and his wife, Priscilla, lived.

As his eyes became accustomed to the glare, Aaron noticed that the star was not a star at all but a bright, luminescent blue-and-silver flying-craft. 'This is a close encounter of the third kind', Aaron told himself quietly, surprised at his own cool head in the presence of an alien invasion. 'We are being visited. I must stay calm.'

Aaron watched metallic poles extend from beneath the amazing machine as it came gently to rest on the lawn. Then a ladder was unfolded from the side and a door began to slide open. A great golden light shone from inside and a figure stood in silhouette against the light.

'Oh My God!' Aaron shrieked, recognising the man instantly and utterly losing his composure. 'It is... I can't believe it... it's The... '

He felt his shoulders shake and then his whole body convulse before the light enveloped everything - his body and soul.

'Wake up', came a familiar voice. It was Priscilla shaking him with one hand and pulling back the curtains with the other to let a stream of daylight into the room. 'It's seven o'clock and time you were stirring yourself. Some of us have been up for over half-an-hour.'

Aaron jolted to his senses, acutely disappointed that his ecstatic moment had been so rudely interrupted. 'I was having the most amazing dream and you've ruined it', he said accusingly.

'Oh yes, what was it this time? Elvis gave you a new Cadillac? You were voted Elvis tribute-artist of the year?'

'No, Elvis was here, on the lawn', said Aaron, pushing back the bed-quilt. 'He was in a flying-saucer, just coming down the steps... when you woke me.'

'Sorry to have intruded but welcome to the real world. It's tomorrow we fly to Graceland. Today, it's work as usual.'

Aaron staggered to his feet, put on his dressing-gown, a gold one, embroidered on the back with the Elvis logo of the lightening-bolt in silver and the letters TCB stitched below in scarlet. He went to the bathroom to take care of the usual morning's business of washing and shaving. He was a man of average looks, height and weight who was moving seamlessly from youth towards early middle-age. He passed the table on the landing with its two framed pictures, Jesus to the left and Elvis to the right. This was where Priscilla lit a votive candle every evening before going to bed and where she said her prayers and read The Bible and her Elvis books.

By now Priscilla was downstairs. The first thing she did every morning was put a selection of Elvis tracks on the player. Soon the gentle sound of Elvis singing *I can't help falling in love with you* seeped through the house.

Aaron had wired the player to speakers in every room so that when he and Priscilla moved around the house, Elvis went with them.

Aaron looked at himself in the bathroom mirror. He checked his hair and sideburns. Yes, black to the roots. As he shaved he hummed-along-with-Elvis. By the time he was in the shower *The American Trilogy* was playing, so he unhooked the showerhead to hold as a microphone for the *Glory Glory Alleluia*, throwing it from hand-to-hand before sinking to his knees in an Elvis pose.

Breakfast was coffee, toast, peanut-butter and lists.

'Passports, dollars, cash and travellers' cheques, empty the fridge, sun cream, disposable knickers...'

Priscilla talked and scribbled away. She was using one of the pencils she had taken from The Vernon and Gladys Burger Bar on their last visit to Memphis and writing on the memo pad she had had in her last Christmas stocking. There was a faint, sepia impression of Elvis on every page. Aaron was still half in his dream-world, mixing the early-morning visit from The King with plans for their trip to Memphis.

'Do you think we'll be able to walk up to the Meditation Garden early in the morning, like we did last year?' he wondered aloud.

'I would think so... Yes... If you wake up in time... Dressing-gown, slippers, spare toothpaste. Will we need spare toothpaste do you think, or can we buy it there?'

'We can buy it I expect and anyway we won't run out in two- or three-weeks. I wonder who we'll meet? Sam and Dorothy were fun - and the two Californians.'

'May do but lots of people come for the anniversary, we'll probably not spot them in the crowd... Socks... Do you want your "We're a Present from Tupelo" socks and your "Worship The King" T-shirts?'

By quarter-past eight, Aaron and Priscilla were in the car and setting off through the morning traffic to their respective places of work. On his way to the animal-research institute where he had a job as a laboratory-technician, Aaron dropped Priscilla at the district hospital where she worked as a medical-secretary. They were both content enough in what they did for a living. They were paid sufficiently well for them to be comfortable, with enough money in reserve to indulge their shared passion for Elvis Presley. One day they would have a family they hoped but they were both young enough to wait a few more years and in the meantime they lived for The King.

Neither could remember when Elvis had not been at the centre of their lives. At school, while his friends thumped their heads to the sound of the latest, ear-splitting, unmelodic craze, Aaron listened to *Jailhouse Rock* and the music of the early Elvis, the subversive rock'n'roll with which he made his name before he joined the army. Priscilla's classmates couldn't understand why, instead of declaring her undying love for the latest boy-band, she pined for a has-been hero from her parents' generation. Yet pine she did and from the very earliest age, pictures of Elvis covered her bedroom wall.

Priscilla's real name was Kellie but she was nicknamed Priscilla at school, because of her devotion to Elvis and the name stuck. 'It's 'cos you behave as if you are married to him', her best friend had once said. Priscilla had brown hair, a pleasant but not distinctive round face and a neat frame which was always well-dressed in the latest, mass-produced, High Street, chain-store fashions.

Aaron changed his name from Keith when he and Priscilla became engaged. He took Elvis's middle name as he considered that to call himself Elvis would have been too presumptuous. It was a Vegas wedding of course, held in a pink wedding-chapel complete with an Elvis-lookalike minister. They exchanged rings and teddy bears and the wedding-breakfast had a Hawaiian theme. The honeymoon was spent in Memphis where they stayed at The Heartbreak Hotel and went on the tour of the Graceland grounds and mansion every day.

They had met through *The Sincerely Elvis Dating Agency*. Priscilla had taken the initiative. 'Lonesome tonight would like to meet handsome Hound Dog to get all shook up.' Aaron responded with a letter signed 'Elvisly yours' and their first date was at the monthly meeting of the local *We Love Elvis Fan Club*. Within three weeks they were an item.

The last day at work before the summer holiday went slowly for Aaron. Half of the lab staff were away staying in French gîtes or cycling through the Scottish Highlands and work was slack, just stocktaking and clearing. At the hospital too it was the same holiday-period but with a very different outcome. When half the hospital support-staff was away, most sunning themselves on Mediterranean beaches, Priscilla had to work twice as hard. Time rushed by.

That evening, after a supper of southern fried-chicken cooked to the Colonel Parker recipe, Priscilla spent some time in front of her Elvis-shrine listening to the sweet sound of *Amazing Grace*.

'We're coming to see you tomorrow', she whispered. 'Please, Jesus and Elvis, keep us safe on the journey.' She lit a light-blue candle and smiled to herself as she remembered Aaron waking-up that morning.

'Sweet dreams', she said to her husband as she snuggled next to him in bed.

It was on the 'plane to Memphis that Aaron had the first inkling of an absurd idea. He had been explaining to Priscilla the new project to which he had been assigned at the lab. 'Real groundbreaking stuff', he said. 'Cloning.'

He went on to explain how Dolly, the celebrated, cloned sheep, had only been the start of a new, scientific era. His boss was now telling him that soon, farmers would be able to order bespoke sheep, cattle and pig embryos from a catalogue, thanks to the work his team would be doing at the laboratory.

'You know how farmers can order semen for artificial insemination from a champion bull', Aaron said. 'If the boss's work goes well, it'll be complete cloned-embryos which will be on the market. And they'll be available for pet owners too. If you want your mongrel to give birth to a Crufts' champion - no bother at all! And all the racehorse owners will be able to order a clone of Red Rum. And maybe if they ever find Shergar... ' He paused thinking perhaps the red wine was making him silly.

Sitting together on a 'plane, after a couple of mini-bottles of airline, red wine, was one of the few times Aaron ever talked about his work. Normally, when he returned home Priscilla's question of 'How was the lab today?' was answered with a casual 'OK', and no further detail offered. Sometimes, after a few drinks with friends he would open-up but usually only to boast how important his job was. 'Cutting edge', he would say, without letting-on that his responsibilities mostly consisted of setting-up apparatus, washing test-tubes and ordering new supplies of rubber-gloves.

The conversation on the 'plane came in fits and starts. When they were trying to get the headsets to work, or they were absorbed in watching a film, little was said. When meals or drinks were served however, conversation started again. Workplace gossip was mixed with potted-science and sometimes the topic changed completely back to their holiday plans.

At one point, somewhere over the mid-Atlantic, Aaron glanced at one of the fan magazines he had brought with him. It was the latest issue of *Elvis Times*. '"Holy relics and souvenirs.

The King comes to London'", he read aloud. 'We could go to that when we get back.'

'Go to what?' asked Priscilla.

'The Elvis Exhibition, it's on from 11th to 30th September. There's a two-page article about it here. They claim it's the biggest travelling-exhibition devoted to Elvis ever. Original Vegas jumpsuits, his first guitar, his GI cap, his wedding tuxedo - even a wart he had surgically removed. Now that's interesting.'

'What's so special about a wart?'

'The DNA of course. Just a smidge of DNA is all they need in the lab to clone a sheep. Think what you could do with a sample snip taken from the wart - clone a new version of Elvis himself.'

'Like Jurassic Park?'

'Well, a bit, though you wouldn't have herds of dangerous Elvises let loose. Just the one.'

'Don't be daft', said Priscilla as she unbuckled her seatbelt. 'I'm going to stretch my legs and go to the loo.'

The 'plane landed on time and the transfer to the internal flight went smoothly. Even the line at immigration-control moved swiftly and efficiently.

'Purpose of visit', they were asked.

'Vacation', said Priscilla.

'We're going to Graceland', said Aaron and still under the influence of the red wine, started doing a Paul Simon impression.

'Aaron', Priscilla whispered sharply, 'behave yourself'.

The immigration-officer's features showed neither sign of amusement or disapproval. 'Have a nice day', she said and waved them through.

Memphis in August is hot. Very hot. It is also very, very crowded. Mid-August is when every Elvis-fan from around the world hopes to be at Graceland. Catholics go to Rome, Muslims to Mecca and followers of Elvis are drawn by an irresistible force to Elvis's home-city each August 16th to mark the anniversary of his death.

Priscilla could still remember the day she heard Elvis had died. Remaining forever fresh in her mind were painful memories of tears, immeasurable grief and the humiliation of being taunted by the bullies. For a while, she was called 'The Widow' by her friends. The first day after she heard the news she could not even go out of the house. She stayed in her room weeping inconsolably. Nothing her mother said brought her comfort. Priscilla was enveloped by wave-after-wave of desolation. The only times she ventured out of her room were to look at the television-news. The images of the weeping fans and the piles of flowers outside the gates of Graceland became etched in her memory.

Aaron had suffered in silence. He had bitten his lip to stop himself crying and ignored the playground taunts on the first day back at school after the holidays. Once, when he had asked for permission to go to the lavatory, the class erupted in mirth. 'Don't let him go Sir, he might die on the bog like Elvis.'

Time heals but in Memphis, in mid-August every year, Elvis-fans still shed tears.

The first morning after their arrival Aaron and Priscilla were awake early. Truth to tell, neither had slept much, both for the excitement of being near Graceland again and the fact that their body-clocks were still half on British time. They got up as dawn was breaking and dressed in silence as if preparing themselves, each in their own separate way, for a special spiritual moment.

On leaving their hotel they were pleased to find that the early-morning weather was tolerably cool. They were staying just over the road from Graceland and as the traffic was light, quickly got across the main road. They walked by the long, stone wall that separates the busy highway from the paddock in front of the mansion and joined a small gathering of other fans at the gates. After a few minutes the silence was broken by the gatekeeper emerging from his office. 'OK folks you can go on up. And stick to the paths.'

The small group made its way up the drive like a line of monks processing to early-morning prayer. Some carried flowers. One carried a home-made card showing Elvis dressed in angelic white-and-gold. No-one spoke. Priscilla slipped her arm in Aaron's and allowed a tear to roll down her cheek.

In a few minutes they reached the Meditation Garden where Elvis's grave is to be found alongside memorials to other members of his family. One fan knelt in front of the grave and placed her flowers on it. Another reached across with her card. Priscilla and Elvis simply stood with their heads bowed. One, five, ten minutes passed. More Elvis-fans arrived. Some were talking to each other in hushed, reverential tones. Some mouthed words of prayer. One party of five came with a wreath inscribed, 'Ohio loves Elvis'.

As the sun rose higher in the sky, Aaron began to look around at the familiar scene. There, to one side, was a statue of Jesus standing with his arms outstretched in front of a cross. On the bar of the cross were the letters IHS, a traditional abbreviation for the Latin phrase 'Iesus Hominum Salvator' - Jesus, Saviour of Men. Beneath Jesus' feet was carved lettering which needed no explanation - PRESLEY.

In the middle-distance was a fountain and beyond that the Graceland mansion. Aaron looked at Elvis's grave and noted, as he always did, the spelling of Elvis's middle name Aron. 'There's nowhere else his name is written with just one letter A', a fan had once told him. 'It's a deliberate mistake - a kinda code - to let his true fans know that it's not really him buried there. He only pretended to die. He's still alive and is going to come back one day.' Aaron had nodded and said nothing. 'If only', he had thought. 'Oh no', Priscilla had said. 'It can't be true. Elvis wouldn't lie to us.'

In time, the group at the grave began to disperse. Aaron and Priscilla walked slowly down the drive.

'Thank you', they said to the gatekeeper in passing. 'My pleasure', he had replied.

They crossed the road and turned right, walking past the courtyard of souvenir-shops to the diner where they always took breakfast when staying in Memphis. Eggs (over-easy), biscuits and beans and plenty of refill coffee.

That day Aaron and Priscilla visited Elvis's grave three times. The first time had been the early-morning 'walk-up', the privileged access given to Elvis-fans 'in-the-know' before Graceland opened for the day.

The second time was when they joined an official tour-party to see the inside of Elvis' house. It was a trip they had made on many occasions before. Each time, as they walked into the house, the same feelings overwhelmed them. This was the real place where Elvis had lived and where his spirit still lingered.

They followed the tour-route through the downstairs rooms. Never upstairs, that was forbidden territory. Upstairs was considered the Holy of Holies.

In Graceland, time has stood still, as if the house is waiting for Elvis's return. As the years have passed, the gadgets that Elvis had used, at the time the latest in technology, have begun to look dated and quaint. A cynic once said of The Jungle Room, 'It cost him a fortune but it ain't worth a dime'. But to an Elvis-fan, this faded, dated, rather-tacky room which Elvis had designed in the very latest Afro-chic, long-before mock bush-animal skins became passé, is hallowed ground. As always, Aaron and Priscilla saw the rifle-range and the paddocks where Elvis had kept his horses. All tours of the mansion end at the Meditation Garden and it was there that Aaron and Priscilla paused again to think about The King.

Their third visit to the graveside was that evening, after dark. It had been during the night on the fifteenth/sixteenth of August 1977 that Elvis had died, alone in his bathroom upstairs at Graceland. Now, some two decades later, thousands of fans converged on Graceland to mark the anniversary, to honour and remember Elvis and to walk, carrying candles and torches of naked flames, through the grounds and Meditation Garden.

It was a ritual which had begun in a smaller way shortly after Elvis had died, after his body had been translated from its first grave in a public cemetery to its permanent resting-place in the grounds of his home. Initially, the gathered fans had been numbered in hundreds. Year-on-year, the numbers grew. That evening, there were tens-of-thousands in the road outside Graceland. Priscilla and Aaron held tight to each other as they waited for the line to start moving through the gates. They shuffled forwards inch-by-inch in the dark. Elvis's music was playing but they couldn't see from where. The atmosphere was part-wake and part-carnival. Friends greeted each other with hugs and kisses. New friendships were made as strangers fell into conversation with each other.

Priscilla found herself talking to a woman who said she came every year as she now lived in Memphis. 'I used to live in Italy', she said. 'I was a teacher and never thought of Elvis. Then suddenly, the day he died, Elvis took over my life. I couldn't get him out of my mind. "I'm going to live in Memphis"', I told my family. "Are you crazy?", said my mother. We haven't spoken since. I bought a ticket and came.

'On my first day in Memphis I just walked around. I passed a funeral-home and knew instinctively that this was where Elvis had been taken. I went in to look. Then I saw the Baptist Memorial Hospital he had been taken to as well. It was as if I was being guided.

'I pray everyday to God through Elvis. He is like a bridge between us and God. I go to Graceland every day and put fresh flowers on his grave.

'I work as a waitress and have a small apartment. Elvis is everything.'

Another woman told Priscilla how Elvis spoke to her. 'He gives me messages', she explained. 'I hear his voice as plainly as I hear you.'

As they waited to go through the gate there was plenty of time for fans to share their personal Elvis stories.

'It's not that we have joined some sort of cult', said one woman rather defensively. 'I read somewhere that serious Elvis-fans behave as if they've started their own religion.'

'It was a university professor's idea wasn't it?' said another fan. 'He talked of the Elvis tribute-singers being like priests.'

'There's a women who says Elvis was some kind of superior mystical being from another planet.'

'How silly.'

'But it's not as if he wasn't interested in religion.'

'He once had a vision of God in the desert.'

'Larry Geller used to give him religious books to read.'

'Larry who?'

'Geller. His hairdresser and spiritual adviser.'

'He was a good Christian boy. Elvis I mean, Larry Geller was Jewish, I think.'

'I have a picture of Jesus and Elvis together', said Priscilla, joining in with the free-flowing conversation. 'They are on a table upstairs at home. Perhaps I shouldn't but I pray to them both.'

'You're so right. Alleluia!' said a gentleman who had been standing next to Aaron on the edge of the congregation. He spoke with a slow, southern accent. 'I think Elvis may really have been The Messiah. I have a book describing how The New Testament is not about Jesus at all - it's foretelling Elvis.' He thrust the book into Aaron's hand.

'Read that when you have the chance.'

Priscilla wasn't quite sure what to make of this unexpected, theological insight but before she could ask any questions their group had reached the gates. They held out their candles to be lit from a burning torch and silence fell over the party.

For the next two hours it seemed to Priscilla that nothing in the world mattered but her intense devotion to Elvis. It was a sacred evening. She felt as if she was enclosed in Elvis's arms, as if they were strolling together under the stars. She held Aaron's hand but her mind was on Elvis.

It was two o'clock in the morning before Aaron and Priscilla were back at the hotel and getting ready for bed. Priscilla's eyes were red from weeping. 'It was so lovely', she said.

The next day was as hot as ever. After a late breakfast, Aaron and Priscilla went for a walk along Elvis Presley Boulevard, walking away from downtown-Memphis. They passed various fast-food outlets, some quiet, suburban streets leading-off the highway, a dentist, a Methodist church, a small shopping-mall. It was their regular, morning walk when visiting Graceland.

'Look', said Aaron, as they approached one particular, empty lot. 'They've started building something new.'

He went to look at a sign set up by the sidewalk. '"Coming soon"', he read aloud, '"The Church of The Latter-Day Elvis." Who on earth are they?'

'We're a new denomination,' came a voice as if from nowhere. Aaron turned round and recognised the man who had spoken briefly with them the night before. He was in his late-thirties, older than Aaron. He was a bit shorter than Aaron's five-foot ten-inches and his brown hair was receding and swept back. 'You're English aren't you?' the man asked. 'I saw you in-line last night. Wasn't it a beautiful night?'

'Lovely', responded Priscilla.

'So are you from this new church?' enquired Aaron.

'Sure am. Allow me to introduce myself. Tim Barker, Major Tim Barker. I'm the assistant to the Reverend Doctor, our prophet and founder. He wrote that book I was talking about.'

'So what are you going to do on this plot?' asked Aaron.

'We're building a cathedral, the first cathedral to be built to honour The King. Are you coming back next year?'

'We hope so.'

'Then you'll see it finished. It'll be a magnificent structure built to the glory of Elvis and all his saints. It's going to be huge. Shaped like a guitar with Tennessee's biggest tapestry at one end - showing the risen Elvis. Glass and gold, nothing spared. It will be ready for Elvis himself. He's coming again you know. He will return. The Messiah will come and very soon. In my life-time I'm sure of that.'

Aaron nodded but said nothing.

'Have a nice day', said Major Barker and turned his attention to another pair of sightseers.

One week in Memphis is always too short a time. Very soon Aaron and Priscilla were packing and preparing, reluctantly, to go home. On their last morning they went again at dawn to stand by Elvis's grave. Priscilla wept of course and Aaron put his arm around her.

'We'll be back next year, won't we?' she asked.

'Of course', replied Aaron.

'I wonder if Elvis will return, like that man at the Elvis Church said?'

'Don't be silly', said Aaron. 'He really is dead and he really is buried. That's his grave.' Then, thinking he might have sounded a bit insensitive, he added, 'But we have his music and his movies and his pictures, so he sort of lives on'.

Waiting for their flight home, Aaron found the book Major Barker had given him a few days earlier during the anniversary vigil. He glanced at the cover. It showed a picture of Elvis with his arms outstretched displaying the stigmata, the wounds of The Crucifixion on his hands and those of The Crown of Thorns on his head. He flipped through the pages and glanced at some of the chapter headings. 'Elvis and the Doctrine of Incarnation'; 'Redeemed by Elvis'; 'The Return of the Risen King'; 'Put your Trust in Elvis'; 'Elvis - the Just One'; 'Eschatology and Elvis';

'The Charisma of Elvis'; 'Elvis and the Elect'; 'Elvis and the Rapture'.

He thought he might try to read the chapter entitled 'Elvis - The Paraclete' but he could only think of budgerigars while the book seemed to be droning on about The Holy Spirit. 'Can't understand a word of it', he said to Priscilla, and when they were called to board the 'plane he deliberately left the book on a seat.

But Priscilla picked it up and smuggled it into her hand-luggage.

CHAPTER TWO

Six months earlier Tim Barker had been a desperate man. After a successful career in the US army, away from the protection and order of the military, his life had gone to pieces. Twice divorced, twice bankrupt and with escalating gambling debts which he had no idea how he was going to control or clear.

Two o'clock one February morning, he had just finished a poker-session which had added a further five-thousand dollars to his problems. He was in the backroom of a bar in downtown-Memphis. As he got up from the table with a vague promise that he would settle as soon as he could, his way out of the room was barred by two, very large men wearing shades and heavy, gold jewellery.

'Mr Carioli wants to see you', they said.

'Mr Carioli?' Barker knew of Mr Carioli by reputation. He was the entrepreneur behind almost every illegal business in the district and owner of the gambling-club where he had just lost again heavily. Mr Carioli was also well-known for his unorthodox methods of debt-collection.

'Shall I arrange to see him tomorrow?' Barker asked, hoping to buy enough time to leg-it out of town.

'He's upstairs now', came the uncompromising reply.

Barker had no option but to allow himself to be escorted by the two men to an office on the second floor.

'Mr Carioli, you have a visitor', they said as they opened the door.

Barker was pushed into the room and left to stand while Mr Carioli, seated behind his desk, looked at him. Barker might have thought he was on the set of a B-movie but for a surge of panic in his guts which told him it was all very real.

'I hear you owe me some money', Mr Carioli said softly, with a hint of an Italian accent.

'Er, yes', Barker stuttered, trying in vain to get a close look at the man speaking to him but he was dazzled by a powerful light coming from behind the man's head.

'A lot of money', said Mr Carioli, leaning forward and looking at a computer screen.

'Er, yes, a lot of money.' Barker shuffled nervously and chewed at his lower lip.

'Can you pay me?'

'No, not just now but I will. Soon. I promise.'

'It's not wise to make promises you can't deliver. The fact is, you don't have a dime', said Mr Carioli. He tapped at his computer keyboard for half a minute or so and looked at the green figures appearing on the screen. He scribbled notes on a pad and tapped some figures into a calculator before looking-up again.

'As well as owing me, you owe eight money-lending companies, plus money for your car. There's rent on your apartment, alimony for two wives, two bank-overdrafts and seven debt-orders - and that's just in Tennessee.'

'How do you know all that?' exclaimed Barker, shocked both by the scale of his predicament when presented with it so starkly and angered by the fact that Mr Carioli had all the details, literally at his fingertips.

'I have contacts', said Mr Carioli. 'People who tell me things.'

The room fell silent. Barker was cornered. He felt his bowels loosen and prayed that he wouldn't utterly disgrace himself. His digital watch sounded the hour. For a full minute, it seemed to Barker an eternity, Mr Carioli said nothing but toyed with a pen.

Then, 'I have a suggestion', he said eventually, finally breaking the silence. 'I've been checking you out and I know you've been in the army and in the business world. You've got talents. In fact, from everything I've heard, if you didn't gamble you'd be a millionaire several times over. So, would you like to do a job for me?'

Barker felt like a drowning man being thrown a lifebelt. 'Well yes - but doing what?'

'Take a seat', said Mr Carioli, and instantly a chair was placed behind him.

One of the two heavies guarding the door put his hands on Barker's shoulders and pushed him into a sitting position.

'Tell me', Mr Carioli said, leaning forward and with a friendlier tone to his voice. 'What's the best way to make money? Huh?'

All Barker could think of was a line his father often used when he was alive. 'Find an oil-well or start a religion', he blurted out.

'Can you find me an oil-well?' Mr Carioli snapped back, changing his tone. 'You own some options in the Middle-East do you? Not that I've heard of them but if you did, with your credit-rating I doubt you could hire yourself a screwdriver let alone a drilling-team.'

'Well, no', Barker replied, beginning to regret that his flippant remark had slipped out. 'I don't think I could lay my hands on an oil-well just now.'

'Then start me a religion', said Carioli, his voice relaxing. 'Me and some friends have some money we need to... er... legitimise. Over the next year or two we will have fifty-million dollars to... er... invest. We need a plan to keep it out of sight and get 10% back legit every year. I want you back here at noon tomorrow with a business-plan.'

Mr Carioli gestured to his security-guards. 'Take my friend Mr Barker home and see he's back here on time.'

Six hours later, after a sleepless night, Barker decided to get a coffee and buy some breakfast with his last twenty-dollar note. It was all the money he had to his name since every one of his credit-cards had now been refused.

Once out on the street, having left the apartment block, he realised he had company. One of the muscular assistants on Mr

Carioli's pay-roll who had escorted him home earlier was following him at a discreet distance.

Barker walked briskly in the cold, winter air to a breakfast-bar he knew. He sat at a plastic-covered table looking out onto the street and ordered coffee and an egg muffin.

What a fool he had been to talk about starting a religion. He had been raised by a devout, Episcopalian mother and had been a choirboy when young but he had not been inside a place of worship for fifteen years, except for funerals. And the next time he feared, might be his own farewell to the world.

He knew how to sell cars and negotiate real-estate. It was just a pity his last two ventures had gotten unlucky as he explained to his creditors. But how do you begin to start a religion?

He was so deep in his own panicky thoughts that he hardly noticed a man joining him at the table. He was not one of Mr Carioli's employees. His minder was sitting at a table on the other side of the bar, ordering waffles and maple syrup on expenses.

'Is anyone sitting here?' the stranger asked.

'No', replied Barker.

'I didn't feel safe sitting near the big fella the other side of the bar. Looks like he might, well, might not like anyone too close.'

The two men sat opposite each other in silence. Barker glanced at his companion briefly, just long enough to guess that he had probably been living rough the night before. His clothes were shabby. He had long hair and an unkempt, white beard. He looked about sixty-years-old. Barker also noticed that he was reading a well-thumbed Bible.

Suddenly the man looked up and caught Barker looking at him. He stared him in the eye.

'It's all here', the man said jabbing his finger at The Bible pages. 'It's all here.'

'Oh, what is?' Barker said hesitantly and noncommittally, diverting his gaze and not wishing to have his precious thinking time commandeered by a Bible-basher.

'Elvis', came the reply. 'The return of Elvis.'

Having allowed the social-ice to be broken, there was nothing Barker could do but listen. In fact, there was no way he could have stopped the white-haired man from recounting his life-story. But he told it well and was surprisingly frank and articulate. He was, as Barker suspected, homeless but he had, he said, once been a priest and a university professor. He had taught theology and, as a young man, had made a name for himself in academic circles as a specialist in Gnosticism. This was an early and supposedly-heretical form of Christianity he explained patiently.

'You'll have heard of the four Gospels - but in fact many more were written which were ruthlessly suppressed. Thomas, James, Mary, Peter, Philip, the Gospel of Truth... lots of others who painted a very different picture of who Jesus was.

'Have you heard of the Messengers of the Light?' the man asked, looking Barker in the eye once more. 'They are sent by God to lift all mankind out of our shared ignorance. There was Adam's third son Seth, the prophet Mani and of course Jesus. But the most important to our generation was Elvis. We can all be saved from our ignorance by listening to the messengers and learning the mysteries of the cosmos.

'For us today, Elvis is The Logos, the word made flesh who came to dwell among us.'

There was a ring of excitement in the man's voice, more of a man-with-a-mission than a no-hope hobo.

The man described how he had lost his university job. 'I could still be there now drawing a regular salary - but I started to ask questions. They said I was having a breakdown but I wasn't. There was a voice telling me that everything I was teaching the students, everything I was supposed to believe in, was mistaken. Could I be a hypocrite and carry on pretending - teaching and saying mass - when I no longer believed? What was I to do?

'They offered therapy to sort me out. They sent me on a vacation and I took a trip out to Sedona. Then, one day as I was walking in the desert, something amazing happened. I heard the voice of God. Only it wasn't exactly God as I would have expected to hear him. It was the voice of Elvis who told me to take courage. "Preach the truth", he said.

'I just stood still on the spot. Rooted. Terrified. "But what is the truth?" I asked the voice, echoing the words of Pontius Pilate to Jesus. "I will teach you", came the reply.

'So I resigned my position. Quit my well-paid and secure job at the university. I had nowhere else to go - but I was free. Free at last. I lost all my income and my apartment and my academic reputation - but I gave it all up willingly to walk the path of righteousness.'

Slowly, Barker became interested in what the stranger was saying. It was nonsense, it was rubbish but it was plausible nonsense and rubbish. Plausible enough, he thought, for some people to want to believe in it. It slowly occurred to him that possibly these odd ideas could be packaged into a religion, one which might attract thousands of paying followers.

'Hell', thought Barker. 'Memphis makes millions out of Elvis-mania and it's only just touching the potential market.' He had often driven past Graceland and seen a growing and thriving enterprise. He had even thought to himself on occasions that some of the Elvis-fans he had met had the zeal of Christian evangelicals.

The more he thought about it and listened, Barker realised that the Elvis-industry had serious, undeveloped market-potential. There was much more to the business than just an aging fan-base spending their pension money. There were young Elvis-fans too and increasingly there were rich Elvis-fans as well. Barker knew the commercial brand was all tied up by the Presley Estate. They had sharp lawyers stopping any other business or individual exploiting the image and memory of Elvis but an Elvis religion would be different, wouldn't it? Register a religion and it gets a special tax and legal status.

Barker began to listen carefully and ask questions. What he thought he understood from his table companion was that Elvis and Jesus were one and the same. Both had been born into humble circumstances and been acclaimed as Kings.

'But their kingdoms are not of this world', said the man. 'They are kings in the spiritual dimension and only very rarely does this world touch on the heavenly plane. And that's when the great, spiritual figures of history walk the earth - Buddha, Moses, Jesus, Mohammed and Elvis. But Elvis's work was cut short by his enemies. So he is due to return to finish his work. It could be any time now. It will be in my life-time of that I am certain. He has told me so in the messages I receive from him in visions. All he asks is that a home be prepared for him. He can't come back to Graceland - that contains too many sad memories. He wants a temple or a cathedral built in his honour so that he can return in triumph to save the world.'

After an hour and several cups of coffee, Barker eventually said, 'I've got to go'. He needed to get back to his apartment and start sketching-out some details of his business-plan. He could not afford to be late for his appointment with Mr Carioli. 'But I like what I hear', he said, quickly adding, 'Never thought of The Bible and religion like that before. Can we talk some more perhaps? Where can I find you again?'

'I'm always here or hereabouts.'

'Breakfast tomorrow, same time?'

'That's a deal.'

They shook hands.

'I too am looking for answers', continued Barker, 'ones which could literally save my life. I think I could believe in Elvis'. He got up to leave. 'I don't even know your name? I'm Tim Barker.'

'I'm Garon. Dr Garon Love.'

'See ya Garon.'

Tim Barker spent two frantic hours back at his apartment making 'phone calls and calculations before heading off to see

Mr Carioli. He wanted to discover just how many fans visited Memphis every year, how much they spent and on what? From those figures he could calculate the potential for expansion and what market-share of that expansion a new religion might expect to take. He telephoned all the possible sources of information he could think of, such as hotels, souvenir-shops, tourist-offices and libraries, sometimes posing as a journalist writing a feature, sometimes as a salesman looking for new markets for a product. He was good at this sort of research and enjoyed the excitement of discovering new facts and assembling them into a business-plan.

He noted there were over five-hundred, Elvis fan-clubs in the USA and that, according to one survey, over 80% of Americans said that their lives had been touched by Elvis Presley in some way. Seventy-percent of Americans had watched a Presley movie, Barker was told by one source; over 40% had danced to one of his records; in-excess of 30% had bought an Elvis record, CD or video; 10% had visited Graceland; 9% had bought Elvis memorabilia; and 9% had read a book about him.

One librarian said there were several books published hinting that Elvis-worship was turning into a religion of its own accord. 'Try looking at Harrison's book, *Elvis People - The Cult of The King*', she said. 'It spells it all out. Visits to Graceland are likened to medieval pilgrimages. Buying souvenirs is compared to collecting the relics of saints. And writing messages to Elvis can be seen as a form of prayer.'

It was all very promising thought Barker and as yet, apart from one or two jokers, he could find no evidence of an Elvis Church which directed all this devotion into a formal religious movement.

As he finished the first draft of the business-plan, he also made a few preliminary checks about what he thought he knew about the tax status of charities and religions, resulting in some initial calculations of potential income. According to one newspaper article read to him over the 'phone by an obliging researcher, it was estimated that on average, every signed-up member of a Christian congregation who tithed 10% of their annual income, raised over $3000 a year for their church.

As noon approached, he began to feel that the sums were stacking up in his favour. He left his desk strewn with papers, jottings and calculations to walk to Mr Carioli's office clutching a single sheet of paper on which he had typed-out the essential points of the plan. He was not surprised to note that he was followed all the way. At 12 o'clock precisely he arrived at the downtown bar but instead of heading for a poker-game, he asked to be shown to the second-floor office which he had entered so reluctantly not long before.

Again, he could only see Mr Carioli against the background of a bright light, this time that of the noonday-sun.

'Have you got me a proposal', Barker was asked.

'Yes', he said and held-up his plan for Mr Carioli to see.

'I don't want no blasphemy', said Mr Carioli. 'My mother's very religious.'

'We're going to build a cathedral to Elvis - here in Memphis', Barker began, hoping sincerely that Mrs Carioli senior was a devout Catholic and not an Elvis-fan. 'It will be the centre of a new Elvis-religion.'

Mr Carioli gestured with his hand just enough to show interest and invite more.

Barker outlined his ideas, marshalling his research data into a convincing presentation. 'I have found someone ready-made to be the guru and prophet. I reckon that by getting just 1% of Elvis-fans to join, and persuading them to pay tithes as congregation members do at lots of other churches, we would have an income of over five-million dollars a year. That's 10% on your investment.'

'Build a cathedral eh?' Mr Carioli thought for a moment. 'Make it good. And... er... I want to approve all the contractors you employ, to make sure we are giving jobs to my friends, if you get my meaning? I know lots of good builders.'

Mr Carioli put his hand in his desk-drawer and took out a wad of one-hundred dollar-bills. 'I want to see you here on the first Monday of every month at twelve-noon exactly. You will tell me what you've done and I will give you the next instalment of cash. I want this religion up-and-running and earning by August next year. And don't talk to nobody about our arrangement.' He paused before adding, 'and if I hear of you playing poker, the deal's off and I'll be asking the boys to collect the money you owe me'.

He dismissed Barker with a gesture of the hand. Barker walked downstairs, amazed at his good fortune and terrified of the challenge ahead of him.

As he walked down the street he caught a snatch of Elvis singing.

The steps that lead to any church form a stairway to a star.
They're part of God and should be trod more often than they are.
I believe in the man in the sky, I believe with his help I'll get by...

The music was coming from a tourist souvenir-shop and he noticed a poster of The King in the window. 'Thanks Elvis', Barker said as he passed by. 'I'll do you proud.'

CHAPTER THREE

It was the first Monday back at work after their Graceland holiday and Priscilla was dropped off at the hospital by Aaron. She made her way to the renal-unit where she worked. She was sorry the trip was over but pleased to be back in a familiar routine. And to bridge the two worlds of Graceland and the National Health Service, she had round her neck both her hospital identity-badge on a chain and her new, Elvis necklace.

She greeted her colleagues with a cheery 'hi' and then went to look in her pigeon-hole for any messages. In and amongst the accumulated collection of hospital circulars, she was surprised to see an envelope marked 'Human Resources'. Inside was a curt message, simply saying that the HR Department wished to see her on her return. There was no clue as to why she had to be seen and Priscilla started to imagine the worst. Had she done something wrong? Was she going to be made redundant in a reorganisation of the health service? Had someone complained about her?

She phoned HR to ask when it might be most convenient to come and see them. 'About two o'clock', said a jolly voice, adding, 'it's nothing to worry about'.

Priscilla wasn't sure whether that was a routine response or a reassurance. It was only just-gone nine and she had five hours of anxious speculation. Did any of her colleagues know what it was about?

'Just something routine I expect', said her friend Daphne. The renal registrar agreed with her.

'Do either of you actually know what it's about?' Priscilla asked.

'No idea at all', they said in unison, rather too quickly Priscilla thought suspiciously.

The morning passed unusually slowly. At last two o'clock approached and at three minutes to the hour Priscilla knocked on the door of the HR Department. 'Come in', came a voice, which Priscilla recognised as the same cheery one she had heard on the 'phone.

'I'm Priscilla', but before she could give a surname, the jolly voice, which had a happy face to match, said, 'yes we're expecting you. Did you have a good holiday? Go anywhere special?'

'Yes, America.'

'Ooh whereabouts? I've always wanted to go there.'

'Memphis.'

'Wow, that's where Elvis came from isn't it?'

'Yes.'

'Did you get to see Graceland? Must be an amazing place. I'd love to go there.'

'Yes, we stayed in the hotel just opposite. We go quite often.'

'Lucky you.'

At that moment an inner-door opened and a smart-looking woman emerged. 'You must be Priscilla, come on in.'

Without any small-talk the woman quickly got down to business. 'I know you have been in renal for five years and from all accounts are excellent at your job. However, the lead medical-secretary at the IVF clinic is going on maternity-leave from next week and we need someone with just your qualifications and experience to cover. Would you be interested in a transfer?'

Of all the possible reasons for her interview, this was not one for which she had prepared herself but it didn't take Priscilla long to make up her mind.

When Aaron collected Priscilla at the hospital that evening, she was bursting with the news.

'You'll never believe it but I got called to HR today... and I'm being transferred, with promotion. I'm going to be lead medical-secretary at the IVF clinic. How about that?'

'More money?' asked Aaron.

'Next grade up.'
'When do you start?'
'Tomorrow.'
'Great, well done, clever girl... we'll have to celebrate. Let's stop-off at the supermarket and get a bottle of bubbly.'

They were on the last glass of special-offer cava, slumped on a settee with Priscilla's head lying on Aaron's shoulder, when a thought occurred to them both simultaneously. They both started to talk together. Then they both stopped.

'You first', said Priscilla giggling slightly.

'No, you', said Aaron.

'No, you', insisted Priscilla.

'Heads it's me, tails it's you', said Aaron fumbling for a coin in his pocket. A fifty-pence piece fell onto the floor, head-side up.

'It's me then. We... I was thinking,' said Aaron with the deliberation of someone trying to marshal his grammar after too much alcohol. 'You know, we'll both soon being, doing the sort of, be doing the same job. Except you'll be doing it for people. Making babies in test-tubes, I mean, while I do it for sheep.'

'That's funny, just what I was thinking. Amazing isn't it. I wonder if I'll actually get to see a baby being made. Do you get to see lambs made?'

'Well they do it with pettettes and piptri dishes... I mean pipettes and petri-dishes.'

'Of course we won't be cloning people', said Priscilla.

'No - but you could I suppose. Same technique. We're all mammals aren't we... people and pigs and things.'

'Well, you are... sometimes... a pig I mean', Priscilla giggled. 'When you eat spaghetti.'

'Time for bed', said Aaron. 'This conversation is getting very silly.'

They went upstairs arm-in-arm. While Aaron was in the bathroom, Priscilla stood in front of her shrine. She bent forward and kissed Elvis and Jesus. 'Thank you', she said. 'I love you both lots and lots.'

Two weeks later, Aaron and Priscilla were sitting on a train on their way to London. It was a Saturday and while they planned to do some shopping, the main purpose of the day-out was to see the Elvis Exhibition which they had read about in the fan-magazine. It was being held at a shop in east-London dedicated to all things Elvis. It was a place where tribute-artists could buy Elvis costumes and jewellery and fans could find the latest Graceland merchandise sold under licence. From the outside, the shop looked a bit rundown and could have been mistaken for a warehouse but inside it was an Aladdin's cave of delights for any dedicated Elvis-devotee.

This Exhibition had been drawn from several, different, Elvis exhibitions around the world. A jumpsuit collector from Las Vegas had loaned eighteen, different suits from The King's later years, including some that had clearly been extended several times around the waist to accommodate the star as he grew increasingly portly.

A collection of scarves had been loaned by a Canadian who had stood in the front-row at twenty-five Elvis-concerts and on each occasion been rewarded with a scarf and a kiss. It had been Elvis's habit to wear several scarves during a performance and hand them out to female members of the audience as each became drenched in his sweat. They became treasured items and few were ever washed.

There was an army uniform, reputedly worn by Elvis in Germany and a display of the typical, military kit that would have been issued to a conscript GI at the time Elvis was called-up.

There was a gallery of Elvis art, from the naïve to the kitsch. A huge, black, velvet curtain hung on one wall depicting a fantasy-Elvis ascending into heaven in all his glory, surrounded by a choir of angels. There were other parodies of Christian icons including an image of Elvis displaying his sacred heart and another depicting Elvis with a halo, carrying a cross.

At the centre of the Exhibition was a selection from an amazing, American museum called *The Everything you need to know about Elvis Show*. All the items were the property of an American artist who claimed a place in The Guinness Book of World Records for the scope, size and extent of his collection. This collection's only rival was the legendary one known as *Graceland Too* run by the eccentric collector and Elvis-fan, Paul McLeod, at his home in Holly Springs, Mississippi.

Only a small proportion of over 30,000 Elvis items had been brought over to London from their permanent home at *The Everything you need to know about Elvis Show* in Florida but the selection included what some fans considered to be the world's most-sacred Elvis-relic, the wart, removed by a US Army surgeon from Elvis's left arm.

It was displayed in a test-tube of preserving liquid. A small, bleached lump of organic matter in a perspex reliquary with a spotlight shining on it. The container was laid on a silken cushion, surrounded by flickering, electric candles and plastic roses. As they passed, some fans bent a knee and made a sign-of-the-cross. Priscilla looked at the wart in awe and, as she moved away to let another fan see the relic, she too found she instinctively crossed herself.

For several minutes Aaron and Priscilla said nothing. It was Aaron who broke the silence. 'It's amazing to think that that little lump of... of... well, matter, contains his entire DNA. Not just all the information about him as a human but everything about who he was: hair-colour, height, facial features and even the sound of his voice', he said. 'The tiniest slither would be enough to create a new Elvis. Awesome.'

Sometimes, lying awake at night, Priscilla fancied she could hear her biological clock ticking. She was enjoying her present life of freedom, just herself, Aaron and no kids. But one day, soon perhaps, she thought how wonderful it would be to have children. Aaron liked the thought of being a dad but was quite happy to put the expense and responsibility off for just another year or two. On the occasions when Priscilla became broody, he readily admitted feeling some paternal urges as well.

'Aaron', Priscilla whispered.

'Uh', he grunted from somewhere suspended in the land between wakefulness and sleep, hoping he might dream of Elvis again.

'When we have a baby', said Priscilla, 'I mean if we had a baby, what would we call him'?

'Assuming it was a him', said Aaron waking slowly.

'Could we call him Elvis?'

'Suppose so... but what if he turned out to be freckly with blond hair and nothing like Elvis and more of a Wayne or a William?'

'Bit of a risk I suppose. Perhaps he could be a William, with Presley as a second name?'

Priscilla thought for a further moment and added, 'but if we did call him Elvis, wouldn't there be things we could do to make sure he was Elvis-like? I mean, dye his hair black, dress him in jumpsuits and give him guitar lessons?'

'Not a good idea to be too pushy, he might grow up to hate Elvis music. Kids often go contrary to their parents. A protest to exert their independence. The only way to guarantee we have a child looking and behaving like Elvis is for him to have the same DNA... and that's not... '

Aaron was about to say the word 'possible' when he paused. But Priscilla immediately took up his train of thought. 'But it is', she said excitedly. 'It is possible. His DNA, it's still preserved. We saw it today. In London.'

'Yes we saw a wart', said Aaron. 'It's a long way from seeing a wart to giving-birth to a baby Elvis-clone.'

'But not impossible.'

'Well, first we would have to steal the wart. Then we would have to take a sample of DNA from it. We would then need access to a fertilised, human egg and remove the nucleus and substitute DNA from the wart. Then we would have to insert the treated egg into a human surrogate-mother and if very, very lucky, after nine-months we would have an Elvis-clone. But it took the scientists who cloned Dolly two hundred and seventy-seven attempts to get it right. And where are we going to get a fertilised, human egg from? And who's going to do the tricky bit of removing the nucleus and putting the new DNA inside?' Aaron finished his scientific tour-de-force hoping he had made himself clear. Cloning Elvis would be well nigh impossible.

'Yes', Priscilla acknowledged. 'Not very easy.'

'No. Goodnight.'

Having been woken, it took Aaron a while to get back to sleep again. He tried counting identical sheep but gave up at number two-hundred and seventy-seven. The notion of producing an Elvis clone gnawed away at his imagination. He began to think how it might be possible to steal the Elvis wart. He ran through some of the practicalities in his mind. Breaking and entry at night would probably set off an alarm and anyway burglary was not his scene. The easiest plan, he thought, would be to take the wart, test-tube and all, and leave an identical one in its place. This would have to be done when the Exhibition was open. And would they really be committing a crime, he wondered, if they had left no evidence behind that a crime had been committed?

He began to hatch a plot. He and Priscilla would need to visit the gallery when it was quiet. Early in the morning on a weekday perhaps? Priscilla would need to cause a diversion while he took the wart off its cushion and replaced it with a replica. They would then sneak out and nobody would be any the wiser. But how would he find a replacement? The wart could be any small lump of flesh, an off-cut from a piece of butcher's meat perhaps? As for finding a suitable test-tube, he was sure somewhere in the lab there would be a perspex tube of the same make, or something very similar. He fell asleep eventually, imagining he was looking through cupboards at work to find the exact match.

The next day in the lab, Aaron took a closer interest than usual in the work going on around him. He started asking questions and one of the PhD students was happy to answer them.

'Why do you need two pipettes?'

'Why does one have to be blunt and the other sharp?'

'So what's a somatic cell?'

'What's a blastocyst?'

'How do you stimulate cell division?'

'What's the success rate currently with somatic cell nuclear-transfer?'

'How do you impregnate a ewe? How do you know the catheter is in the right place inside the uterus?'

The answers from his mix of theoretical and practical questions gave Aaron a much clearer idea of the whole business of cloning. He discovered how his lab's pioneering refinements to the techniques used to impregnate Dolly were producing dividends.

'We're almost there', he was told. 'Ninety-percent success rate, high enough to start industrialising the production of embryos.'

Once, when the PhD student was peering through a microscope at a petri-dish to execute the removal of a nucleus from a cell taken from a ewe's udder, Aaron asked if he might have a look.

'Yes of course - and if you've got a steady-hand, see if you can insert the sharp pipette to suck out the nucleus.'

Aaron nervously took the pipette. When his hand had steadied he watched through the microscope as the pipette touched and then penetrated the egg. The student took a look and assured him he was on the right track.

'I've done it', Aaron said after a few minutes. 'What do I do next?'

Over the next few days he became quite expert at the job. The lab was glad of his help. Even the professor was content to have a technician relieve his specialist-staff of some of the chores involved in the laboratory's work.

Priscilla discovered that moving to a different hospital-department gave her a renewed interest in her work. Five years in the renal-department had been very enjoyable but she was beginning to find the work repetitive. There was a slow changeover of patients in the dialysis unit and an even slower turnover of staff. She had wanted something new to stimulate her interest and the IVF clinic provided it.

She liked the contact with the hopeful mothers-to-be who found her both efficient and understanding. She got on well with the other secretaries in her team and with the medical staff. She also found the science interesting and began asking useful questions.

She learned about egg-retrieval and embryo-culture. Maybe fifteen eggs would be taken from a mother and ten would be fertilised.

'Some of them don't get any further so we don't keep them', she was told.

'Just chuck them out?'

'Yes, they're not babies, just eggs that wouldn't have developed. It happens in nature all the time, eggs get fertilised but never grow in the womb.'

A lucky egg that divides and grows will, after five-days, become a blastocyst Priscilla was told and she was allowed to look at one under a microscope.

'Think of it', she said, 'I might be looking at a new Beethoven or Einstein or Elvis'.

'Or perhaps a Myra Hindley - or Adolf Hitler?'

'Most likely an accountant or call-centre worker.'

Priscilla asked question after question and soon had a clear, overall picture in her mind of the clinic's work. She impressed everyone with her enthusiasm and interest.

She also discovered that what gave everyone in the clinic a special buzz was receiving birthday cards from the children who would never have been conceived but for their work. Before long, Priscilla came to share the same sense of pleasure and pride as she came to know more and more of the patients and hear how, after years of hoping for a child, they became pregnant at last. The sense of satisfaction was similar to the one she had known when renal-patients came back to the unit in rude health after a successful transplant.

'I think it might be possible', Aaron declared out-of-the-blue the next Sunday morning. He had seemed to be in deep thought for a while, staring at the same page of the Sunday paper for a long time.

'What might be possible?' Priscilla asked, looking up from her magazine.

'It might really be possible to clone Elvis.'

'Go on.'

'We could get DNA from the wart and I've got access to all the equipment we need at the laboratory', Aaron explained. 'I've been watching very closely how they clone animals and I'm now quite practised at removing nuclei from cells and replacing them with new genetic material. All we need is a supply of human eggs. As long as you're prepared to be Elvis's mother of course?'

Priscilla didn't reply immediately. She wasn't either surprised or shocked by Aaron's suggestion because many of the same thoughts had already occurred to her as she had gone about her work at the hospital. She had secretly hoped that Aaron might say something on those lines. She delayed her reply to give herself some time to reflect. Did she truly want to commit herself to the project, to become the mother of Elvis? It was all very well to make far-fetched plans but to carry them out?

'Sorry', said Aaron thinking he had misjudged the issue and the moment. 'Perhaps it's a daft idea.'

'I think', Priscilla said, slowly and deliberately, 'I think I could get the human eggs. There are often some going spare at the clinic'.

Aaron squeezed Priscilla's hand. 'We would have to call him Elvis, if he was Elvis', he said.

Nothing further was said that day but both Aaron and Priscilla knew an important decision had been taken. That night Priscilla spent extra time over her prayers. She looked at her pictures of Elvis and Jesus. She reflected on how she might become the mother of the new Elvis. For a while, recognising neither the irony nor the absurdity of the situation, she even thought of Jesus' mother Mary and the story of the Angel Gabriel and how Mary gave birth in a stable.

'Can you get a weekday off work?' Aaron asked her at breakfast next day.

'It might be difficult. I've only just started working at the clinic and don't have any annual-leave owing. Why?'

'If we are going to get hold of the wart it would be better not to try at the weekend. Too many people.'

'We could go up on Saturday and get there very early. It opens at nine-thirty I think?'

'It's the last weekend too, so we don't have much option. But I'll need to go up beforehand and have a look around. Just to check what sort of test-tube it's in and to see if it's alarmed in any way. I've got a half-day owing. I'll take it tomorrow.'

It would have been the perfect day for the crime. When Aaron arrived at the Exhibition it was almost deserted. The room where the wart was on show was empty for a full thirty-seconds at one point as Aaron inspected it carefully, took photographs with his camera and looked underneath the display-table for signs of an alarm wire. If he had had a test-tube and a substitute wart with him he could and would have done the deed there and then.

He surveyed the scene carefully, rehearsing every move in his mind. Making a replica wart would not be a problem he concluded. He would get a small, fatty piece of beef at the butcher, cut off a lump of fat and whittle it down to the right shape and size. The test-tube was a slightly unusual design but he felt sure that at the lab there would be a convincing replica. Aaron wondered how long it would be before anyone noticed the switch? The Exhibition was due to be dismantled and sent on to Paris on its world-tour within a week. Someone would spot it then, surely? Maybe, Aaron thought, he should just take a sample and return the original as soon as possible? It would hardly be fitting for future fans to cross themselves reverently in front of a slice of butcher's dripping.

That Friday evening, while Priscilla prepared a roast-dinner, Aaron sat at the kitchen table with a sharp knife, a lump of raw beef-fat, several pictures of the wart and a selection of test-tubes he had borrowed from work. As the Yorkshire puddings were being brought out of the oven and Priscilla was telling him to clear the table so they could eat, he let out a cry of triumph. 'Done it.'

Priscilla looked at his handiwork and then at his photographs. 'Very good', she said. 'I can hardly tell the difference.'

'Now all we'll need tomorrow is the substitute wart, a sharp blade, a small dish in which to put the sample of the real wart and a fair share of luck.'

'Luck? But you said the plan was foolproof', Priscilla asked nervously. 'What would happen if we got caught? Can you go to prison for stealing a wart?'

'It's not stealing a whole wart', said Aaron. 'Taking a small slice on loan. We will repay the world with Elvis. And anyway nothing can go wrong. Trust me.'

Priscilla didn't sleep much that night thanks to nervousness, excitement and Aaron snoring. She rehearsed everything in her mind. She and Aaron would get to the Exhibition early. If the room with the wart was empty, she would keep-watch by the door while Aaron swapped the test-tube containing the wart for the one with the lump of beef-fat. If they did not have the room to themselves, she would cause a diversion by pretending to faint or 'accidentally' knocking into the one of the jumpsuits on a display-stand. This would give Aaron time and opportunity to make the switch. Then Aaron would hide the test-tube in his coat pocket and sneak away to the lavatory to remove the wart. He would use the blade to take the required sample, put it into a special container, replace the wart in its original reliquary and return to the exhibition-room. Once the coast was clear again, he would replace the mock wart with the genuine article and they would leave. Nothing could go wrong, could it?

CHAPTER FOUR

The morning of the DNA snatch did not go entirely as planned. The first thing to go wrong was that their train was delayed and Priscilla and Aaron did not arrive at the Exhibition until ten-fifteen, just as a mini-bus from the Wolverhampton *We are always with you Elvis Fan Club* was arriving.

Aaron, hoping for anonymity, was greeted by the security-guard at the entrance as a long-lost friend. 'Back again? Saw you in the week. Never forget a face. You must be a big fan.' Aaron muttered a muffled 'yes, a big fan, sure', and he and Priscilla scuttled-in as fast as they could.

They pushed ahead of the Wolverhampton party and made straight for the wart. It was exactly as Aaron had seen it the day before and there were only two other people looking at it. They were examining it closely and somewhat sceptically.

'It can't really be his', said one. 'No-one keeps a wart. Like keeping toe-nail clippings. Who'd bother?'

'I expect someone's got his.'

'His what?'

'Toe-nail clippings. They're that daft about him. I just like his music myself.'

'I wonder how it came to be saved? When I had my appendix out the surgeon told me it went straight in the bag for the incinerator.'

'Same with my tonsils.'

'Though the dentist gave me my tooth.'

'That was worth something, a shilling in my day from the tooth-fairy.'

'Perhaps the surgeon thought the wart would be worth a shilling or two, as a sort of relic.'

'He could have snipped off a lock of hair when Elvis was under, instead of keeping the wart.'

'He'd have had it removed under a local anaesthetic and would've noticed.'

'Most-likely one of the theatre-nurses was a big fan and kept the wart back from being incinerated.'

'Yeh. 'Spect you're right. Do you think bits get kept from other operations on celebs? Has someone got the Pope's prostate or the Queen Mother's fish-bone?'

The speculation trailed-off as, eventually, the two sceptics moved away and the room became empty. Priscilla stood at the door. 'All clear', she whispered.

Aaron took the replacement wart out of the pocket of his anorak and stretched out his other hand to lift the phial containing the true Elvis-relic. He deftly made the switch and nodded at Priscilla. Just at that moment he spotted a CCTV camera positioned above the door. Its red light flickered. 'Oh damn', he muttered. 'I never saw that yesterday.'

Knowing there was little he could do if he had been seen, he said nothing to Priscilla as he went past her to the Gents. Initially, it appeared that all the doors to the cubicles were closed. However, he realised with relief that one was unoccupied. He pushed it open with one hand since his other was holding the wart, safe under his coat.

While she waited, Priscilla pretended to show interest in a signed-photo of *The Jordanaires*, Elvis's backing-singers. Barely a minute later the security-man came into the room. He walked purposefully over to the table with the wart.

'I could have sworn I saw someone trying to nick it', he said partly to himself and partly to Priscilla. 'On camera, like. But there's nothing missing. I must have been seeing things. And I forgot to put a tape in the machine so I can't look at it again.'

Priscilla smiled weakly and her knees began to shake.

In the lavatory cubicle Aaron was all fingers and thumbs. The top of the test-tube seemed stuck fast. He had to find the pliers he had secreted in his jacket to twist it off. Once removed the test-tube let off a horrendous smell of preserving fluid. He had to poke the wart out with a wire and then put it onto a flat surface. With the lid of the lavatory-pan down, Aaron knelt in front of it. He put the wart on a tissue, found the blade he needed and took a delicate slice from the back.

He heard sounds outside the cubicle. He thought it might be the security-man from the glimpse he had of black, polished footwear. There was a knock on the cubicle door. The security-man had spotted the soles of Aaron's shoes. The owner of the shoes was obviously not in the usual sitting or standing position adopted by cubicle users. Perhaps he was unwell and had collapsed on the floor?

'Is everything alright?' he asked.

'Yes', said Aaron, wanting to reassure him as briefly and confidently as he could.

'Just checking', said the security-man. I suppose that must be the direction of Mecca, he thought to himself.

Aaron continued with his delicate task. He took care that the area of the wart from which he sliced the minute sample he needed was on the side no-one normally saw when it was displayed. He put the precious, DNA sample in a small, plastic container, put the lid on and placed it safely in his pocket. He returned the wart to its original test-tube and pressed the top firmly into position. He put the test-tube into his inside coat-pocket, stood up, pulled the handle to flush and unlocked the cubicle door.

He was washing his hands when the security-man joined him at the row of hand-basins.

'Odd smell', he said, sniffing the air.

'Toilet-cleaner, I expect', said Aaron a little nervously.

'The janitors must be using a new brand. Funny thing happened just now', he added chattily. 'I glanced at the CCTV in the office and could have sworn I saw someone nicking that wart. Went to have a look and nothing missing at all. I must be imagining things in my dotage.'

'And who'd want to steal an old wart anyway?' said Aaron with a false laugh, trying to sound as casual as possible.

'Well there are always nutters around. It would have been kidnapping, I expect. They'd have been demanding a ransom for its safe return.'

'Like people stealing valuable paintings.'

'Yup, or it could have been a theft ordered by a mad, wealthy Elvis-fan living the life of a recluse and wanting the ultimate Elvis-souvenir. Then there's terrorists. Who knows what the next IRA plot might be?'

'Who knows?' agreed Aaron.

'But thankfully, no harm done. Well I must be off. I forgot to put a tape in the recording-machine this morning so I'd better go and do that and if anyone so much as touches the wart again, we'll have evidence.'

The moment Aaron got back into the exhibition-room Priscilla grabbed him.

'You were seen', she whispered.

'I know', said Aaron. 'But we're not suspected. I've spoken to the security-guard.'

'Did you get a piece of wart alright?'

Aaron tapped his pocket. 'All we need to do now is put the real wart back and scarper.'

There were three people in the room, two lookalikes wearing 'Gays for Elvis' badges and a thin young woman in red with a stud through her eyebrow.

'I think we need a diversion', said Aaron. 'We've got to be quick before he gets a tape in his machine.'

Priscilla had rehearsed this moment in her mind many times the previous night. She swung her arm against a stand and it, plus the Vegas jumpsuit on it, fell across a display of rare, Elvis-magazine covers, knocking several on the floor. She shrieked as she did it, 'Oh no... how could I have been so clumsy?'

It was not an Oscar-winning performance but it bought Aaron the time he needed. While all eyes were on Priscilla wrestling the stand upright and then grovelling on the floor to pick up the magazines, he removed the test-tube containing the globule of beef-fat from the display cushion and replaced it with the genuine wart.

If he had taken a second longer he would have been caught red-handed, for just as he finished the security-guard came in. 'What's up?' he demanded. 'Everything OK?'

'Sorry, I'm so sorry', apologised Priscilla. 'I banged against the stand and it fell and knocked the magazines onto the floor. And I...'

'Don't you worry dear', the security-man reassured her. 'Could have happened to anyone.'

Out of the corner of her eye she saw Aaron give her a thumbs-up sign. A tear of relief trickled down one cheek.

'Don't you cry dear', said the security-man offering her a large, red handkerchief. 'It's not your fault. I told them it was a stupid place to put a stand and someone was bound to knock it over. All's well that ends well. No harm done.' He put his arm round her shoulder. 'You need a nice cup of hot tea. I'll get you one in the office.'

There was no way out. For the next twenty-minutes Aaron and Priscilla sat in the security-office drinking sweet tea and making reassuring noises that Priscilla was fine and they ought to be leaving. Occasionally they glanced at the bank of television screens and on one they watched a steady stream of visitors paying homage to the sacred wart.

Later in the day, the security-man wondered again who would want to steal a wart. He put two and two together and made five. 'Terrorists', he thought. 'Now, they might be after it. And someone did try and nick it, I saw him with my own eyes. And I know for sure there were foreigners in today. I saw one of them praying. I'd better check the room again, just to be sure.'

Once home, Aaron took the precious sample from his pocket and placed it on the kitchen table.

'Mission accomplished', he said with satisfaction.

'That was the easy bit', said Priscilla. 'Next, you have to smuggle the equipment we need out of the lab and I have to get hold of a human egg.'

'I'll get the lab equipment bit-by-bit through the week. The pipettes and petri-dishes won't be a problem, there are always plenty around. I'll need some batteries and copper wire. A microscope will be a bit trickier. Perhaps I can borrow that officially. I could say I want to show a nephew some bugs swimming in river-water as part of a school-project.'

'But your only nephew is in Australia.'

'I know that but they don't know at work.'

'It's not every day they have discarded eggs at the hospital', said Priscilla, 'and I'm not always working in that part of the clinic when they get chucked in the bag for organic-waste. I'll try and get one on Friday so we can do the business at the weekend but I can't promise. It could be tomorrow or any time'.

Priscilla feared that all through the week she would be on such tenterhooks that someone would get suspicious. 'No-one will guess what we're doing, not in a million years', Aaron reassured her.

On Wednesday afternoon, Priscilla had her chance. One of the junior-doctors had just been examining a batch of eggs under a microscope when his bleeper sounded. 'Can you do us a favour?' he asked Priscilla who was just passing. 'Put these in the waste. We're not going to need them. None of them has fertilised and the mother is already expecting triplets.' With that he dashed to the 'phone, called a number, then dashed again for the exit. 'Bit of an emergency', he muttered by-way-of explanation.

Priscilla had ample time to empty the contents of the dish into a small container she had in her pocket for just such an opportunity and slip the container into her trouser-pocket. From there it was transferred to her handbag and that evening it was placed next to the wart in the fridge, between the bacon and the butter.

The professor in charge of the animal-research laboratory had no hesitation in letting Aaron borrow a microscope. He even gave him a wall-chart of river micro-organisms for his nephew to put up on his bedroom wall. By Friday evening everything was in place.

Aaron set up the microscope on the kitchen table under the bright, central light. He put the eggs from the clinic in a petri-dish and examined them closely. 'The first step', he pronounced, 'is to select one and enucleate it. For that I need the two pipettes. The blunt one holds the egg and with the sharp one, I suck-out the central nucleus. Done it on sheep and it doesn't look very different'.

He selected what, to him, looked like the largest of the eggs and made a skilful extraction of the central material. He looked-up and smiled. 'Now for the wart.'

He examined the wart under the microscope for several minutes.

'What's wrong?' asked Priscilla anxiously.

'Just trying to detach a complete cell. There's some deterioration. Not surprised over the years.'

After another couple of minutes he looked up from his work with an expression of pleasure on his face. 'Just need to rinse it through with some saline solution to remove any of that chemical preservative.'

He delicately placed something which, to Priscilla's eye, seemed quite invisible into a third petri-dish.

'Now', he said. 'I have to put the cell from the wart inside the enucleated cell and leave them together overnight with a mild electric-current to stimulate a fusion. Then tomorrow, all being well we will be ready for the implantation.'

Again, that night Priscilla was too nervous and excited to sleep much. She crept downstairs twice in the night to look at the dish with its wires and batteries sitting on the side. On both occasions, on her way back to bed, she paused in front of her Elvis table. 'Dear Elvis', she said, 'I do love you so much. Please, please, please make this work'.

But as she lay in bed in the dark small hours she began to have doubts. For the first time, she was not rehearsing the practical difficulties but having ethical doubts. Were they really doing the right thing? Was it selfish of her to want to have a baby like Elvis? Was taking the egg and the sample of the wart stealing? 'Please Elvis', she found herself praying, 'tell me if you approve?'

She decided to listen to some music and, so as not to wake Aaron, she selected an Elvis track at random on her Walkman in the dark. It was Elvis's answer.

Well, that's alright, mama,
That's alright for you.
That's alright, mama, just anyway you do.
Well, that's alright, that's alright,
That's alright now mama, anyway you do.

For the final hours of the night Priscilla slept soundly.

When she woke it was eight o'clock. 'Time for the final stage', declared Aaron as he stood by her bed. He had placed the petri-dish on the dressing-table and was holding a catheter in his hand. 'I've looked at the egg under the microscope and everything seems alright.'

Aaron was apprehensive about performing the impregnation. It was a procedure he had watched many times with sheep and had asked the lab vet lots of questions but he had no hands-on experience. Priscilla had watched an IVF implant and had also asked questions. They had pooled their knowledge and hoped that after all their hard work in getting as far as this, they wouldn't make a mistake.

'TCB', said Aaron.

'In the bathroom cabinet', said Priscilla.

'No B, not P. Let's Take Care of the Business.'

Aaron let Priscilla rest most of the day. It was now up to nature to take its course.

Some weeks later, Priscilla spent most of the weekend in bed. On the Friday, she had felt unusually tired and was beginning to worry she might have picked up a sickness-bug. That night she was sick. On the Saturday morning she felt so nauseous that she was quite sure she had caught a dose of some nasty gastric-'flu doing the rounds. On Monday, she went into work but by lunchtime was feeling quite washed-out.

'Are you feeling OK?' her boss, the consultant, asked her.

'Not very', Priscilla admitted.

'Come into the office and I'll take a look', she offered sympathetically.

After a few questions and a short examination came the verdict. 'It takes our patients years of effort and intervention, and you've done it without any bother at all.'

'Done what?'

'If I'm not mistaken - you're pregnant.'

'I'm what?'

'Don't sound so surprised. It's not a disease. You are expecting a baby. You are in the club, as they say.'

Priscilla head suddenly felt woozy. She nearly fell off her chair in a faint. The next thing she heard was her boss's voice again.

'You'd better go home and have a rest - and congratulations.'

Aaron was as pleased as any new father could be when he heard the news, although strictly speaking he wasn't the father, just the means to the end.

'Any idea when little Elvis will be born?' he asked.

'Sometime in June, I'd guess', replied Priscilla, counting months on her fingers.

The new year arrived quickly and the spring in next-to-no time. Week-by-week Priscilla got larger. 'I think I felt Elvis kicking', she announced one day.

'Swivelling his hips I expect', said Aaron.

They bought a pram, a cot and everything else needed for a new baby.

'We'd better call the nappies, diapers', said Aaron. 'Elvis is an American after all.'

'But he'll actually be British', said Priscilla, 'and he'll talk with an English accent'.

'He'll look like Elvis though and sing like him when he's older.'

'We hope.'

The first time Aaron saw an ultrasound picture of little Elvis in the womb, he swore he could see the tiny child give an Elvis-style curl of the lip.

'Do you want to know if it's a boy or a girl', the doctor had asked, continuing, 'we can easily have a look'. She had paused and begun looking-closely at the flickering-screen. Priscilla had a sudden moment of doubt. What if the baby was a girl and had been conceived quite normally and the whole business of trying to clone Elvis had been a sad failure? What would her feelings be? Would she love her own little girl as much as Elvis?

'Boy it is', came the verdict after a while. 'Fine, healthy boy.'

One day in late April, Priscilla was at the hairdresser. On the pile of magazines left for customers to read was one with a story headlined on the front cover that immediately roused her interest. She grabbed at it, found the relevant page and started reading.

'Shape your new baby's musical tastes. Research has shown that mothers who listen to music when pregnant can strongly influence the kind of music their baby will prefer when he or she grows up. Babies in the womb develop a good sense of hearing. Mozart played all day in the final two months of pregnancy will give your baby a love of the classics.'

That evening Priscilla took two strips of sticky-tape and attached the earphones of her Walkman to her growing bulge.

Rock-a-hula baby
Rock-a-hula baby
Got a hula lulu from Honolulu
That rock-a-hula baby of mine.

Six weeks before the due-date Priscilla started her maternity-leave. The clinic held a small party in her honour. 'See you again soon', said her boss. 'If not back at work, then in the maternity ward!'

At every ante-natal check-up, Priscilla had been pronounced fit and well. She went to classes with other mothers-to-be and learned about the birth-process. She practiced her breathing exercises conscientiously and from mid-May onwards had a bag packed at home all ready for her trip to the hospital.

June was very hot and Priscilla felt very heavy and uncomfortable. 'I'm just like an elephant', she told Aaron.

'Be thankful you're not', he said, a little unsympathetically. 'They gestate for twenty-two months.'

If Aaron and Priscilla thought they had everything planned for the birth with military precision, Elvis had other ideas. It was the longest day and therefore the shortest night of the year. The dawn-light was seeping through the window when Priscilla woke with a start. She had grown used to back-pain and all the other discomforts of carrying a large child with a penchant for rock'n'roll but this was a new feeling all together. A few minutes later it came again.

'Oh my God', she shrieked, 'contractions!'

Then she felt a warm, wet feeling around her bottom.

'Oh my God, my waters', she shrieked again! 'Aaron, Aaron, wake-up. Elvis is on his way!'

He leapt out of bed and started to dress himself. Priscilla heaved herself upright and began to look for her clothes. Suddenly she collapsed back onto the bed.

'Another contraction', she said groaning. 'Quick, quick get me to the hospital.'

'They said the first baby took hours to come', said Aaron. 'Don't panic.'

'I'm not panicking', panted Priscilla, even more fraught. 'I don't care what first babies usually do. Elvis is in a hurry.'

She tried dressing again. After a few minutes of struggling with her clothes, she was forced to sit down on the bed again. 'Please Aaron, hurry.'

Aaron had the hospital-bag in his hand. 'I'll put this in the car and come back and help you downstairs.'

But the moment he opened the front-door Aaron himself started to panic. In the half-light of dawn he noticed that the car headlights had been left-on. They were glowing a dull yellow, drawing the very last ounce of power from the battery. Aaron put the key in the ignition and turned. Just as he feared. The starter-motor whimpered briefly and died.

He rushed back inside just as Priscilla felt a new contraction overwhelming her body.

'I'm going to 'phone an ambulance', he shouted. 'The car won't start.'

Priscilla was too preoccupied to get angry. The next contraction was the biggest yet.

'Emergency? Yes. Ambulance. My wife is having a baby. Twenty-eight Mulberry Avenue. Yes, The Woodlands estate. How long? We'll hang on. The door will be open.'

Aaron had prepared for every eventuality except delivering Elvis himself. The operator had assured him it would only take ten minutes for the ambulance to reach them but the wait seemed like an eternity. Priscilla lay on the bed, sweating and writhing. 'He's coming, he's coming', she eventually yelled. Aaron took a look and indeed there was the top of a head.

Not long after there was a baby. Aaron and Priscilla felt a moment of amazing, mystical, calm. The room became bathed in a flickering, blue light and Aaron lifted the child carefully and placed him on Priscilla's breast. He made a cry and screwed-up his face. That instant Aaron and Priscilla fell in love with Elvis for the second time in their lives. They looked at him, his face glowing in the all-pervading, pulsating, blue light and Aaron recalled hearing the story how, when Elvis Presley had been newly-born, his father Vernon had said that a similar light, as-if from heaven, had illuminated their home.

Suddenly, two paramedics were in the room. In their moment of joy at the arrival of Elvis, neither Priscilla nor Aaron had heard the ambulance arrive, with its emergency-light flashing.

The paramedics quickly took control. Elvis was wrapped warmly and carried with Priscilla to the waiting ambulance.

'Had some problems finding your house', one of the paramedics said to Aaron during the short journey to the hospital. 'That's why we took so long. You're Number 28 aren't you? But you don't have your number on the door. We had to work it out - find Number 30 and Number 26 and go to the house-in-between. But did I see it's got a name?'

'Yes', said Aaron. 'It's called *Tupelo.*'

'Like where Elvis was born?' said the paramedic.

'Yes. Are you an Elvis-fan?' asked Aaron.

'You bet.'

CHAPTER FIVE

After counting Mr Carioli's money, Tim Barker was astonished to discover that he had a first-payment of thirty-thousand dollars in used, $100-dollar bills. This was serious money and he realised he had to research the project quickly, and in detail, and get it right.

His usual urge when he had money to spare was to find a game of poker. Yet somehow the attractions of a mere card game seemed very small in face of this huge gamble with his life. Not only might it make his fortune, Barker was pretty sure that if he failed and lost Mr Carioli's money, he would quickly join the real, dead Elvis in the-life-beyond.

His first move was to ensure that he could persuade Garon Love to be part of the plan, so it was all-important that he showed-up at the breakfast-bar as arranged. Barker had primed himself with questions. He wanted Garon Love to believe that he'd found his first disciple.

Barker arrived in good time and sat waiting with a coffee. The minutes ticked by and there was no sign of the stranger he had met the day before. He began to fear the worst. Had Garon Love had been arrested? Taken into psychiatric care? Died during the night? If so, all his plans would be back at square one.

Much to his relief, after half-an-hour, Barker saw him walking past the window. Garon Love came through the door with a worried look on his face. Until he saw Barker gesturing to him, he could not let himself believe that his luck had really changed and he had, perhaps, found his first disciple.

'Is there an Elvis Church I can join', Barker asked him as an opening-gambit, once they had ordered food.

'There are some churches of Elvis', Garon Love explained, 'but none can claim to be taken seriously. They are just out to mock. Jokers and cheap comedians blaspheming'. Barker described how he had been brought-up as an Episcopalian but that as an adult, nothing had quite made sense. He explained how he loved Elvis's music, which lifted his soul and spirits in a way a Christian church-service never had. He asked if there was anything he could read on the subject?

'It's all in here', said Garon Love pointing to his head, 'and here', he added, clasping his heart.

'But I can't read that. Could you not write down what you know?' asked Barker in his most-earnest and sincere-sounding voice.

'I don't even have a home. How can I do that? I am a mendicant destined to wander the earth.'

'May I help you?' Barker enquired tentatively. 'I have a bit of money and could find you a place to stay where you could write.'

'Why would you want to help me? You don't know me.'

'I know very little about you and everything I do know has come from you. But I have an instinct about people. I feel I can trust you. But more importantly, I have been searching for the truth and think I may have found it with you.'

'Are you serious?'

'Very serious.'

The two men shook hands across the plastic table just as the waitress arrived with two breakfasts, eggs, ham, sausage, muffins, jelly, hash browns. Garon Love had hardly eaten for twenty-four hours and Barker had said he would pick-up the check.

'You two look as if you've just struck a deal', she said as she put the food down.

'We sure have', said Barker emphatically while Garon Love smiled broadly.

'Enjoy. Have a great day.'

Breakfast took well over two hours. There was so much to talk about. Barker promised to find an apartment for Garon Love within a mile of Graceland. He would set him up with a word-processor and visit him daily, bringing food and supplies.

Garon Love could not believe his good fortune, not only had he found a disciple, he had found a benefactor as well.

Neither could Barker believe his luck. All religions need their scriptures, he reasoned, and soon the Church of Elvis would have its very own Bible.

They arranged to meet for breakfast again the next day when Barker would hand over the keys to an apartment and the writing could start.

'In the meantime', said Barker, 'I'll check you into a hotel'.

Barker had a flair for organisation. It was only his own life he had previously found difficult to manage. Central to the success of the project, he thought, would be to find the right site for the cathedral. He drove around the city looking at vacant plots. He discovered there were several, downtown sites available. He initially thought the cathedral could be built by the river and rival The Memphis Pyramid. Then, he reasoned, lots of fans who come to Memphis don't go anywhere else but Graceland therefore, his cathedral would have to be as close as possible to Graceland, right at the heart of Elvisland. There, fans could easily discover it for themselves while those who already knew about it could combine a visit to the cathedral with one to Graceland.

Barker spent several days walking up-and-down Elvis Presley Boulevard, looking and asking about property. Luck was again on his side. Two fast-food outlets, side-by-side and next to the highway, were up for sale, together with their car-parking space. With Mr Carioli's money he had little problem in buying them. Some of Mr Carioli's 'supporters' helped him evict the owners of two single-storey homes behind and the owner of a further adjoining piece of wasteland found himself persuaded to sell.

Altogether, Barker accumulated five acres of real-estate which he proceeded to clear. He commissioned an architect to draw-up plans, and to liaise directly with building contractors, craftsmen and artists, all names approved by Mr Carioli. Barker quickly caught-on to the principles behind money-laundering. Limitless supplies of ill-gotten money could be purified by spending it, so long as the contractors being paid had legitimate businesses and were on Mr Carioli's list of friends and relations. The money went into the system tainted but came out the other side clean and untraceable.

By Elvis Week in mid-August, six months after Barker and Mr Carioli had struck their deal, everything was in place for the construction-work to start. Garon Love's book was finished too and Barker had had thousands of copies printed. The paperback showed the image of the stigmatised Elvis on the cover. Under Barker's instruction, the designer had deliberately blurred and combined Christian and Elvis imagery. However, the hardbacks were bound in black mock-leather with gold-lettering, to give them a distinctive, Biblical feel.

The book was long, dense and scholarly. Barker skimmed through, looking for good quotes to display as poster-slogans on billboards along the highway.

'We know not the time or the place but it is written Elvis will return in glory.'

'He is God's chosen-one and all the nations of the world will know his name.'

'And the world will be shaken-up by the sound of the golden voice of heaven.'

Barker took full advantage of Elvis Week to sow the first seeds. He mingled with the crowds at Graceland and handed out copies of the paperbacks to any fan who showed an interest. He struck-up conversations whenever the opportunity arose and began to spread the good news of the return of Elvis. A sign was erected on the building-site about the Elvis Church and its new cathedral and a steady stream of curious fans began to turn-up to see for themselves what was happening.

Garon Love had had no difficulty writing the new Elvis scriptures. He worked day and night, barely sleeping for weeks on end. Such was his prolific output that Barker provided him with a secretary to take dictation. His mind was overflowing with ideas. He had an encyclopaedic memory for Biblical references in Greek, Latin and Hebrew as well as English. He recalled every word his troubled and disorientated self had ever heard from Elvis in his visions. He collated the Elvis sayings and compared them with those of Jesus drawn from the Biblical and Gnostic Gospels. From the wealth of material at hand he produced an incomparable and scholarly concordance. The task he had set himself was to give followers of Elvis ready access to the words of The King, both those he uttered in his lifetime and those later revealed to his prophet, himself.

Even when the book, called *The Good News of Elvis*, was finished and had been handed over to Barker for printing, Garon Love still did not stop writing. By way of commentary, he wrote a companion-volume, going into even-greater detail.

When this second book was finished and published as *The Elvis Revelation*, Tim Barker organised a round of publicity. The first seeds of the religion had already taken root. More and more fans were asking questions about it. Soon the American media began to sense a story. Garon Love was invited on to local-radio shows to talk about his ideas. Often the DJs and shock-jocks put him on air simply to laugh at him but Elvis-fans listening felt drawn to the message. 'Repent, The Kingdom of Elvis is at hand.'

Barker issued a press-release saying that the Church of The Latter-Day Elvis had awarded Garon Love the title of 'Reverend Doctor'. And as the Reverend Doctor's public profile rose, so did the structure of the Church's cathedral.

Every month Barker reported back to Mr Carioli. On each occasion the routine was the same. He would present himself at the office and be escorted up the stairs. Mr Carioli always contrived to sit with a bright light behind him and although Barker could get an idea as to his size and general appearance, he could never get a clear impression of his face. Mr Carioli was not someone who wanted to be recognised by too many people and from Barker's perspective, as long as he stayed on the right side of his benefactor and employer, what did it matter what he looked like? Barker was just relieved that every time he went to see Mr Carioli to report on the project's progress, Mr Carioli expressed himself very satisfied and produced a new wad of notes from his desk drawer.

Work on the site went on twenty-four hours a day, seven-days a week. Floodlights were used at night so there would be no let-up in the activity.

All Mr Carioli's friends were eager to help. Barker could call on every specialist and skilled craftsman and woman he needed. Masons hammered; carpenters sawed; painters, plasterers, electricians and plumbers swarmed over the site. Some of America's finest artists were commissioned to provide paintings, sculptures, tapestries and stained-glass. A huge organ was built, by far the largest in the state, and twelve bells cast for the tower. The idea was that on the hour, every hour, they would chime the tune of an Elvis hit.

If neighbours complained of noise and disturbance, Barker visited them with a thick wad of $20-notes and two of Mr Carioli's larger friends. Few complained more than once.

The work in progress had to be inspected from time-to-time to ensure it was meeting safety regulations but generally red-tape was applied with a light hand. Was this city policy, or did Mr Carioli have friends in high-places? Barker did not ask too many questions. He became quite a specialist in city and state tax-breaks and any other financial-incentives for which he could apply to make Mr Carioli's money go further.

To help grow the congregation needed to fill the cathedral when it was finished, Barker instigated a recruiting-drive. He got the

Reverend Doctor to stand by the gates to Graceland to distribute leaflets and preach the word. To begin with, the Graceland-guides and security-guards viewed him with mild amusement. But as the days went by, and more and more fans became interested in what he was saying, the Graceland officials became irritated and tried to move him on. Eventually a compromise was reached and he was allowed to stand on the sidewalk, by the wall at the far-end, away from the gate. But he continued to attract attention. Some fans even came specially to hear him.

Every Saturday, an open-air service was held in front of the growing-cathedral. Barker recruited the best musicians in the state and devised an Order of Service and entertainment which he knew would draw the punters. He discovered he had quite a gift for showmanship.

Seven months before the opening of the cathedral, a Special Service was held to mark Elvis's birthday. It was a cold day in January and Barker raised a huge tent which he warmed with enormous, gas-fired blast-heaters. He hired the celebrated, Elvis tribute-singer, Tad Masaka, and a full-orchestra. The Reverend Doctor preached inspirationally. Barker's only mistake was to underestimate the crowd he would draw. The tent overflowed and his helpers were overwhelmed in their task of gathering as many names and addresses as possible for the Church's database of supporters. Barker had timed the start of the service carefully and hundreds of fans who been to the Graceland celebrations had had time to walk the short distance to the cathedral-site to enjoy a second Elvis-event. This one in the warm.

The service ended with the cutting of a gigantic, pink, Elvis birthday-cake in the shape of a Cadillac. Everyone went away with a piece packed in a special Church of The Latter-Day Elvis souvenir-box.

Later, when inputting the collected names into his computer-database, Barker noted that he had already exceeded the estimate of members he had written into his original business-plan. Reporting back to Mr Carioli at the beginning of February, he was able to make some very encouraging, new projections. Before long, new members were so numerous that a special office had to be built in the grounds of the cathedral and more land had to be bought for another car-park.

The office was equipped with the latest computer-technology to drive a ruthlessly-efficient marketing-programme. Members were sent regular, personalised mail-shots. Birthdays, anniversaries and other family events were recorded on the computer-database and letters, apparently signed by the Reverend Doctor himself, were sent on every special day.

'The perfect birthday-gift! Show your love for Elvis by buying an Elvis replica-scarf, personally blessed by me, your friend, Garon Love.'

'Did you know that your happy day coincides with a particularly-sad one for one of our most-devoted Elvis-fans? It's the anniversary of the day her beloved-husband went to be with Elvis in heaven after a hit-and-run accident. Now she is a widow, struggling to raise four children on welfare. Can you help with a donation?'

'So what there ain't no real widow?' Barker replied to the Reverend Doctor, when he queried the pitch. 'Elvis needs the money now. We'll give the money to widows and orphans later.'

As the summer arrived, Tim Barker was confident that the building would be ready for the great inauguration to be held in Elvis Week. By this time, the Reverend Doctor was a familiar figure in Elvis circles as a latter-day prophet. Barker encouraged him to keep his hair and beard long and to wear clothes to look the part. He was always dressed in black and usually in garb resembling that of a monk. Barker's idea was to project the image of the holy man of Elvis. The Reverend Doctor continued to hear the voice of Elvis and wrote down everything he heard which Barker published in a weekly newsletter for the growing band of loyal believers. And it was from this growing number of disciples that Barker recruited a team of volunteer-vergers to welcome visitors to the cathedral and show them around. To look after security-matters, he strengthened the team by recruiting a few of Mr Carioli's more-worldly believers.

The one thing the completed cathedral would lack, Barker realised, was a genuine Elvis-relic. He'd read that many of the great churches of Europe had been built to house the remains of saints. Elvis's cathedral should follow in that tradition. He had also discovered, in the course of his researches, that medieval saints were often dismembered after death and the body-parts distributed to churches raised in their honour. Notwithstanding all of Mr Carioli's influence, Barker realised there was no way he would persuade Graceland to exhume the body of The King and let him have a finger. He did discover, however, that there was a wart somewhere in the world that had been removed from Elvis and was still preserved. If nothing else was available, he decided, he would have that and put it on-show as the centre of attention and a focus for pilgrimage.

However, after eventually tracking it down, he found the owner initially reluctant to part with the most-prized item of his lifetime's collection, especially since it had become the centrepiece of several, successful travelling-exhibitions. 'It's on-tour around Europe just now', he remonstrated. 'I can't get it back that quickly.'

But a package of $100-bills, and a veiled threat that the whole of the rest of the collection looked somewhat 'flammable', proved very persuasive.

The wart arrived in a FedEx package, marked 'medical organic matter' for the purposes of customs-control, and was immediately moved to a beautifully-decorated, glass-fronted monstrance for display, surrounded by flowers and candles.

By now Tim Barker had dropped his title of 'Major' and become 'Archdeacon'. He had been ordained by the Reverend Doctor in a simple ceremony and had an illuminated Certificate of Ordination drawn-up to display in his office. The Reverend Doctor now likened himself to St Paul, the first Christian author. He referred to Barker as his Barnabas, his faithful companion, travelling with him on the spiritual road.

As Elvis Week approached, and with it Mr Carioli's eighteen-month deadline, Archdeacon Barker was satisfied that everything was in place. He had had a cathedral built which was the talk-of-the-town and which had become one of the wonders of the state of Tennessee. He had a prophet signed-up who was feeding the faithful with a regular diet of spiritual revelation. He had a large and growing list of followers who were eager to buy merchandise, put money in the collection-plate and pledge to tithe a tenth of their earnings to the Church. He had booked a top Elvis-act for the Opening Service and signed-up a choir and orchestra. Orders of Service were printed, vergers were ready and trained to guide visitors around the cathedral and sign them up as Church-members. The builders had cleared the site. The bills were paid. Nothing had been left to chance.

CHAPTER SIX

Priscilla's stay in hospital lasted less than twenty-four hours. She was quickly declared fit enough to go home. Elvis had been prodded and examined and declared 'a fine young thing' by the brisk and efficient midwife on-duty.

'What's he to be called?' she asked.

'Elvis', said Priscilla proudly.

'Lovely', said the midwife, before bustling out of the ward muttering, 'ridiculous, whatever next?' to herself.

Aaron had slipped home during the day to get the house ready and recharge the car-battery. He prepared the crib, changed the bed-linen, put on a wash and checked the nappies were ready for use in position next to the changing-mat in the bathroom. He chose a frozen-meal from the freezer and had it ready to cook. Finally, he found the bottle of champagne they had been keeping for the day and put it in the 'fridge to chill.

There can be no training and no adequate preparation for the responsibility of bringing home a newborn baby. First-time parents fret and worry at every stage. Aaron and Priscilla were no exception. Is he breathing properly? How much feeding does he need? Should we leave him to cry? Is he warm enough or too hot?

Language deteriorates too. It took millions of years for human communication to evolve into a sophisticated system of vocalisation to convey important information and subtle feelings. Within minutes of having a baby in the house it degenerates into a succession of 'coochy-coos' and 'who's got lovely toesie-woesies?'

Everything about adult-life after a birth is different from adult-life before. Time loses all sense of dimension. Domestic standards plummet. New smells pervade every living space, pleasant baby-smells and often unpleasant, nappy odours. But by-far the most overwhelming sensation felt by new parents with their first baby is exhaustion. No wonder, for what does a mother have to endure after nine-months carrying a child and the hard work of labour? Week-after-week of sleep-deprivation.

Elvis quickly found his own, demanding routine. He remained awake much of the day with only brief naps at regular, two-hourly intervals. At night, although he went to sleep without protest, he woke to demand parental attention or food in the same, regular pattern.

By early-August, as a gaunt Aaron sat across the breakfast-table from a haggard and utterly-weary Priscilla, neither could summon-up any enthusiasm for what, in previous years, had been the highlight of their annual calendar.

'We've got the tickets', said Aaron. 'We booked them at the special-rate, six-months ago.'

'Memphis will be so hot. And travelling with a baby, is it wise?'

'Shall we cancel it then?'

'We won't get our money back and we've paid for the hotel as well... '

'It's not as if we've never been to Graceland... '

'But we do always go... '

'Perhaps it's just what we need. A holiday. A break in the routine. And for baby Elvis, it'll be coming home.'

Perked-up by that last thought, Priscilla agreed. In all the upheaval and exhaustion of having a baby, she had never forgotten who the baby really was. She constantly looked for similarities between her Elvis and her King.

When his hair started to grow, she checked it was the right colour for Elvis. She watched-out for eye-colour and any giveaway-look in his face. She was convinced he would grow to be the spitting-image of The King.

Baby Elvis was barely six-weeks-old when he made his first trip to America. 'I can't believe how much extra luggage we have', said Aaron as he loaded the trolley at the airport. 'All this baby-kit. It's like moving an army.'

Everyone goes gooey at the sight of a new baby. 'Isn't he cute?' said the woman at the check-in. 'I could eat him up', said the girl running the security-check. 'What a gorgeous little bundle', said the flight-attendant. Fortunately, the flight was not delayed and Elvis enjoyed flying, at least, he fell asleep for most of the journey, giving his parents their longest stretch of uninterrupted sleep since his birth. They could scarcely believe so much had happened in a year. Just fifty-two weeks earlier, when they had taken the same flight across the Atlantic, the idea of making their own Elvis had been a ridiculous fantasy.

As they were driving to The Heartbreak Hotel, where they had a reservation for the next week, Priscilla started to take Elvis from his car-seat to hold him up to the window.

'You can't do that', said Aaron, who was driving their hire-car. 'What if I have to brake suddenly?'

'Oh - but I want him to see Memphis. I thought he might recognise some of the places we go past.'

'Don't be silly, he might have Elvis's DNA but he hasn't inherited Elvis's memory.'

'I know', said Priscilla. 'He's got a lot to learn.'

Priscilla was settling the baby back in his seat and didn't notice the billboard they drove past. It was an advertisement for The Church of The Latter-Day Elvis.

'Elvis is coming back', was its message.

The next morning, to start his education, they took baby Elvis on their early-morning walk to the Meditation Garden. Priscilla carried him in a papoose.

He had a large sunhat on his head and a good breakfast of mother's milk inside him.

A large, matronly woman walked alongside them.

'Mighty-fine little fellow', she said. 'What's his name?'

'Elvis.'

'Why, Praise the Lord', she exclaimed! And turning to her friend she added, 'did you hear that? He's called Elvis! Ain't that just so appropriate'?

Her friend turned to another. 'Did you hear that? This little baby's called Elvis.'

Soon the new Elvis had his own fan-club as a gaggle of Presleyites stood around Priscilla in admiration.

In due course, the fans dispersed to go about their own devotions and Priscilla stood in front of the place where four Presleys are said to lie. 'That's your grandma', she whispered to baby Elvis, pointing at the grave of Minnie Mae Presley. 'And there's your Ma and Pa', as she nodded towards the graves of Vernon and Gladys. 'Except of course, we're your Mummy and Daddy for now.'

'And that's you', Priscilla then whispered, looking at the inscription *Elvis Aron Presley.* 'Well sort of.' She suddenly felt rather self-conscious and hoped no-one had overheard her.

'I think he likes it here', she said to Aaron. 'Do you think he finds it, sort-of, familiar?'

Aaron smiled and nodded indulgently, then gently rolled his eyes heavenwards.

'When do you think we should tell him who he really is?' Priscilla asked on their way back to the Graceland gate. 'It'll be a bit like telling him he's adopted. They say a child should grow-up knowing.'

'Oh, we'll cross that bridge when we get to it', replied Aaron. 'Maybe he'll never need to know. After all, we're his parents on the birth-certificate. It will be our secret.'

'But won't he realise something one day? He'll look like Elvis won't he?'

'Perhaps not-exactly. But no need to worry about it now.'

But the worry persisted in Priscilla's mind. How was she to explain all this to her baby in years to come when he started asking questions? Aaron however, had closed his mind to the problem. Everything would sort itself out in due course, wouldn't it?

Later that afternoon, to pass the time before the evening's candlelit vigil, the family wandered along Elvis Presley Boulevard.

They could not fail to notice the astonishing, new building that had arisen on one of the empty lots since their last visit. 'Welcome to The Cathedral of The Latter-Day Elvis', announced a huge sign.

Aaron and Priscilla stood and gawped in amazement. It was a truly-huge and lavish structure, set-back from the main road beyond a luscious, green lawn on which a water-sprinkler was creating rainbows in the sunlight. There was stained-glass, marble, and glittering gold in profusion. The front of the cathedral was columned with a flight of seven steps leading-up to a pair of copper doors, twenty-feet high, decorated with a relief-sculpture of a kneeling Jesus paying homage to Elvis. On the roof, surmounting the magnificent dome, there was a statue of Elvis, a golden copy of the one which fans seek out in The Holy Land, not far from Jerusalem.

Aaron and Priscilla and the sleeping-baby in the papoose ventured towards the building. They noticed a smaller entrance to the left of the big, copper doors and walked-up the steps towards it.

A notice on these smaller doors invited visitors to 'Enter this sacred-space, dedicated to the name and glory of Elvis, The Messiah'. They pushed the doors and went in. They were instantly overwhelmed by what they saw and heard.

First of all the immense size struck them. It was as big as any cathedral they could recall. At the farthest-end, above a high altar with an altar-cloth on which the words ELVIS LIVES were embroidered, was a magnificent work-of-art, a great, colourful tapestry soaring at least one-hundred feet. It depicted Elvis-in-triumph, blessing the world. To the right was a huge bank of candles. Some people were standing silently in-front of them. Others were bending-forward to light new candles from the old. The murmuring sound of prayers mingled with the gentle sound-track of a recording of Elvis singing *Love me Tender*. The high ceiling was painted a dark, deep blue and speckled with stars to resemble the night-sky, as if in a planetarium. All the stars revolved slowly around the Blue Star of Orion which Elvis himself had once said was his true home.

The windows to left and right were of coloured glass. All were picture-windows and each one, Aaron and Priscilla soon realised, told the story of an Elvis song. The *Hawaii* window was the first they noticed, next to the one dedicated to *The Blue Suede Shoes*. Then, beneath the windows they noticed a series of side-chapels. The first they spotted was the one dedicated to *Suspicious Minds*. 'Pray here', said a sign, 'to rid yourself of envy and jealousy'. Beside another, a sign asked, 'Are you feeling down and depressed? Come and cry in the chapel'.

The whole building was pervaded by a warm smell of candles and incense. It was full of visitors wandering slowly and appearing suitably-astonished by what they saw. Unlike a Christian cathedral, rising from a cruciform ground-plan with a nave, transepts and choir, the Elvis Cathedral was built on a guitar-shaped floor-plan. The entrance led into a circular-area connected by a short-but-wide nave to a second circular-area, above which rose the magnificent dome, and around which, one-hundred-feet above the ground, ran a gallery, rather-like the Whispering Gallery at St Paul's in London. The whole design of the cathedral had borrowed freely from famous, European, religious buildings. The idea for the Elvis-in-triumph tapestry, at the end of the long choir-cum-sanctuary which stretched off the second circular-area, clearly came from Coventry Cathedral in England. The bank of candles which Aaron and Priscilla had noticed on entering, was inspired by the basilica of St Thérèse-of-Lisieux in France. There, behind the candles, was a relic on display in a glass-fronted, jewel-encrusted case. Not a withered-arm, as is the case with St Thérèse, instead a small phial containing the Elvis wart.

'Look! Priscilla, look!' Aaron exclaimed excitedly as they approached. 'It's the wart. They've got the wart.'

'We certainly have', came a voice from behind them. They turned and immediately recognised Major Barker. He was dressed in a purple cassock with a lightening-bolt badge on which was printed his name, 'Tim Barker'. But instead of the prefix 'Major', he now had a new title, 'Archdeacon'. He didn't appear to recognise them. Since they had last met twelve months ago, he had not only encountered thousands of other Elvis-fans but had also been responsible for the intense building-programme that had ensured the cathedral rose from nothing in just eleven-months and thirteen-days. It was hardly surprising that he didn't recognise these two, not-apparently-special, British visitors.

'It's the only-known, surviving, bodily relic of The King', he told them. 'It had been in a touring, Elvis exhibition but was kindly gifted to our ministry by the owner. A beautiful and generous gesture for which the heavenly rewards will be great.'

'What an amazing place', responded Priscilla, looking around.

'All in Elvis's honour - Alleluia.'

Archdeacon Barker handed Aaron a leaflet. 'Do come tomorrow', he said. 'It's our Official Opening. The Reverend Doctor will be preaching. Our choir will be singing. It'll be the greatest, holy show in Memphis.'

'Thank you, we'll try and be there.'

'And have you had your little baby Elvised?'

'I beg your pardon?' asked Aaron hesitatingly, not quite sure if he had heard the Archdeacon correctly.

'Elvised. We can arrange an Elvising for your baby.'

Aaron's uncomprehending face prompted the Archdeacon to further explanation.

'You'll have heard of a Christening? An Elvising is a bit like that - but we dedicate new babies to the service of Elvis.'

Priscilla and Aaron looked briefly at each other before Priscilla found the words. 'Yes, we'd love to do that.'

'Tomorrow then, after the service. Find me in the Teddy Bear Chapel and I'll see if the Reverend Doctor himself will do the honours. If I recognise your accents, I think you must be British and you'll be our first Elvising from England... Oh - boy or girl?'

'Boy. He's called Elvis.'

'He must be very special.'

'He is.'

The new Elvis Cathedral was the talk of all the fans as they gathered outside Graceland for the annual, candle-lit procession. Aaron and Priscilla listened to the snippets of gossip and conversation around them.

'Who paid for it? That's what I want to know?' came one voice.

'I think it's the Scientologists', said another.

'No it's a secretive billionaire.'

'It's the Illuminati, the secret controllers of the world.'

'It's not real of course. The marble's all painted on, like a film-set.'

'Don't believe it. I saw them back in January bringing in huge slabs of real marble on trucks.'

'Are you going to the service tomorrow? I am. They say that Tad Masaka will be there.'

Aaron and Priscilla immediately recognised the name. Tad was a well-known and highly-regarded Elvis tribute-artist. *The next best to the real thing* was his slogan. Fans swore they could close their eyes during a performance and imagine they were listening to the real Elvis Presley. Those who kept their eyes open said he mimicked the moves and swivels of Elvis to perfection.

'We'll have to go', said Priscilla, 'and get Elvis Elvised'.

Aaron and Priscilla arrived twenty-minutes ahead of time for the scheduled service to find the cathedral bursting to the seams. Whether drawn to worship, or simply out of curiosity, hundreds of the fans who had gathered the night before at Graceland were now there. The organ was playing a medley of Elvis hits. Aaron, Priscilla and baby Elvis were shown to two seats in the central-nave between the two circular-areas of the guitar floor-plan.

They looked at the Order of Service they had been given by a verger in a sequined jumpsuit. There was to be music from *The Elvis Rainbow Gospel Choir* and a musical tribute from Tad Masaka. There was promised a Gospel reading from *The Good News of Elvis* and an act-of-communion during which members of the congregation would be invited to come forward to receive scarves. There was also to be something described as 'an exposition of, and devotion to, the sacred, relic-of-Elvis', as well as the inaugural-sermon to be preached by the Archbishop, The Most Reverend Doctor Garon Love.

No Elvis-fan would have been disappointed. The service lasted almost two hours and everyone stayed to the end. Baby Elvis sometimes slept but mostly seemed transfixed by every sound, smell and sight. He only cried once.

The splendour, the choreography, the sheer showmanship of the occasion could not have been matched by The King himself. The one-hundred-strong *Elvis Rainbow Gospel Choir* opened the service by singing *How great thou art*.

Tad Masaka's *American Trilogy* was the ultimate show-stopper. As he sang, he was to Aaron and Priscilla just a tiny speck in the distance but his voice filled the building and he was shown in close-up on giant screens. The screens had been erected specially for the occasion in key positions around the cathedral so that no-one could miss a single detail of the worship in colour and close-up.

Tears were streaming down Priscilla's face as she heard the words.

So hush little baby
Don't you cry.
You know your daddy's bound to die.
But all my trials, Lord, will soon be over.

She was not quite sure what emotion had overtaken her. She recalled the comfortable feelings from her childhood when her favourite grandmother, now long dead, had taken her to Mass. She looked at little Elvis and wondered what sort of life he would have. What trials would he suffer and endure? But before she could let her mind imagine the worst, the mood of the song changed. Tad was joined by *The Elvis Rainbow Gospel Choir*. The organ thundered. Trumpeters in a distant balcony lifted the words of the *Glory, glory Alleluia* to heaven and Priscilla was certain that she was truly in the presence of Elvis The King.

Archdeacon Barker, wearing gold and scarlet vestments, read a passage from *The Good News of Elvis*.

'In the beginning was Elvis and Elvis was the Word and Elvis was with God. He was born into a house little bigger than a stable and at the moment of his birth, a shining blue light from the heavens shone over the place where the tiny child lay... '

The reading finished with the words, 'and he died in ignominy betrayed by his friends. But for us and all true followers and disciples of Elvis he never died. He lives for ever and will return.'

'Give me an E', Archdeacon Barker shouted, punching the air with the fist of his right hand.

'E', shouted back the congregation.

'Give me an L.'

'L', came the response.

'Give me a V.'

'V', Aaron, Priscilla and a thousand voices shouted back.

'Give me an I.'

'I', came the return shout, even louder than before.

'Give me a S.'

'S', the congregation erupted with sound.

'Who's going to live for ever?'

'Elvis, Elvis, Elvis, Elvis, Elvis, Elvis, Elvis, Elvis, Elvis, Elvis... ' Such was the noise that Priscilla cradled her baby tightly, covering his ears with her hands. And only when Archdeacon Barker thought he had the congregation roused to a state they could not exceed, did he give the signal for the collection to be taken.

As *The Elvis Rainbow Gospel Choir* swayed to the sound of *All Shook Up*, the vergers moved through the cathedral with huge plates. 'Give for Elvis', implored the Archdeacon. 'The more you give, the greater your reward in heaven. The more you give, the more lavish will be our welcome for The King when he returns. The more you give, the more we can give to the charities Elvis loved. You want a new car? A new home? Money for medical bills? Give to Elvis now and you will be rewarded a hundred-fold.'

In contrast to the finery worn by the Archdeacon, the choir, the subdeacons, priests and acolytes, Archbishop Garon Love wore his usual simple, monastic habit. He had long, white hair and a flowing, white beard in the style of a Hollywood, Old Testament prophet.

His address was given without notes, standing in front of the Elvis high-altar. Again, Priscilla and Aaron would have only had the briefest of distant glances of him if he had not also been shown in close-up on the giant screens. He spoke about the theology of the incarnation and both Priscilla and Aaron were rather lost by his apparent erudition.

The doctrine of the incarnation, he claimed, was central to Christian belief and had been so for almost two-thousand years. Christians had come to believe that Jesus was God and that God had chosen to come to earth in the form of a human being to live alongside those he had created in his own image in order to suffer with them and ultimately offer forgiveness for their sins through his own sacrificial death.

'But the Christian doctrine was based not on history but prophesy', the white-haired Archbishop declared. 'The life of Jesus, as told in its familiar Gospel form, had a divine purpose. That purpose was, and is, to prepare later generations, including all of us here today, for the true coming-to-earth of God in human form. I speak of Elvis.'

A ripple of *Alleluias* washed through the congregation like a Mexican-wave of sound, followed by cries of *Praise the Lord* and *Praise to Elvis*.

'But who was Elvis? And who is Elvis?' the Archbishop demanded with a rhetorical flourish. 'Was he the Son of God like Jesus? Was he an alien as many have suggested - whose destiny was to come to our planet to share the wisdom of a higher civilisation?

'I am telling you today - he is both an enlightened alien from space and the Son of God. He is both the reincarnation of the Biblical Adam and Jesus and an immortal, wise person. See the hundreds of clues Elvis left behind to help us discover the truth! Read Elvis's life-story in The Holy Bible! Find out how the Great Pyramid in Egypt is a monument to Elvis! Did not the Mayans and Aztecs believe in the great, white God-who-was-to-come? And the Druids of ancient Britain, were they too not awaiting Elvis? He was to land in glory in Wales at a place which today carries the name of holy Elvis, or Saint Elvis. Read how the great seers Nostradamus and Edgar Cayce prophesied Elvis's appearance and disappearance! Discover how astronomy, astrology, numerology, scripture and ancient folklore all foretell Elvis's coming into the world at this late hour of human history!

'And these are not just my words. Others have seen the light. I have quoted one, Cinda Godfrey, and there are many others in this present day who have seen the Elvis light.

'Did you know that in 1958, an eleven-year-old girl from Michigan was visited by an archangel and given an astounding prophecy about Elvis Presley? A prophecy that finally makes sense of the Secret of the Seventh Seal of the Book of Revelation. Read! Study! Learn for yourselves! Open your minds to the gift of truth. When you understand all the facts you will see heavenly correlations not diabolic coincidences and realise that the odds of Elvis Presley being anyone but The Messiah are mathematically impossible!

'Elvis gives us all the clues', reiterated the Archbishop, 'especially in *The American Trilogy*. Like Jesus as recounted in the ancient Gospel stories and recalled in the Catholic Mass, Elvis tells us he is of this earth and of this place. Incarnated. He is rooted in the land of cotton. Like the Jesus of the Bible stories, he knew his destiny was to die. *Hush little baby... you know your Daddy's bound to die.* But it ends in glory, triumph and resurrection. *Glory, Glory, Alleluia.* Elvis is risen and will come again'.

'I don't know exactly what I make of all this', said Priscilla, 'but I think there's something in it'.

'Load-of-nonsense', replied Aaron and would have dismissed the old prophet as a complete nutcase except for his final words.

'I say to you today, on this important day when we inaugurate a house for Elvis's glorious return, that Elvis is alive! He is on this earth again in human form. I don't know where he is or when he will reveal himself. It might be tomorrow, or he might still be just a little baby in his mother's arms unaware of his great calling and vocation. But that Elvis has returned as The Matraya for our age, I am utterly convinced.'

The congregation fell silent. The fans who had come to the cathedral out of loyalty for their dead hero were stunned. Many were disbelieving, others nurtured a sneaking hope that the preacher might be right. The world needed Elvis.

The silence was broken by a loud baby's cry that echoed around the building. Baby Elvis had woken-up and wanted some food.

At the end of the service, as the congregation dispersed, Aaron, Priscilla and Elvis moved through the crowds towards the Teddy Bear Chapel. It was a perfect octagon in shape and in seven of the eight walls were picture-windows showing worlds populated by cuddly-toys. One window was of a New York street-scene. The cops were bears and so were the taxi drivers. A panda was selling newspapers called *The New Bear Times*. There was a shop selling honey and another advertising *The Bear Essentials - all you need for your picnic*.

The next window illustrated a woodland scene, a clearing where a large blanket had been laid-out for a picnic. There were plates and sandwiches and cakes and cups of juice and lots of excited bears all-around. A third-window depicted a snow-scene with bears loading presents onto Santa's sleigh. The fourth portrayed the jungle. The bears were joined by cuddly monkeys and colourful parrots, Dumbo-elephants and a large but friendly-looking lion. The fifth window showed a party of teddy bears enjoying a fun-fair. The sixth was a picture of Noah's Ark, with Noah and all his family represented by teddies. And the seventh-window showed dozens of bears in a toy-shop, boy-bears dressed in blue playing with train-sets and girl-bears in pink playing with dolls.

On the eighth-wall there was no window, just an impressive, baroque-style altar, lavishly decorated with golden carvings of bears posing as cherubs. Each bear had a tiny pair of wings on his back and was blowing a trumpet. In the centre of this tableau stood a golden Elvis, carrying a bear.

Around the walls of the chapel there were seats and in the centre was a font set upon the shoulders of four Winnie-the-Pooh bears.

Aaron and Priscilla had had plenty of time to look at all this while waiting since it was at least thirty-minutes before the Archdeacon arrived.

'So glad you are still here', he said without apology but smiling broadly. 'My, what a service. Didn't you just feel so uplifted by Elvis?'

'It was wonderful', answered Priscilla.

'Now, the Reverend Doctor will be along in just a minute. He is so keen to meet visitors from England.' And still smiling, he added, 'and can I have your credit-card now please? We have to charge a small fee to cover costs and any profits go to one of Elvis's favourite charities'.

Aaron had not been expecting to pay for the Elvising ceremony. 'How much?' he spluttered.

'To give and not-to-count the cost was what Elvis used to say', responded Barker. 'Usually we charge five-hundred dollars but because you're our first couple from England, we'll say three-hundred this time.'

There was no way-out. A small crowd had gathered around them. To have backed-out at that stage would have been very embarrassing. Most English people do not like to make a scene. Aaron handed over his card and Barker inserted it into a slot in the side of the font. After a few seconds, a slip of paper emerged from another slot. Aaron signed his name where shown.

'This will be the most important day of your child's life', intoned the Archdeacon. 'Today he becomes a member of the great Elvis family. He will have a certificate signed by the Reverend Doctor himself. Glory be!'

A moment later the Reverend Doctor arrived. He was dressed in a monk's habit as before but now had a priest's stole around his neck. 'I am delighted to meet you', he said gently, 'and to welcome your child into the world in the name of Elvis'.

He indicated that they stand around the font and gestured to the on-lookers to gather round them. The Archdeacon gave Aaron and Priscilla a printed Order of Service.

'We are gathered together today in the name of Elvis. Like Vernon and Gladys before them, the parents of this new child come to give thanks for their precious gift and to declare before you and this gathered congregation the name by which this child shall be known.'

On cue, Aaron and Priscilla declared together, 'he shall be called Elvis'.

A round of applause broke out. There were by now at least one-hundred people standing in the Chapel. 'Glory be!' some said. 'Alleluia', shouted one woman.

The Reverend Doctor prayed for peace and prosperity for young Elvis before taking him in his arms. He dipped his hand into the water in the font and made the sign of a lightening-bolt on the baby's head.

'I name you Elvis in honour of Elvis, The King.'

There was more applause. Baby Elvis chuckled. He seemed to be thoroughly enjoying himself at the centre of attention. He took a handful of the Reverend Doctor's beard and stuffed it in his mouth.

'Lord, now let this baby grow in peace', the Reverend Doctor prayed. 'May he live to see your word fulfilled, and see the light to lighten all the nations of the world when your servant Elvis returns.'

As Aaron walked out of the cathedral he was not in a good mood. 'If I'd known we had to pay... huh... what a waste of money', he said angrily to Priscilla. 'It only lasted ten minutes. We should have checked first before agreeing. It's not that we can throw three-hundred dollars away.'

In truth, it had not occurred to either of them in advance that they would have to pay for the Elvising ceremony. And three-hundred dollars was daylight robbery! Aaron said nothing more but vowed never-again to return to the Cathedral of The Latter-Day Elvis.

Priscilla was less-concerned than her husband about the money. The Elvising of her child was for her the culmination of a greater experience. Perhaps her Elvis was destined for great things?

CHAPTER SEVEN

As Elvis grew from baby to toddler, schoolboy to teenager, he was both a source of pride and disappointment to his parents.

In physical appearance he was undoubtedly a Presley reborn. Priscilla could tell that from the photographs of the original Elvis as a child. The big, dark eyes, the smooth skin, the chubby cheeks and sleek, dark hair, they were all shared by her own son. As his voice lowered from boy-treble to that of a young man, the tone and the pitch was that of Elvis. Admittedly, this Elvis spoke with an English accent but when he mimicked the sounds he heard on his mother's CDs, he adopted a southern drawl and he became The King.

When Aaron and Priscilla first took her Elvis to a meeting of the *We Love Elvis Fan Club* he was dressed for the occasion in dungarees and a large hat just as the original Elvis appeared in one of his childhood photographs. He won that month's Elvis-lookalike competition hands-down and drew so many admiring comments that Priscilla almost gurgled with pride.

'But he looks so like Elvis he could almost be a clone', one fan-club member said unwittingly.

Priscilla felt her face turning red with embarrassment as she was unexpectedly reminded of the extraordinary and unusual circumstances of her son's conception. With all the responsibility and work involved in parenthood and their life generally, there had been little time for such reflection. Neither she nor Aaron had ever mentioned anything to their only child about his origins and Priscilla was rather hoping they might never have to. To be reminded by a casual remark took her by surprise. Surely no-one suspected, she thought anxiously. She told Aaron about the remark later when Elvis was in bed.

'Do you think she suspected?'

'Impossible. How could anyone have any inkling?' he reassured her.

Despite the undeniable resemblance between their son and the original Elvis, Aaron and Priscilla had reason for some disappointment. As the boy grew older and more independent, he increasingly refused to behave like Elvis.

He had always hated the taste of peanut-butter. When Priscilla had first given him some to taste he spat it out in disgust, much to her horror. But as a young teenager, he developed a dress sense far removed from that of The King. He preferred to keep his hair long and made every attempt to adopt the Gothic look. And while as a young child he learned every Elvis song at his mother's knee, by his thirteenth birthday his bedroom pounded with the sound of heavy-metal.

His was a classic rebellion. Like the son of a preacher who declares himself an atheist, or the child of an English teacher who swears never to open a book, for several years in his early teens Elvis was a revolting child. He was in open revolt against everything held dear by his parents. He argued and challenged and disobeyed and refused.

Where once he had happily raised and clapped his hands as the fan-club members danced to the Elvis number *Let Us Pray*, as he approached his teens, he refused to go near the club and its 'sad f***ing wrinklies'. How could her Elvis be so unkind to her Priscilla wondered, when the great Elvis himself had loved his mother so dearly?

At secondary-school, teenage Elvis hated sports and music with an intense loathing. He had once been a promising-guitar player but once a teenager, he had stopped going to lessons and sold the guitar. His mind focussed on just two interests, computers and the mock-medieval, parallel universe he could inhabit via the internet. At home, he spent hours on his computer playing on-line games in fantasy worlds of dragons, gremlins and trolls.

He had first become interested in this nether-world after a visit to the hairdresser. Larry, as he was known by all his customers, specialised in the Goth look, especially black dyes, black eye-makeup and chalk-white faces for his female clientèle. He also offered unisex tattoos and body-piercing. Larry's salon was full of pictures of vampires, zombies and bats and the reading-matter was not *Hello!* and *Cosmopolitan* but magazines dedicated to the occult and the dark-sciences of fantasy-games.

When Elvis had been one-year-old, Aaron and Priscilla decided to give their annual trip to Graceland a miss. It was a financial decision as much as anything. Priscilla, as a new mother, was no-longer working full-time at the hospital and with all the additional expense of looking after the baby, finding the extra cash for a holiday in the USA was not easy.

Instead they organised a holiday in Britain. They borrowed a friend's caravan and drove north to Scotland. They visited Edinburgh and Loch Lomond, Glencoe and St Andrews, Culloden and Skye. They looked in vain for The Loch Ness Monster and went on a tour of a distillery. The highlight was their detour to Prestwick airport where they saw the site of Elvis's one-and-only visit to Britain. He had stopped-off briefly at Prestwick when flying with American troops between Germany and America.

Priscilla took a photo of Aaron holding baby Elvis by the hands as he stood tottering on the very spot where the first Elvis had once stood.

By the time Elvis was six-years-old, Aaron and Priscilla could once again afford a holiday in Memphis. With Elvis at school, Priscilla was able to work regularly, part-time, to supplement the family income. A picture of young Elvis was taken for the family-album. He was dressed in a jumpsuit, with his dark hair quaffed and sleeked back, posing by the Graceland Gates.

They walked past the Cathedral of The Latter-Day Elvis and noticed streams of people going in and out. 'They'll be minting it', said Aaron as he watched. 'It's just a money-grabbing fraud.'

Priscilla told Elvis how, when he was a baby, they had all been to a service at the Cathedral and had met the Church's leaders. But now, she explained, it was too expensive to even look inside. Just to enter, visitors were charged five-dollars each.

When Elvis was twelve, shortly before his rebellious nature came fully to-the-fore, he had still been content to accompany his parents to Elvis gatherings and visit Graceland every year. Aaron had used his new digital-camera to take a photograph of Elvis writing a message on the long wall outside Graceland. *To Elvis - Hi from Elvis from England* he wrote in a bold-hand with a black, felt-tipped pen.

Despite booking months ahead, they had been unable to get a family-room at The Heartbreak Hotel so, on that occasion, they were staying at the In-the-Ghetto Hotel, half-a-mile away from Graceland itself.

Late one afternoon, Aaron and Priscilla were sitting under a parasol at a table by the pool. Aaron was dozing and Priscilla reading a five-day-old copy of *The Mail on Sunday* given to her by another guest who had only recently-arrived from England.

She was engrossed in an article about Lisa Marie when she suddenly thought, 'where's Elvis?' He had been in the chair next to them earlier but now she couldn't see him anywhere.

'Aaron', she demanded. 'Have you seen Elvis?'

'I wasn't asleep', he protested sharply as he woke-up. He looked around. 'No idea. I know he was here earlier. He'll be OK.'

'No, we've got to find him', Priscilla insisted. 'Go and look.'

Aaron reluctantly heaved himself out of his chair and headed for the hotel. He took the elevator to the fifth-floor and went to their family-suite. He opened it with the key-card and expected to find Elvis inside lying on the bed, watching a movie on television. But there was no sign of him. He went through the connecting-door to Elvis's bedroom. It was empty too. 'Are you in the bathroom?' Aaron called out. There was no reply.

He walked back along the corridor and went to the hotel games-room. There was a dance-machine there and a racetrack-simulator. Both were in use but there was no sign of Elvis. He went to the internet-room. Perhaps Elvis was emailing a friend back home? But again, there was no sign of the boy.

Aaron returned to the pool and reported. 'He's not in the room and I've had a good look around in the lobby and games-room.'

Priscilla put her newspaper down. She was anxious. 'He must be somewhere. I'll look inside again and you walk round the grounds. See you at reception in ten-minutes.'

When they next met, Priscilla had become very worried. She quizzed the receptionist. Had she seen a twelve-year-old boy answering to the name of Elvis?

'They all answer to the name of Elvis round here', she replied unhelpfully.

'But he's a very special Elvis... ' Priscilla started to explain.

'To you maybe', the receptionist came back, 'but to me, he's just another lost kid who'll turn-up again'.

'Thanks for nothing', snapped back Priscilla and stormed-out to the pool again.

'Elvis', she called. 'Elvis, Elvis. Where are you?'

She got some strange looks from her fellow-guests.

'He won't hear you', said one wag. 'He's up at Graceland, six-foot-under.'

'I'm looking for our son, Elvis. He's just twelve and he's gone missing.'

'Oh... I saw a kid about twelve, some half-an-hour ago', responded the man helpfully. 'He wandered-off in that direction', he continued, nodding towards the next-door hotel. 'Where the music's coming from.'

Priscilla and Aaron half-ran and half-walked towards the sound of Elvis-music. As they came though the lobby of the hotel, *Jail House Rock* hit them between-the-ears. There was a karaoke-bar and there in the bar, strutting-his-stuff and swivelling his pelvis, was their son.

For the first time, they realised there was something different about young Elvis's voice. It had matured from treble to the exact sound of Elvis Presley. His voice had broken, or rather metamorphosed into a replica of the most-famous voice in history. It had happened so unobtrusively that his parents had not noticed the important but subtle transition. When the music finished, the room exploded into wild applause.

'That kid's got it', marvelled a large woman in a vast, pink smock adorned with a picture of Elvis. 'He's going to be the greatest tribute-artist there's ever been. My! What talent! And don't he look like Elvis?' Her friend agreed.

As Elvis left the stage, women hugged him and men shook him by the hand. 'Wow, what a performance!'

Suddenly his eyes met those of his mother. Young Elvis immediately realised she was not best-pleased. 'We've been looking for you everywhere. Hunting high-and-low. We've been frantic with worry.'

'Is this your kid?' said the woman-in-pink. 'Don't get so cross. With a voice like that, don't you know he's got to be going about Elvis business?'

Priscilla relaxed. 'Next time, just tell us where you're going', was all she said, enormously relieved to have found him.

'They want an encore', said the woman-in -pink.

'I'll sing this one just for you, Mum', said Elvis. He took the stage, the lights dimmed and he sang *Amazing Grace* with such feeling that a number of people in the audience, including the woman-in-pink, began sobbing uncontrollably.

The next day, when the family was taking a walk along Elvis Presley Boulevard, they noticed that outside the Cathedral of

The Latter-Day Elvis there was a new sign. 'Worship Elvis today - Here at 10.30am - Entrance Free.'

It was Barker's latest marketing-ploy. If, once in a while, he let the punters in free of charge he could fleece them for even more than the entrance-fee once they were inside.

It was twenty-past-ten, and a steady stream of worshippers was proceeding up the steps.

'It's free today', said Elvis. 'Can I have a look inside?'

'There'll be nothing free about that place', said his father with feeling. 'It's just one, big, cash-making con.'

'But let me just have a look inside', Elvis pleaded.

'Well, OK', relented Aaron, 'but just for a few minutes'.

The cathedral was every bit as opulent and lavish as Aaron and Priscilla had remembered.

'Wow!' said Elvis as he looked around, gobsmacked. 'Cool or what?'

They were ushered to seats and before they realised what was happening, a service had started and they were blocked-in by late arrivals.

The smell of candles and incense was as strong as ever they recalled. They saw again the blazing colours of the windows as the sun shone through the stained-glass on the south-side. The vergers had seated the family on the north-side of the cathedral, in the centre where the nave narrowed. They were close-by a new addition to the building, a recess resembling the lady-chapel of a medieval church. It was dedicated not to Elvis but to Princess Diana. A single candle burned on the altar and its flame flickered in the light breeze caused by a hidden electric-fan. On the wall by the entrance, a plaque simply read '*The Candle in the Wind* Chapel dedicated to the memory of a Holy Lady.'

The service lasted over an hour. *The Elvis Rainbow Gospel Choir* sang and Archdeacon Barker read from *The Good News of Elvis*. Then, just as Aaron and Priscilla remembered from their first visit, he whipped the congregation into a frenzy with his shouts of, 'give me an E, give me an L, a V, an I and an S. Who's going to live for ever?'

'Elvis, Elvis, Elvis, Elvis... '

When the collection-plate reached them, Aaron deliberately refused to give anything. 'Gave them enough first-time', he muttered. The verger holding the plate scowled disapprovingly but could do nothing.

The Reverend Doctor preached and against her better-judgement, Priscilla found him mesmerising.

He told the story of the young Jesus. Of how his parents had lost him on a visit to Jerusalem. 'They searched everywhere. As time went by his mother got more and more worried. Then she found her son arguing and debating with the scholars. They were amazed at the boy's talent and learning. "Where've you been", Mary scolded. "Didn't you know that I have to be about my father's business?" responded Jesus.

'The Bible', continued the Reverend Doctor, returning to his favourite theme, 'is prophecy. It foretells the return of Elvis. And Elvis has returned. I am certain of that. Fact. I don't know when he will be revealed but surely in my lifetime. I am an old man and cannot live many more years. You will see Elvis returned in glory. Today, like Jesus, he too may be a young man who will go missing. His parents will hunt for him. When they find him, he will rebuke them with the same words'.

Priscilla recalled the events of the previous day and a shiver went down her spine.

'That's uncanny', she said to Aaron.

'What is?' asked Elvis, overhearing.

'Oh nothing, nothing', she replied quickly. But he could see in her eyes that something the preacher had said had shaken her to the core.

Two months later, the pubescent hormones which had tuned Elvis's voice to perfection were on the rampage. Priscilla and Aaron were quite unprepared for the ferociousness of the ensuing rebellion. He became moody, sulky, argumentative, objectionable and decidedly un-Christ-like (or un-Elvis-like), in his behaviour. His teachers found him difficult and his parents found him impossible. To communicate with any figure of adult authority, he developed a code of stroppy-sounding grunts. As for singing like Elvis? Forget it.

For five, stressful years, life at *Tupelo* was domestic hell. Teenage Elvis spent hours on his computer with his on-line, role-play games. He seldom washed, never tidied his bedroom, stayed-up most of the night and slept much of the day when he did not have to go to school or college. When he went out with his friends, his choice of dress and hair style got weirder and weirder.

Priscilla blamed Larry the hairdresser. 'He's encouraging him to believe such nonsense', she complained to Aaron.

She was thoroughly shocked one Saturday when he came home with his head shaved and a stud in his tongue. He always wore black and liked macabre jewellery. He had an iron ring on the third-finger of his right-hand adorned with a miniature, human skull. He often put a pentacle-pendant around his neck. He had long grown out of his *My Parents went to Memphis and all they got me was this lousy T-shirt* T-shirt and it had been replaced by a shredded, black number emblazoned with the slogan *Son of Satan*. He was the devil's own teenager. Priscilla, who had imaged that her son would dote on her with almost Oedipus-like devotion, as Elvis had on his mother Gladys, felt deeply hurt.

For five, long, testing years Aaron's life was non-stop, shuttle-diplomacy between his wife and his son.

'Your mother says will you be in for supper?'

'Ugh!'

'Your mother wants to know what time you'll be back tonight and should she leave the front-door off the latch?'

'S'pose.'

'Your mother says can she have your clothes to wash tonight.'

'Whatever.'

Many times Priscilla cried herself to sleep at night, moaning, 'we should never have done it. He's a monster. We've created a Frankenstein monster'.

'He'll get over it', Aaron reassured her but not-quite certain whether he believed what he was saying himself. 'You'll see. He'll grow up. It's only a passing phase. It's just his age.'

And quite suddenly, on Mother's Day when Elvis was seventeen-and-three-quarters, everything changed.

He had recently quit college and Aaron and Priscilla were in complete despair. He was about to become a legal adult and he had no prospects, no qualifications and no income. The night before Mother's Day, Priscilla had sobbed herself to sleep with worry.

But that Sunday morning she was woken by a knock at the bedroom door and it was Elvis carrying a tray.

'Happy Mother's Day', he announced cheerfully. 'I've brought you breakfast-in-bed. Tea, orange juice, croissants and honey.'

He was wearing the smart shirt Priscilla had given him for Christmas, for which he had previously given no thanks and which, until that moment, so far as she knew he had never unpacked.

Elvis laid the tray on her lap as she sat up and gave her a kiss on the forehead.

'Enjoy!'

Priscilla and Aaron felt as if they had burst into the sunlight from a dark, interminable tunnel.

By Elvis's eighteenth-birthday he was a totally-transformed character. The morose, unkempt Goth had become a well-spoken, witty, pleasant and devastatingly-handsome young-man.

His hair was kept long but clean and he sported a neat, black beard. With earnings from his new job at a local supermarket, and his evening work as a barman, he contributed weekly to the housekeeping and still had money spare to buy new clothes. His astonishing resemblance to the original Elvis was not apparent to anyone other than Aaron and Priscilla since his choice of fashionable, twenty-first century clothes was nothing-like the fifties and sixties style the first Elvis had popularised. He took up cycling, running and healthy eating.

On his eighteenth-birthday, Elvis announced that he wanted to see the world. He had it all planned-out. He had the money to fly to America and enough to let him cross the continent by Greyhound bus, staying at youth-hostels on the way. He would then fly to Australia and get himself a job to earn the cash to return home via India, Egypt and mainland-Europe. 'I want to see The Grand Canyon, wild crocodiles, the Himalayas, The Taj Mahal, the pyramids and The Coliseum. After that I shall do my A-levels in a year and go to university. I'm going to be a teacher. A geography teacher.'

After the horrendous teenage-years, all Priscilla and Aaron could do was listen to his plans in astonishment and wish him good luck.

'It's all planned then?'

'Yup. I'm going to book the tickets on-line tonight. I've found a way of doing it really cheaply.'

'And when will you leave?' Priscilla asked.

'All being well, next week.'

'By yourself?'

'Yes-and-no. Roger, a friend at work, is finishing his gap-year and wants to see America before starting at uni, so he'll be with me for the first-leg but he'll have to fly-back from LA. After that, I'll be on my own.'

'Good luck, son', said Aaron, shaking him by the hand and giving him a big hug. There was the start of a tear in his eye. It was the moment few parents are ever quite prepared for - the day their chick prepares to fly the nest.

Roger was the supermarket clown with a particularly-imaginative gift for practical-jokes. There was the day he carefully placed a Singing Billy-Bass on the wet-fish counter, surrounded by ice and fresh-mackerel. The realistic-looking fish was actually a novelty-toy, programmed to burst into song when prompted. Its head and tail also swivelled in-time to the music. At least a dozen customers were taken by complete surprise at the apparently-dead fish suddenly bursting-into life. Soon the fish-counter had gathered quite a crowd.

The store-manager called for Roger to report to his office. As it was April Fool's Day he took a relatively-lenient approach to the offence. Roger kept his job.

Ten weeks later Roger was not so fortunate. The incident with the radio-controlled mouse in the breakfast-cereal aisle resulted in instant-dismissal - and gave him the extra holiday he decided he'd been looking-for to visit the USA.

Elvis found Roger an amiable travelling-companion. They had two days in New York before taking the bus to Washington DC where Roger posed for a photograph outside The White House wearing a pair of President Obama novelty-ears. Elvis kept his parents up-to-date with their movements with brief, daily text-messages and 'phone-pictures.

It had been a spur-of-the moment decision to travel to California via Memphis. They were sitting by The Lincoln Memorial, eating hotdogs and discussing the next-leg of the journey, when Elvis remarked casually.

'Fancy seeing Graceland?'

'Why not?' replied Roger.

'Thought it would be nice to see the place without the parents', confided Elvis. 'I'm telling you it's weird. All these wrinkly Elvis-fans and lookalikes with big bellies. Some really sad cases. But like Mum and Dad, it's their, well, religion. Freaky. Instead of going to church they go to Elvis-clubs. And in

Memphis there's this amazing Elvis Cathedral. It must have cost megabucks to build.'

So they caught a bus and twenty-five hours later arrived in Memphis having travelled via Charlottesville, Lynchburg and Nashville. Every three or four hours the coach had stopped and the two lads had a five-minute walk, a quick-trip to the bathroom and bought themselves a coke and burger each.

Elvis did not care much for junk-food. 'Don't they sell anything else over here?' he complained.

'No. This is the land of the free', answered Roger quickly. 'The free-foot-wide backside!'

It was early-evening when they arrived, just as the sun was setting over the city's impressive Pyramid. Memphis was packed-solid for Elvis Week. They found a cheap hostel with some difficulty and crashed-out but woke early and decided to wander-up to Graceland to see the early-morning fans at the graveside. By the time they'd realised their hostel was five-miles away from Graceland, and had worked out exactly how the Memphis bus-system was organised, it was mid-morning before they were standing by the wall outside the mansion.

Roger was intrigued that every square-foot of the wall was covered in graffiti. 'They clean it off from time-to-time', said Elvis, 'but it's still always full. I wrote something here once when I was a kid but I expect it's been scrubbed-over dozens of times since'.

'I've got to write something', said Roger, 'but I can't think of anything dafter than what's here already. Look. "I heard the call, I made the pilgrimage, I came to Graceland", and this, "Only two people have moved the world so much, Jesus Our Lord and Elvis Our King". This is fruitcake-land! And this one, "Elvis is a God"'.

Roger walked along the wall reading out the messages. 'I like this one - "Elvis if you read this I know you are alive". "Coming back from Lubbock, I thought I saw Jesus on the 'plane. But it might have been Elvis. They kinda look the same". "Elvis the world needs you to return".'

'Rog, look at this one. It actually says Elvis will return. It's signed by someone called The Prophet. "Elvis is here. He will make himself known on the anniversary of his death this year. Make yourself ready for the return of The King"'.

'They're dead right', replied Roger quickly. 'Elvis is here but the wrong one. Must be funny seeing your name written everywhere like this. Imagine if Vernon and Gladys had called him Roger. "We love Jesus and Roger", "Our Roger who art in heaven".'

'Don't talk blasphemy', said a fearsome-looking, sixty-something Elvis-fan who had overheard. 'You'll be sorry when Elvis and Jesus come back. That'll be judgement-day and young-men like you will go to hell.'

'Thank you ma'am', said Elvis in his most-polite, English tones. 'We'll bear that in mind.'

'You do that.'

'When is Elvis going to return by the way? This message says it'll be on the anniversary this year.'

'No-one knows the time or place', said the fearsome fan, 'but the Reverend Doctor from the Church is quite certain it'll be very, very soon'.

Earlier, they had decided not to spend any money going inside the Cathedral of The Latter-Day Elvis though Roger had been much-intrigued by what he saw from the outside.

'They'll let us go in free tomorrow', Elvis had told him after reading a notice-board. 'There's a big Elvis Anniversary Service. *The Return of The King. Are you ready?* it says.'

'Cool', said Roger.

Thinking now they would rather have some beer-money for the evening than spend their dollars on the formal-trip around Graceland, Roger and Elvis wandered over the road to the shops in search of free entertainment.

'I've been round Graceland lots of times before', said Elvis, 'and don't need to see it again'.

'I'm not fussed', replied Roger.

That evening they were sitting in a bar in Beale Street. With them were two, Scottish girls, Fiona and Kirsty, in America on a gap-year tour. The four had met while wandering around the souvenir shops opposite Graceland and got-on well. They were all staying at the same hostel, so they decided to spend the evening together, getting to know each-other and downtown-Memphis. There was the easy sound of a jazz-band playing somewhere in the distance and Elvis felt mellow and contented.

Fiona was slim with a mane of red hair. Kirsty was shorter and slightly plumper, with dark hair, pale skin and vivid, blue eyes. They had been school-friends in Edinburgh and both had been offered places at Stirling University. Kirsty had been born-and-bred in the Scottish capital but Fiona had moved there at the age of ten when her father had been offered a post as a teacher. She was originally from the Shetland Isles, Britain's most-northern group of islands and her accent, though largely central-belt, had occasional echoes of the far-north. They had arrived in America a fortnight earlier and picked up an economy hire-car at Newark airport before meandering west.

It was on the third-round of beers, while eating a pork-pull from the barbecue, that Roger had one of his wild ideas.

'I reckon', he said thoughtfully, 'that Elvis kind-of looks-like Elvis... if you get what I mean? Like Presley, The King? Put him in Elvis-clothes, shave-off the beard, cut his hair short and smarm it back... and, hey presto! I reckon he could win a lookalike competition!'

Roger grabbed a handful of Elvis's hair and pulled it back.

'Look - he's got the eyes, the bone-structure, the features... '

'But can he curl-his-lip like Elvis and give the sexy-look?' asked Fiona.

Elvis duly obliged.

'You're right, he does look like Elvis', exclaimed Kirsty in astonishment. 'But can he sound like Elvis too?'

Elvis stood up, swivelled his hips and drawled, *I ain't nothing but a Hound Dog.*

'God, he can sound like him too', marvelled Fiona. 'It's brill!'

'Well then, this is the idea', began Roger, inventing the practical-joke to upstage even the singing supermarket-fish. 'Tomorrow, they say Elvis will return. We are going to make it happen. A dramatic entry into the cathedral with our Elvis looking and sounding the part. They will go nuts!'

CHAPTER EIGHT

For eighteen-years the Church of The Latter-Day Elvis had been a great success and Mr Carioli had been very pleased with his investment. But, as time went by, the flow of income began to slacken-off. Mr Carioli noted he was not getting his full 10%-return and started to ask questions. Tim Barker started to feel anxious.

Starting a religion is easy enough but how do you finish with one, he wondered. He looked at the options. It was not as if it could be put on the market for sale as a going-concern with assets and goodwill. To strip the cathedral-building of its valuable materials, its gold-leaf and marble, would fetch some money. So would the site as a plot of real-estate. But would Mr Carioli get all his money back? Barker doubted it.

There was only one, feasible option he concluded. Have a last, massive income-drive, then liquidate the assets rapidly. That course of action would generate just enough money, Barker calculated, for Mr Carioli to have his original investment returned to him and therefore have no reason to complain. Already, he had had almost twice his original investment back in annual-income.

Barker devised his plan. He would use the approaching Elvis anniversary to whip-up a sense of acute anticipation. He needed the fans to believe that Elvis was really going to return - and imminently. If he could persuade them that the end was truly nigh, they might even cash-in their life-savings and pension-funds. Why would they need money stashed away for the future when the future was Elvis?

Over the years, Barker had researched the opposition carefully. He had noticed how support for the Christian, end-time churches typically peaked and troughed. He had observed that during periods of revival, when 'The Rapture' and 'Judgement Day' were expected at any moment, church-incomes shot-up. 'What do you need your savings for?' the preachers would thunder. 'You can't take your money with you to heaven. Give it to God.' He had also noted that church-incomes inevitably fell-back as hopeful anticipation turned to acute disappointment when the faithful realised that nothing significant had happened.

Barker recognised that the key to engineering the required expectation, such as would increase the Church's income so substantially that his exit-strategy would be successful, was to fix a date for Elvis's return. Then, as long as he had planned his financial and personal escape-routes correctly and he could get out just-before the faithful came to realise their hopes had been falsely-raised, all would be well.

There were other reasons too, unrelated to the Church's finances, which made Barker want to get out. No religion can survive for long without attracting enemies. As the Elvis Church grew and prospered, it came under increasing attack. In fact, for most of the eighteen years of its existence, it had attracted as much hostile attention from outsiders as it had loyalty from its members.

Committed Christians hated the Church and everything it stood for. To link Jesus and Elvis was to them a blasphemy, the ultimate, unforgivable blasphemy against The Holy Spirit according to several, well-known tele-evangelists. The whole idea was wicked, absurd and unbiblical they said. However, attacking the Reverend Doctor on biblical grounds was often a mistake as several preachers discovered. Dr Love was, however bizarre his views, a first-rate, Bible scholar.

Barker recalled the day the Reverend Doctor had been hijacked by three, Christian ministers on a live television-show.

They had harangued him relentlessly and fiercely, brandishing their Bibles and quoting text-after-text. They had used verses from The Bible as verbal-cudgels.

The first-minister glared accusingly. '"Beware of false prophets, which come to you in sheep's clothing, but inwardly they are ravening wolves." Those are the very words of Jesus from Matthew, Chapter 7 verse 15... '

Then, the attack was taken up by the second, as if rehearsed. '"And many false prophets shall rise, and shall deceive many", says Matthew again, in Chapter 24... '

The third-minister joined-in. '"Take heed that no man deceive you. For many shall come in my name, saying, I am Christ; and shall deceive many"', he quoted. Jabbing a finger forcefully in the Reverend Doctor's face, he added, 'You, Dr Love, are a deceiver. The Good Book says, "There shall arise false-Christs and false-prophets" and you are without doubt one of them'.

As if on-cue, the three preachers all turned the pages of their Bibles. Instead of quoting from The Gospels, they began to quote from The Epistles.

'Galatians, Chapter One. "There be some that... would pervert The Gospel of Christ... "', began the first-preacher.

The second-minister took-up the attack. '"The antichrist, whereof ye have heard that it should come; and even now, already is it in the world... " One John, Chapter 4... '

'"Let no man deceive you by any means... "', continued the third. 'Chapter 2 of Two Thessalonians. "For that day shall not come, except there come a falling away first, and that man of sin be revealed, the son of perdition; Who opposeth and exalteth himself above all that is called God, or that is worshipped; so that he as God sitteth in the temple of God, shewing himself that he is God."'

Once more, the apparently-synchronised preachers turned the pages of their Bibles together, this time switching from the New Testament to the Old Testament.

'"If there arise among you a prophet, or a dreamer of dreams..."', commenced the first...

'"Saying, Let us go after other gods, which thou hast not known, and let us serve them... Thou shalt not hearken unto the words of that prophet... "', continued the second...

'"That dreamer of dreams, shall be put to death; because he hath spoken to turn you away from the Lord your God"', concluded the third.

Then, they thundered together in unison, 'Deuteronomy Chapter 13. What have you got to say to that?'

After a pause, quietly and with great dignity, the Reverend Doctor looked the first-minister in the eye and asked, 'Which church do you represent?'

'I am from The Bethel Preaching Ministry.'

'And you?' said the Reverend Doctor to the second-preacher.

'I am an Elim Pentecostal.'

'And you?'

'I am from The Peniel Tabernacle.'

'How very interesting. Elim was a special place God gave the Israelites to rest.

'Bethel was the name given by Jacob to the place where he had his famous dream. It means House of God, as you will read in Genesis, Chapter 12.

'And if you look at Genesis, Chapter 32, you will see Peniel means Face of God.

'In The Bible you will find the word "Elohim", an ancient expression of the divinity. And the word "Elyon", referring to "God most high". And in Psalm 80, another "El" word is found, meaning "cedars of God". In Psalm 36, there is yet another use of "El" to talk of "the Mountains of God". You will have read of Eleazar who was the third son of Aaron and of the prophets Daniel, Elijah, Elisha. What do all these words have in common? They all contain the letters, "El", the ancient term for "God". I stand before you like Aaron. A priest of God, of El and in particular, of El-vis.'

After a stunned silence, one of the preachers sneered, 'so what does "vis" mean? Where's that in The Bible?'

'"Vis" as in vision perhaps? Or, in a modern setting, as in "vis-à-vis", meaning, "face-to face". St Paul says in One Corinthians, "For now we see through a glass, darkly; but then face to face...

When I was a child, I spake as a child, I understood as a child, I thought as a child: but when I became a man, I put away childish things". We, at the Elvis Church, have grown-up. God is speaking to us in the language of today. The Children of Israel were not allowed to see God's face. Today, through Elvis, we are adult-enough to be given that privilege.

'To visualise is to see, and to have a vision is to see beyond ourselves. Elvis came for us to see God face-to-face. It is all there in The Bible.'

It was an expositionary tour-de-force, which left the three ministers huffing-and-puffing with indignation. But what the Reverend Doctor then added was so outrageous that it left them livid with rage.

'And I ask you also to read again the words of St Mark and his description of the crucifixion. In his last words, as he died in agony, Jesus himself called to God. I will quote you the passage. "At the ninth-hour, Jesus cried with a loud voice, saying, *Eloi, Eloi, lama sabachthani*? which is, being interpreted, *My God, my God, why hast thou forsaken me*?" I believe that *Eloi* was the weak and strangulated attempt of a dying-man to call on Elvis.'

The three ministers rose from their seats together, as if to make a physical attack on their adversary. Before the end-credits rolled, there was time for just one, final exchange of texts.

'From the Prophet Jeremiah, Chapter 5', roared the minister from Bethel. '"A horrible thing is committed in the land; The prophets prophesy falsely, and the priests bear rule by their means; and my people love to have it so... "'

'From St Matthew's Gospel', the Reverend Doctor instantly responded. '"They shall call his name Emmanu - EL, which being interpreted is, God with us... and she brought forth her firstborn son: and called his name JESUS".'

Barker chuckled to himself at this memory of what he still considered to be the Reverend Doctor's finest hour. He remembered the telephones ringing in the cathedral-office all the next day. Half the callers were outraged Christians, the others were new members, signing-up to have their names on the Church's database along with their all-important, credit-card details.

More bothersome than the opposition from the Christian fundamentalists had been the trouble emanating from those describing themselves as the true-followers of Elvis. Barker knew that his brand of Elvis devotion would only ever be of interest to a minority of Elvis-fans. However, he'd calculated that, to make a profit on the venture, only 1% of the devotees needed to become loyal members. The other 99% could believe and do what they liked as far as he was concerned so long as they didn't cause him any bother.

One such group of true-followers, *The Elvis Truth Society*, was a permanent thorn in the side of the Church. Their message was simple and summed-up what most Elvis-fans themselves thought, that Elvis was a great singer but a flawed character who had made no claims to divinity. Elvis-fans should enjoy his music and films, said *The Truth Society*, and forget the religious nonsense. Members of the society frequently picketed services at the cathedral with banners and leaflets, trying to dissuade fans from attending.

Also outside the cathedral on special occasions, were the Elvis-never-died brigade. Many had read Gail Brewer-Giorgio's book, *Is Elvis Alive?* and believed her theory that he had faked his own death. It was their belief that Elvis was still alive but had opted-out of stardom to lead a quiet, untroubled life. He was now, depending on which version of the story was told, currently-living upstairs at Graceland as a hermit; camping alone in the forests of western-Canada, living off the land; a waiter in a restaurant in Manhattan; or an honorary-member of one of the indigenous tribes of Australia.

One small faction of the Elvis-never-died group had deliberately established affiliations with the Church. They were the ones who believed that after his self-imposed exile, Elvis was planning to return to resume his career. They hoped he might announce himself during one of the cathedral services and they were determined to be there.

Randy Jones of SKEPTICS-r-US had also been a nuisance. He particularly targeted the Elvis Healing Services which had proved to be highly popular with many of the fans. Every week, a congregation of cancer-sufferers, disabled-children, grieving-partners and victims of road-traffic-accidents converged on the cathedral in search of a miracle. In cathedral-publicity, Barker claimed amazing cures. *Come to the place where the blind find sight and the lame leap for joy* said the advertising-fliers. Randy Jones was always asking Barker for evidence.

'Come and see for yourself', Barker would say.

'I've seen what happens', Jones would respond with ever-increasing exasperation. 'What I need are names and addresses, doctors' reports, the opportunity to follow up the cures you claim. I want to make a proper investigation.'

'I'm not stopping you', Barker would say.

'But you're not helping me either.'

Barker also had his own personal reasons for wanting his life to move-on. He was growing tired of the pretence. He was weary of the whole constant charade. He supposed he felt very much like a priest who had lost his faith but didn't want to lose his job. He exhorted and encouraged the faithful with sweet words but felt empty inside. Barker could never admit to any of the faithful, and certainly not to the Reverend Doctor, that he had no personal belief in Elvis as Messiah and that it was all a money-making scam. Even his time away from Memphis on vacation was never entirely stress-free. He knew that at any time he might be hailed by some passing Elvis-fan who had seen him at the cathedral and knew him as the loyal and devout Archdeacon of Elvis.

Another personal reason for wanting to escape needed addressing urgently. Whilst he had given-up gambling, Barker had not given up all his vices. The one he found hardest to resist was the one which tempted him daily and his position at the cathedral gave him every opportunity to indulge it. Barker was a lover-of-all-women and a serial-philanderer. His status as Archdeacon at the cathedral gave him the aura of a man of power and glamour. The thousands of women who had fallen in love with Elvis as teenagers and who remained faithful, loyal and eager for the consummation of their passions, saw Barker as Elvis's vicar-on-earth. They sent him risqué notes, samples of underwear and, in some cases, literally threw themselves at his feet. Barker's apartment was conveniently placed alongside the cathedral and his office contained a sofa which, over the years he had treated as the ecclesiastical version of the casting-couch.

After eighteen-years, Barker had had so many affairs, flings and one-night-stands that it was astonishing no scandal had gone public. The vergers had a shrewd idea what was going-on but they had no evidence and those with connections to Mr Carioli hardly considered it their business to pry. Indeed, some were taking a similar advantage of their position and were not averse to dalliances of their own. Fortunately, there had been no unwanted pregnancies and no scenes from jealous husbands but Barker did not know how long his luck would last.

And for how long too would he want to keep up that sort of life-style? He feared that as a middle-aged man he was beginning to lose some of his libido and uncharitably, he increasingly thought that some of the most-persistent women who fawned at his feet were approaching their sell-by-dates.

Barker had many reasons to quit while he was still ahead.

He began to prepare for the final-push and grand-finale. He left strange messages on fan-websites and on the Graceland wall. 'Elvis will return and soon.' 'The end is coming and the end is Elvis.' He signed them, The Prophet. As Elvis Week approached, the messages started to get more specific. They hinted strongly that Elvis would return on the anniversary of his death that year. A buzz of expectation went around the international Elvis-community.

Then, one day, the Reverend Doctor dropped his bombshell. He and Barker were talking together in the Archdeacon's office when he broke the news.

'I am going to be leaving', he said.

'You are going to be leaving?' Barker repeated the words to make quite sure he had heard correctly.

'Yes. Tomorrow.'

'What? Before Elvis Week?'

The Reverend Doctor nodded. 'It is eighteen-years since we started this work and I think I need to be on the road again.'

'But... ' and Barker paused. He could hardly admit to the Reverend Doctor that his departure would ruin his plans. He needed him there to give authenticity to his campaign. He was an essential ingredient. He was the innocent but crucial public-face of the whole scam.

'Why?' Barker asked. 'Why now, just as everything is going so well and so many young people are coming to Elvis and acknowledging him to be their personal saviour?'

'The trouble is I am no longer hearing what Elvis wants me to do. "Leave everything and follow me" were his first instructions, and I did. But now I have become too settled and too comfortable. Elvis no longer speaks to me.'

Looking-back on the hints of the previous year, Barker realised he should not have been taken by surprise. He had noticed that the Reverend Doctor was losing his touch. His sermons were beginning to ramble. He was repeating himself and stumbling over his words. But Barker had suspected it was simply old-age, not a crisis of vocation.

'Can't you stay just until we finish with Elvis Week?' Barker pleaded. 'There are so many rumours going around that this truly is the date for his return. You must have heard what people are saying.'

'People are gossiping. But I have heard nothing from the voice of Elvis himself and I will believe nothing until I do. There will be many false-dawns. We know not the day nor the hour. One will be taken, one will be left. I take my directions from Elvis and while I live here, pampered, fed and warm, he no longer speaks to me. My calling is to the highways and byways, to the lame and the halt, to the troubled in mind and spirit. I have become fat and content. I am going tomorrow. That is my decision.' He rose from his chair and left the room.

There was nothing quite like a crisis to kick-start Barker's grey-cells. Ever resourceful, within minutes he had a plan. All he needed was a mini-disk recorder, a small, portable loudspeaker-system and to call on Tad Masaka at his hotel.

Tad was staying at The Peabody Hotel in the heart of Memphis. Barker arrived just as crowds were gathering around the central-fountain in the lobby to watch the daily ritual of the hotel-ducks.

'Crazy', marvelled Tad, as he watched from an upstairs-balcony while the ducks waddled to the elevator to be taken to their night-time home. 'Just crazy!'

'Can you do me a favour?' Barker asked, getting straight to the point. He had seen the duck-routine dozens of times before and to him it was not a novelty.

'There's this little girl who's been in touch', he explained confidentially, taking Tad by the arm and leading him away from the crowds. 'She's a huge fan of yours and of Elvis. She is dying of leukaemia and would really love a personal message for what she thinks will be her last birthday. She's not afraid of dying and hopes to be with Elvis soon.'

Tears welled up in Tad's eyes as Barker told his story. He didn't for a moment suspect it was entirely untrue.

'She wants you to say something to her in your best Elvis-voice. I've written something out and I've got a recorder with me. Can you record it for me... or rather her? Then I can give it to her and it will lighten her life and bring her true joy at the end. Will you do this for a dying child?'

Barker wondered whether his plea might have been a bit over-the-top but the soft-hearted Masaka was so moved by the story that he was entirely taken-in.

'I'll say anything you ask. Come up to my room where it'll be quiet. Show me what you've written.'

"Hi there Melanie. This is Elvis speaking. It's really Tad Masaka but I feel as if I am talking for Elvis himself. I have a special message for you from heaven. My twin-brother, Jesse Garon, and I both send you all our love. Do not be afraid. Hold tight, don't go yet but prepare for the great day. I am with you. One day we will all be returning to our father-in-heaven. I will be here to greet you. Whether it is today or tomorrow or many weeks or months to come, I will be there at heaven's gate to welcome you. Do not be afraid. Jesus and Elvis will be with you."

Tad gave the performance of his life. Barker thanked him profusely and said how happy he would make a very special and brave young lady.

He rushed back to his office and downloaded the recording into his computer. Using his audio-edit programme, he made a few subtle changes. Then he waited until later that evening when he knew the Reverend Doctor would be asleep in his apartment. He had a key, let himself in and placed a loudspeaker just outside the bedroom door.

He switched it on. Tad Masaka's voice gently roused the Reverend Doctor from his sleep.

'Hi there... this is Elvis speaking... '

Barker heard the Reverend Doctor stir.

'Elvis, is that you?'

Barker played the tape again from the start.

'Hi there... This is Elvis speaking. I have a special message for you from heaven... Garon... Do not be afraid. Hold tight, don't go yet but prepare for the great day. I... will... be returning...

tomorrow... I will be there... Do not be afraid... Elvis will be with you.'

'Great God and Elvis be praised!' The Reverend Doctor exclaimed. Barker heard further noises as if he was getting-out of bed. He quickly pocketed the recorder and speakers and left. As he gently closed the apartment door behind him, he heard the old man let out a cry of joy. 'Alleluia!'

The next morning, the Reverend Doctor was a man transformed. He could scarcely contain his enthusiasm when he found Barker. 'I have heard Elvis', he rejoiced. 'He spoke to me last night. It is today. He will be returning today.'

'How do you know?' asked Barker, feigning disbelief.

'He spoke to me last night. As clear as I hear you now. He spoke to me. "Do not be afraid. Hold tight, don't go yet but prepare for the great day." Those were his exact words. I wrote them down immediately in case I forgot them. My memory isn't as good as it was.'

'Are you sure you heard Elvis?'

'Totally, no mistaking.

'Then, if you're sure, we'd better spread the word.'

Barker quickly arranged a slot on *The Memphis Elvis Radio Breakfast-Show* for the Reverend Doctor. The enthusiasm in his reinvigorated voice was infectious. 'I heard him last night - Elvis returns today.'

Barker tipped off the local television-stations and newspapers. 'Don't miss the story of the century', he urged the news-editors.

Barker's plans were going well. It was a simple strategy. Get the punters in, get them worked-up into an apocalyptic frenzy, separate them from their money in huge quantities and get the hell out of town.

Just to be on the safe-side, he decided he should pay Mr Carioli a visit to give him a final briefing although it was not the usual day for making his report. If he was leaving Memphis, he did not wish to be pursued by any of the heavies so he considered it important that Mr Carioli knew about all the details in advance. When he had previously explained that he thought the Church-scam had probably run its course, and had given an estimate as to how much money would be left over-to return, Mr Carioli had raised no objections to his proposals.

He agreed to see Barker and after listening carefully, said, 'You've done very well'. And in a rare moment of generosity added, 'and you can keep the final-collection yourself'.

Barker walked back to the cathedral a happy man. He had settled his debts and would soon be a wealthy and free man, so as long as Elvis didn't really return of course. And the chances of that happening, Barker reassured himself, were billions-to-one against.

CHAPTER NINE

Back at the hostel, Fiona took charge of the transformation.

'You need the young-Elvis look', she said and leafed through a pile of books and magazines she had bought. 'You want to look like Elvis did when Sam Phillips first discovered him and he made his first record. No jumpsuits or high collars. A checked shirt, open collar, fifties-style jacket with padded-shoulders and jeans. And cowboy-boots of course.'

'So where do we get the clothes from?' Roger enquired. 'We've only got twelve-hours to get Elvis ready.'

'What time do the shops open tomorrow morning?'

'Nine o'clock. Which leaves us just ninety-minutes to find the right stuff, buy it, get Elvis dressed and get up to the cathedral. Can't be done.'

'It might be worth going to the all-night mall - could be something there.'

'But not genuine fifties-stuff.'

Kirsty had meanwhile been looking through some more of the Elvis magazines. 'Look at this', she suddenly said. 'It's Elvis back in 1955 giving a live concert at The Overton Park Shell. He's all in black. Getting a black shirt and some tight black jeans at the mall shouldn't be difficult.'

Fiona and Roger grabbed the magazine to look at the picture. 'Who's got the brains, Kirsty-girl', said Roger, giving her a hug.

'But it's going to cost us', said Elvis, struck by a sudden moment of realism and doubt. 'I don't have much cash to spare.' He began to wonder if Roger's idea had been such a great one after all and would not have been sorry if the joke had been scrapped there and then.

'Plastic', said Fiona confidently. 'Let's go.'

They set off for the all-night mall and began trawling the lines of clothing for the right look, colour and fit.

They bought a black shirt, black jeans and a heavy, large-buckled belt. Elvis went into the changing-room to try everything on. He twice sent Fiona off to find tighter-fitting jeans. 'They mustn't be baggy.'

He emerged to a comment of 'pretty good', from Kirsty. And 'cool', from Roger. Fiona said nothing and just looked thoughtful. She paid with her credit-card but still said nothing.

She only broke her silence back at the hostel. 'It'll do', she said cautiously. 'But first thing in the morning I'm still going to go and have a look at that odd store we saw on Beale. I have a hunch it'll have exactly what we want.'

Before meeting Elvis and Roger, Fiona and Kirsty had found a time-warp of a shop that sold everything, including clothes, and probably hadn't updated its stock since the 1950s.

With that agreed, Fiona took control of the next stage in the transformation. 'Right, Elvis', she ordered. 'Go and shave. That beard comes off and then I'll cut your hair.'

For the next hour, Roger and Kirsty watched as Elvis, sitting in his underpants with a towel over his shoulders, was transformed into - Elvis. Taking the beard off made a huge difference. Cutting his hair was a revelation. Fiona shaped it with gel to give it the fifties-look. 'Now get changed into the black', she commanded, 'and don't look in the mirror - yet. And you two', she added, looking at her audience, 'go and get us some coffees. And knock before you come back in so I can tell you if we're ready'.

Elvis went into the bathroom to change. His earlier misgivings had faded and he was getting back into the swing of things again. Fiona joined him to supervise. She fiddled and fussed over the details. How many buttons to leave open? At what angle to best-display the belt-buckle? When at last she heard a knock on the door, she quickly called out 'coming' and then left Elvis to look at himself in the mirror for the first time.

He could not believe what he saw in front of him. He stared in amazement at his own reflection. But it wasn't himself in the mirror! After years of living with Elvis Presley via his parent's obsession, here he was, apparently face-to-face with their idol. The likeness was uncanny.

'Hurry up, let's look at you', Roger was calling. Elvis emerged to applause!

'Woooow', exclaimed Roger. 'Jesus Christ!' swore Kirsty in astonishment.

'Not bad, eh?' said Fiona. 'And if I find some better clothes in the morning, it'll be perfect.'

Just before nine o'clock the next morning, Fiona was outside a store called Schwartz. Just after nine o'clock, the doors opened. The store boasted that it dated from 1876 and Fiona could quite believe it judging from the state of some of the things on sale. There's no place quite like Schwartz and no smell quite like that of the dirt and ancient merchandise which hits the visitor on entry.

Clothes were on sale on the third-floor alongside hardware and household-goods. Fiona found a wide stairway at the back of the shop with rusty metal-pipes for railings. On the uppermost storey, she made her way through aisles with boxes piled high on both sides, treading on squeaky floorboards with only a few naked-bulbs to light the way.

The clothes, when she found them, were covered in the dust and grime of years of neglect. The women's clothes were in the fashion of the 1970s, and the men's clothes even earlier. After several minutes wandering around, Fiona saw a jacket on a hanger, one of the few garments offered the protection of a transparent, plastic cover. It had broad padded-shoulders. It was two, maybe even three sizes too big for Elvis but that was what she had had in mind. It was in a startling light-brown check with just a hint of green thread. She thought it was perfect. It was a bargain too as the price-tag appeared to date from the early-sixties. This jacket, on top of the black outfit, would complete her re-creation and transformation of her new friend.

Fiona rushed back to the hostel to find Elvis. She had left him in bed but now he was up and changed and looking the spitting-image of the youthful King.

'Try this', she said thrusting the jacket at him.

'But it's far too big', Elvis protested.

'Exactly. You look at the early Elvis-pictures. He always wore large, loud jackets that no-one else would have dreamt of wearing. It was how he invented his look.'

Elvis put the jacket on, looked at himself in the bathroom-mirror and instantly knew Fiona was right.

Roger glanced at his watch. 'Forty-five minutes to go. What I suggest is, Elvis puts an anorak on top of everything, with the hood up. We can't spring the surprise too early. We've got to wait for just the right moment - then wham!'

They arrived at the cathedral with five-minutes to spare. The place was packed. Every seat was taken and crowds were standing in almost-every available space. Elvis started to feel rather nervous. He was beginning, once more, to have second thoughts about the whole project. Putting a singing-bass on a wet-fish counter was one level of joke. This was a whole, new ball-game. Not only were there crowds of eager Elvis-fans, there were several television crews as well, with their satellite-transmitter trucks parked on the road outside.

'Rog', he whispered. 'Do you think... er... I mean... should we go ahead with this?'

'Are you chickening out?' Roger whispered back.

'Well... no... um... I mean... maybe... All these TV-cameras and all these people... I can't get up and march to the front like Elvis with everyone watching.'

'That was the point of the gag', said Roger. 'Anyway you can't go wrong.'

'But it's a bit like the Americans invading Iraq', said Elvis. 'Nothing can go wrong at first - but what do we do afterwards?'

'Oh... I hadn't really thought about that', admitted Roger. 'You just disappear into the crowd I suppose, leaving everyone guessing.'

'Disappear? Looking like this?'

'We'll be behind you, with the anorak.'

By this time Roger, Elvis, Fiona and Kirsty had been pushed by the crush of people into an area at the back of the cathedral. The service was about to begin and Archdeacon Barker came forward to make an announcement. 'I'm sorry folks', he began.

Good, thought Elvis. Perhaps he's cancelling everything.

But Barker continued. 'I'm real sorry folks but we can't fit any more of you inside the cathedral. Would anyone who is not already through the door, kindly remain outside. As you know, we are relaying everything outside and no-one will miss a word.'

There were a few grumbles from the head of the line but most realised there was no possible way of getting-in.

Over the tops of hundreds of heads, Elvis saw a Gospel choir in procession. He could also see them close-up on the giant screens. They were singing *Amazing Grace.*

Behind the choir came two lines of Elvis-lookalikes, the priests and canons of the Church. Taking up the rear was the Reverend Doctor. He was dressed, as always, in his simple, monastic habit but he was also carrying a shepherd's crook to signify he was also a bishop, indeed, the Archbishop, the Shepherd of his Church.

There was a reading from The Bible, the promise of the coming of a Messiah from the Book of Isaiah. Then the same words were sung by the choir, accompanied by the full-orchestra, in the version made famous by Handel.

For unto us a child is born, unto us a son is given: and the government shall be upon His shoulder: and His name shall be called Wonderful, Counsellor, The mighty God, The everlasting Father, The Prince of Peace.

It was an uplifting moment, raised to even-greater heights by the entrance of Tad Masaka to sing *The American Trilogy*.

'Look, it's Elvis', exclaimed some of the more short-sighted fans in the congregation, followed by murmurings of, 'No it's not. It's only Tad'.

The Reverend Doctor's sermon was an inspired piece of oratory. He borrowed liberally from all the great preachers he had heard.

'I have a dream... that one day Elvis will return to earth... I have a dream... that Elvis will once more walk-the-walk at Graceland... I have a dream that...'

Then later, 'Ask not what Elvis can do for you but ask what you can do for Elvis...

'And Elvis of the people, with the people and for the people shall not again perish from the face of the earth.'

Some moments his voice was raised triumphantly, at other times he spoke in a whisper. When he described how he had heard the voice of Elvis the night before, the congregation erupted in applause with shouts of 'Elvis'.

'As sure as I am standing here before you - I heard Elvis. And he said, "I am coming back." No ifs or buts. No equivocation. "I am coming back." I have written down every word. "Prepare for the great day. I will be returning tomorrow. I will be there. Do not be afraid. Elvis will be with you".'

At that point Archdeacon Barker leapt to his feet with a shout of 'Alleluia'. He announced the collection. 'This is for Elvis', he urged, 'to fund his mission when he returns.

'From today all your needs will be met. You no longer need to store-up your cash in banks where moth and rust and the avarice of the bankers will corrupt and lose it. Give it to Elvis.'

While the orchestra played and the choir sang, substantial collection-plates were passed from row-to-row. They quickly filled with green bills of all denominations but Barker had anticipated this. There were spare-bags ready to hold the cash.

Teams-of-vergers were also equipped with mobile card-machines. 'You can also give with your cards', the Archdeacon reminded the congregation. 'Help us to gather the greatest-harvest-ever for Elvis on this wonderful day of his majestic return. His coming-in-glory. What you give today will come back to you one-hundredfold.'

The congregation had started to chant. 'Elvis! Elvis! We want Elvis!'

Barker was beginning to feel rather nervous. Judging from the response, he calculated that the collection would set-him-up for years as long as he could make a safe getaway.

As the congregation grew more frenzied, Elvis turned to Roger. 'I'm definitely out of this', he said. 'Call me chicken if you like but this is heavy shit. I'm not doing it. It's not safe. Look at the mood they're in. If I go up-front now and they think I'm genuine, they'll trample me to death in a stampede of love. But if they think I'm an impostor, they'll rip me limb-from-limb in a frenzy of anger.'

Roger nodded. What might have been a bit of fun was looking a bit too serious.

'Yup, you're right. Let's forget it. This is scary.'

Bit-by-bit, the mood of the congregation was changing. It was tipping from joyous expectation to impatience. Barker was seen speaking in the Reverend Doctor's ear.

'Tell them Elvis isn't here but will arrive in Memphis later... sometime before midnight. Tell them to go to the Pyramid for midnight. That's it... he will descend from the sky at midnight.'

'But I can't do that. Elvis hasn't spoken to me again.'

'If you don't do something, we won't get out of here alive.'

Barker pushed the Reverend Doctor to his feet.

He raised his hands to silence the crowd. 'Elvis will return today', he started but the congregation were interrupting him, shouting angrily. 'When? When? When? When?'

Before the Reverend Doctor could say another word, Barker had grabbed the microphone. 'He may be here with us now - or he might be waiting for midnight when the Blue Star of Orion will be seen over the Mississippi river. We'll gather there at midnight.'

The TV news-crews, sensing an anticlimax, relaxed. 'That's a wrap', one reporter said to his cameraman. 'It looks like we've got a late-night tonight.'

The congregation too relaxed. A few started shouting, 'Elvis Now! Elvis Now! Elvis Now!' but the chant never picked-up momentum. Barker started to breathe more easily. By midnight, he would be two states away.

'At midnight', he repeated firmly. 'Let us gather at midnight by the Mississippi river.'

The Reverend Doctor sat down in his chair. He could not understand why Elvis had let him down. He had been certain that it would be at the climax of this service that Elvis would make himself known. He listened to Barker addressing the crowd and, for the first time in eighteen years, began to wonder if the Archdeacon was really the sincere disciple he had assumed.

'Elvis was a humble man', Barker had continued, soothing the congregation with reassuring words. 'It is possible that he won't announce himself in any spectacular way. That he won't arrive in splendour. Maybe we, who have stayed faithful to him, have to find him. So keep your eyes open. If you see a stranger in town, look to see if he's Elvis. He may even be here with us now, just waiting for someone to recognise him and welcome him home. We must open our eyes as little children do when they see the wonders of the world for the first time.'

Elvis quickly put one hand up to cover his face and looked anxiously at Roger. His three friends all kept close to him.

A small girl stood on the chair in front of them. She had been fidgeting and constantly asking when it was time to go home.

'Not long now', said her mom. 'Elvis ain't gonna be here today.'

'What does he look like?' asked the little girl.

'Well... just like you see in the pictures', replied her mom.

The small child turned round and looked at Roger for a while and then at Elvis. He had kept his hood down as far-as-possible but the girl, being so much shorter than him, could look right-into his face.

'Mommy', she said, 'Elvis is here'.

She tugged at her mom's sleeve. 'Look, mommy', she said. 'Look behind you.'

Her mom turned-round just as her daughter made a grab at Elvis's hood and pulled it back.

Her mother gasped. Her neighbour, who had turned with her, cried-out. Others nearby looked to see what was going-on. By then, Elvis's hood was right off his face.

Someone shouted loudly, 'It's Elvis'.

A space had rapidly cleared around him and one of the vergers quickly stepped forward.

'It's The King', he marvelled. 'Welcome back!' And taking Elvis by the arm he firmly manoeuvred him into the central-aisle.

Elvis had no idea what else he could do but go-along with events. He was escorted up the aisle towards the Reverend Doctor. Someone had dragged at his anorak and pulled it off to reveal the Elvis-clothes beneath. For many seconds the congregation was silenced by astonishment. Then someone shouted, 'Elvis has entered the building', and a great cheer went up.

The Reverend Doctor, who had been sitting slumped in a mood of increasing disappointment and disillusionment, leapt to his feet and rushed forward to meet Elvis. They stood looking at each other for a moment and then the old, white-haired man put out a hand to touch Elvis's cheek.

Then he spoke. 'Elvis, let now your servant depart in peace, according to your word. For my eyes have seen your return which you promised to all people. You have come to be a light to the world.'

Stepping to one side and turning Elvis by the arm to face the congregation, the Reverend Doctor declared, 'This is Elvis'.

'Bugger-me', said the cameraman who, just a minute before, had been about to put his equipment away.

'Did you get it?' asked his reporter anxiously.

'Every word. The news-desk is gonna love this.'

The astonished Archdeacon hadn't prepared for this eventuality despite all his planning. He needed time to think. He thrust a microphone into Elvis's hand and gestured to the orchestra that they should start playing *The American Trilogy*. The orchestra began to play the opening bars and Elvis had no option but to sing. He knew every word of the song - and every gesture - and his performance, although made under-duress and a little half-hearted, was totally convincing.

The music kept the congregation in their seats and gave Barker the time to work out what to do next. All his careful plans had exploded in his face. Who was this kid? What was he playing at? As the last chord echoed around the cathedral and faded away, Barker noticed people rising from their seats and moving towards him and Elvis. The adoration on the faces of the women looked dangerous.

His instinct for self-preservation kicked in. He quickly grabbed Elvis and pulled him off-stage into the vestry, then through to his office. He shut and locked the doors as he went.

Safe in his inner-sanctuary, Barker snapped. 'What are you up to? Where do you come from? What's your name?'

'My name is Elvis', he replied truthfully.

'Like hell it is.'

'I'm really called Elvis. I'm from England and my mate Roger thought it would be a good joke for me to dress up as Elvis to come to your service. And so we found some clothes and had my hair cut and... '

'Skip the details', Barker cut-in angrily, looking at him closely. Then he reached down a book from a shelf. It was a picture-biography of Elvis. He looked again at the young man in front of him and then once more at the pages of the book.

'You're the most darned-realistic Elvis-impersonator I've ever seen. You could be the boy.'

Barker and Elvis heard a thumping on the door. It was some of the vergers looking for them.

'OK, OK', shouted Barker and then turned to Elvis. 'You stay here. Don't let anyone in except me. I'll go and make an announcement to calm things down. We're going to have to get out of this somehow. We'll call a press conference when things have quietened-down and say it was all a case of mistaken identity. The old man's eyes ain't too good and he mistook a lad from England for the real thing. An English Elvis? Huh!"

Roger, Fiona and Kirsty found themselves caught up in a manic crowd. Everyone surged forward. In the mêlée, no-one noticed the Reverend Doctor sitting back in his seat with a great smile of peace and tranquillity on his face. Only much later was it realised that he had died peacefully within minutes of seeing Elvis, satisfied that his life's work was at an end.

The vergers tried to keep order. 'Elvis will be back. He's just talking to the Archdeacon. Please go back to your seats.'

There had been two police-cars parked outside throughout the service. Four cops had been assigned to keep an eye-on-things generally and make sure the traffic kept-moving. Noticing the commotion via the relay, they ran up the cathedral steps to see what was going on. They found a near-riot inside.

'Elvis is back', they were told dozens of times. 'He's here. He is risen! Alleluia!'

They radioed for help. It took the four-of-them, with substantial reinforcements, at least an hour to clear the building and restore order. The situation had been eased a bit by the announcement Barker made when he returned to the cathedral.

'Don't get too excited yet folks', he had said. 'We've got to make some checks. Can't have just anyone claiming to be Elvis.

Got to make sure he's genuine. It's a big responsibility. There'll be a press conference at three o'clock. So watch the TV for news.'

Within minutes, the return of Elvis Presley became headline-news around Tennessee, the USA and the rest-of-the-world. The sensational affirmation by the Reverend Doctor that Elvis was 'The true Elvis' was played over-and-over-again on CNN, BBC 24 and all the round-the-clock news-stations.

Reporters grabbed voxpops with witnesses who were only too keen to confirm and embroider what they'd seen.

'I could see a kinda heavenly glow over his head as he walked forward.'

'He sung exactly as I remember Elvis singing when I saw him myself all those years ago.'

'He was the young Elvis in all his glory! Praise be!'

'We don't know how he got there, some say there was a shooting-star the night before from the region of Orion. He could have been in a UFO.'

As soon as he heard the news, Mr Carioli was on the 'phone to Barker who was back in his office with Elvis. 'I'm watching CNN. What's going on?' Mr Carioli asked without any preliminaries.

'Just some kid having a joke', replied Barker trying to sound reassuring.

'Some joke', said Mr Carioli. 'Sort it out.' And he put the 'phone down.

Elvis had overheard the conversation. 'Who's that?' he asked.

'Someone I know', answered Barker. 'He's just seen you on TV.'

'Has it been on TV already?' asked Elvis incredulously.

'CNN - it'll go worldwide.'

'Will they see it in England?'

'Shouldn't be surprised.'

'What are you going to do?' said Elvis getting even more anxious than before. He was worrying now about his parents and what they would do if they recognised him.

'We've got a press conference fixed', said Barker, 'and you are going to eat humble-pie and kill the whole story dead. Then, if you follow my advice, you'll get your ass out-of-town'.

Just then Elvis's mobile-phone rang. He fumbled to find it in his jacket pocket.

'Who knows you're here?' demanded Barker.

Elvis looked at the number. 'It's my friend in the cathedral. What shall I say?'

'Tell him to be at the press conference and have a car round the back for you to get away. Now turn that 'phone off. Until we speak to the press, you ain't speaking to no-one.'

As soon as Elvis had relayed the message, Barker snatched the 'phone from him and switched it off. He handed it back with strict instructions. 'Keep that switched-off. From now-on just do what I tell you and we both might get out of here alive.'

CHAPTER TEN

Aaron and Priscilla were sitting comfortably in front of the television with the BBC Ten o'clock Evening News playing.

Neither was really focussing on what was being said but the brief headline, 'Extraordinary scenes from America. It's claimed Elvis has returned to Memphis', must have half-registered with Priscilla.

'I wonder how our Elvis is', she wondered aloud. 'He'll be in Memphis today. I wonder if he went to see Graceland again. Isn't it nice that he's got his old interests back again?'

Aaron nodded. He had one ear on the television and the other on his wife but his brain was in neutral somewhere in-between.

It was about twenty-five minutes past ten and the main stories on the news were being followed by some less-serious items. The Memphis-story was sandwiched between one about The Queen's corgis and a report on the sacking of a football-manager.

'What's this?' Aaron suddenly exclaimed, his whole attention switching to the screen.

'In Memphis, a short while ago, police had to be called to one of the city's main attractions, The Cathedral of The Latter-Day Elvis, when riots broke-out following a claim by Church leaders that a reincarnated Elvis Presley had returned to earth. The Church's Archbishop, the Reverend Doctor Garon Love, pronounced a young Elvis-lookalike to be the reincarnated Elvis. Some of those present believed the claim; others thought they had been duped. Since his brief appearance, the Elvis-claimant has not been seen again. We are told a press conference will be held later to throw some light on the matter.'

The voice-over was accompanied by shots of police and an animated crowd, plus a brief glimpse of the Reverend Doctor presenting Elvis to the congregation.

'I wonder what that's all about?' said Aaron. 'Isn't it the place where Elvis was Elvised. Rip-off I call it.'

'I expect Elvis will tell us when he texts us with his news. I wonder if he was there', asked Priscilla.

'Let's give him a call on his mobile.'

'That's a good idea.' Priscilla picked up the telephone and key-punched Elvis's number. After a while she said, 'that's funny. It's switched off. It's not night-time, is it'?

'No, they're six or seven hours behind. It'll be afternoon. Leave a message then', said Aaron.

'No, I won't bother him. We'll hear from him in the morning.'

Elvis had been left in Archdeacon Barker's office ever since he had been rapidly steered-off the stage. Barker came in-and-out constantly. He was organising, arranging and reporting-back on what was going-on outside. But each time he left Elvis alone, he locked the door.

'It was a riot out there', he told Elvis when he came back to the office to send a couple of urgent emails. 'But the police have cleared most of the people out now.'

A little later he returned again. 'Very sad news. The Reverend Doctor seems to have had a heart attack. The police and paramedics are there.'

He didn't seem overly concerned and went straight to his computer.

'Who was he?' asked Elvis.

'Don't you know? He is - at least - he was the Archbishop of the Church.'

'Oh!'

'Well, actually, he was just an old man I met years ago who imagined he talked to Elvis', Barker continued. 'A distinguished Bible-professor in his time but something flipped. I got him to write all the theology-stuff about Elvis that folks here like to believe-in.' Barker could see no reason to sustain any pretence with someone he thought was a fellow-imposter.

'Happy way to go', he mused. 'Never suspected anything.'

And with that, he left the room again and Elvis heard the lock click.

When Barker was not in the room Elvis watched himself on television. He was getting increasingly apprehensive. He flicked from news-channel to news-channel and kept seeing the same sequence. He saw himself walking forward, looking exactly like the original Elvis Presley. The Reverend Doctor looked at him closely and touched him on the cheek. 'This is Elvis', he declared. Then the news-reports cut to shots of crowds getting restless and police turning-up. Most of the channels finished with a snatch of him singing and sounding just like the original Elvis and sound-bites from enthusiastic members of the congregation, including an ecstatic, 'I was there and I saw Elvis!'

Shortly before three o'clock, Barker unlocked the door and came into the office to announce, 'everything's ready', adding, 'the Reverend Doctor's been taken to the hospital-mortuary and there are six TV-stations and at least twenty journalists out there for the press conference'.

'Is Roger there?' Elvis inquired anxiously.

'Yup, and there's a car out-the-back with two girls in it.'

Barker looked nervously at his watch. 'Five minutes to go, and make sure you own-up clean. You're an English kid having a joke. Have you got that?'

Elvis nodded meekly. If this was what he had to do to get out of trouble, so be it. He would explain to his parents later.

The 'phone rang for Barker.

'Yes Mr Carioli. All set, the kids going to own-up live on TV.'

Elvis watched as Barker's face turned from looking-satisfied that all was efficiently arranged, to bafflement and confusion with a hint of panic.

'You want what', questioned Barker after a while. 'You want the kid to say what? Why? There's more money in having a real Elvis in the cathedral? You can't be serious?'

But Mr Carioli was serious and the call ended abruptly with Barker in no doubt about his new instructions.

For a moment, he simply looked shell-shocked.

'What's up?' Elvis asked.

'Kid, we've got a change of story. My boss says you've got to tell them you are Elvis. And no-one ever argues with Mr Carioli.'

'Mr who?'

'Mr Carioli. In case you hadn't guessed, this Church ain't what it seems. The Reverend Doctor was genuine... well, a genuine nutcase at least. But the cathedral is a front to launder money for the local mob. Don't ask any more questions but if you don't put on a convincing show as Elvis when we go out there, we're both dead.'

'What? What do you mean?'

'You heard of organised crime?'

'Yes - but only in the movies.'

'This ain't the movies.'

There was a knock at the door. Without waiting for an answer, it was opened and one of the vergers came straight in. He was one of the more menacing-types on Mr Carioli's payroll.

'Have you spoken to the boss?'

Barker nodded.

'So you're on message. Then let's go', said the verger. 'We're ready.'

'What do I do?' asked Elvis.

'Leave me to do the talking', responded Barker swiftly. 'You just mumble, humble-like... "yes" and "no" like Elvis did... and call everyone "Sir" or "Ma'am". Got it? And sound American, not like a Brit. If you don't, we're dead. We're both dead - and I mean that. We're not playing games.'

Elvis got the message.

The press conference had been set up beneath the dome. There was a table covered with microphones with two chairs behind it. In front of it but some distance away, were rows of reporters. There were bright lights shining and a line of television-cameras all set-up.

'Ladies and gentleman... ' With Elvis sitting next to him, Barker began to speak. 'Thank you for coming to the Cathedral of The Latter-Day Elvis. You will have many questions I am sure but first I have a short statement to make. Sadly, our leader, the Reverend Doctor Garon Love, cannot be with us. He has had a massive and fatal cardiac-arrest caused by the joy of seeing Elvis return. As those of you familiar with his ministry will know, he has been preaching for many years that Elvis Presley is the true Messiah and will come back to earth again. Today I can announce that Elvis is indeed with us again.'

'You must be joking!' came a voice from the back of the media-pack.

'I certainly am not.'

'You gotta be kidding?' said another sceptic.

'No. I mean exactly what I say. I believe this is the true Elvis.' Barker put his hand on Elvis's shoulder.

'So where's he been hiding? Why's no-one seen him before?' came another voice.

'I cannot answer that question. I am as baffled as you are. I only saw him myself for the first-time today.'

'Can the kid talk for himself?

'I can do, Sir', said Elvis nervously, remembering to speak in a convincing, Elvis voice. 'You believe the Archdeacon.'

'Can you solemnly and truthfully declare that you are Elvis?' a woman reporter called out.

'Yes Ma'am. I am called Elvis', replied Elvis truthfully. 'My name is Elvis.'

'Will you swear to that on The Bible?' she persisted.

'Yes Ma'am I will.'

'Get him a Bible.'

Barker looked towards a verger who quickly found one.

Elvis stood-up and put his left-hand on The Bible. He held-up his right-hand as if a witness in one of the American courtroom-dramas he had seen on television.

'Repeat after me', said the woman. 'I swear on The Holy Bible that my name is Elvis.'

'I swear on The Holy Bible that my name is Elvis', repeated Elvis, clearly but quietly.

'That is the truth, the whole truth and nothing but the truth.'

'That is the truth, the whole truth and nothing but the truth.'

'So help me God.'

'So help me God.'

It was great footage and over the coming hours was shown repeatedly on news-channels around the world.

Barker was drawing the short press conference to a close, asking a final, 'any more questions?' but hoping sincerely there would be none. He had spotted Randy Jones from SKEPTICS-r-US in the second row and had avoided eye-contact. But Jones did not wait to be called. 'I have a question', he said. 'If he is Elvis, you will presumably have no objection to him giving a DNA sample?'

Barker had not expected this. He fumbled for an answer. 'Well... that's perhaps something to think about... when it can be arranged... '

'I can arrange it now', Jones replied immediately.

'Where are you from?' Barker was trying to gain time and was working on the basis that attack might be his best form of defence. 'What paper or news-channel?'

'I'm from the on-line magazine SKEPTICS-r-US.'

'This is a press conference for the bona-fide media, not amateur webpages.'

'We have fifteen thousand hits a day, we're hardly an amateur outfit. And I have a DNA test-kit with me. I just need a swab from Elvis's mouth. That's all.'

'Certainly not. Conference over.'

But the press-pack quickly sensed tomorrow's story in-the-making. 'Give him the DNA', shouted one journalist. 'If Elvis is genuine, prove it.'

'How are you going to test it?' said Barker, floundering.

'We've been promised a DNA cross-match by The Graceland Estate, taken from the bathroom upstairs where he died. And you have, I understand, the Elvis wart. So if you want to check our tests you are free to do so. We will be announcing our results on line tomorrow, assuming Elvis co-operates.'

By this time Randy Jones had moved forward and was at the table. The television cameras were recording every word and movement. He held out two, small, plastic pots and a couple of cotton-wool swabs on sticks. 'Just smear this around the inside of your mouth', he said, giving a swab to Elvis. 'And here's another stick. Do a second one so you can have a sample yourself to test.'

Elvis obeyed without saying a further word, then turned and walked towards the vestry. Almost immediately Barker was behind him clutching the plastic pot containing the second, DNA sample tightly in his fist.

'Asshole', he yelled once he knew the press couldn't hear him. 'You'll have blown the whole story. This time tomorrow, Mr Carioli will want your head on a plate and your balls in a bag.'

Once inside the vestry, Barker went into his office to call Mr Carioli and tell him about the DNA complication. In his panic he left Elvis alone and while he was on the 'phone, Elvis took a sneak view out into the cathedral.

The journalists were packing up and leaving.

'Psst', he spotted Roger loitering. 'Psst, I'm here.'

Roger moved towards him, being careful not to be noticed. Elvis pulled him into the vestry.

'What was all that crap about saying you were Elvis Presley?' Roger wanted to know.

'I'll tell you later', said Elvis, 'but now we've got to get out of here fast. This is an organised-crime racket and there's a mob leader out to kill me'.

'You're kidding.'

'No - I'm dead serious.'

Roger had kept hold of Elvis's anorak after spotting it on a chair in the cathedral. Elvis put it on quickly and lifted the hood over his face. 'Right. Let's get to the car, and I'll tell you what's happening once we're on our way.'

Just a few minutes later, Elvis, Roger, Kirsty and Fiona were heading-out into the traffic of Elvis Presley Boulevard. At the same time, Barker emerged from his office.

Mr Carioli had been surprisingly understanding. 'Maybe we just go back to our first plan. We've got twenty-four hours to close everything down and when they publish the DNA and prove the kids a phoney, you'll be miles away. And get a DNA-test on the wart to protect your ass in case they try anything smart. Leave an agent to sell the real-estate and valuables and tell him to send the money on to one of my legit investment businesses. A real Elvis would have made us some more money but it was a gamble. Quit while we're ahead. Tell the kid to get back to England and keep his mouth shut.'

But the kid was nowhere to be seen. Barker searched inside the cathedral. He went out the back and found the car gone. He shrugged his shoulders. If Elvis had gone before being told to go, he thought, Mr Carioli would never know the difference. If he had any sense, the kid would be buying a ticket home right now.

Elvis and the others headed for the hostel and checked-out swiftly. They were all shocked by what had happened in the cathedral and agreed they wanted to get out of Memphis as fast as possible. Back in the car, they crossed the Mississippi river and headed west on Interstate 63 to Little Rock in Arkansas.

He tried to sound brave but Elvis was very shaken by his experiences. He explained how he had been locked in the office, and how Barker had told him the truth about the Elvis religion.

'Sorry', said Roger, when he had heard all about Mr Carioli and the mob. 'It was my fault. I just thought it would be a laugh.'

'We weren't to know that child would point you out like that', said Fiona.

'I know', replied Elvis.

'But if what you say is true', said Kirsty, 'you know too much. And you left without permission. So they could soon be looking for you. We're going to have to do something about your appearance. We don't want people reporting sightings of Elvis at the next gas-station we visit. You've been all over the telly-news.'

'I'll pull over at the next junction', said Fiona, 'and we'll find somewhere for you to change your clothes. Pity you can't grow an instant beard.'

Randy Jones of SKEPTICS-r-US was also heading west but by air. He was on his way to Los Angeles with his precious DNA sample. For comparisons to be made, he had arranged to take it to the same LA Biosciences Testing Laboratory which had already been sent the profile of the sample of DNA from Graceland.

He was delighted with his scoop. His web-magazine was all about the use of modern scientific techniques to unmask false religions and supernatural hocus-pocus. He felt confident that with the media interest that would follow his revelation of the great Elvis-hoax, his webpage hit-rate would double.

He was a true born-again, evangelical sceptic, a founder-member of the Californian Dawkins Chapel and fanatical in his opposition to all things irrational. He couldn't believe his luck - at least, he wouldn't have done so had he believed in such a thing - that the day he had gone to Memphis on quite unrelated business should coincide with claims of a second-coming of Elvis, The King.

'You'll never believe it', he had told his colleagues on the 'phone, 'but a kid claiming to be the real Elvis is giving a press conference. And I'm going to ask him for a DNA specimen. I can get a swab at any drug-store. He can't refuse. Can you guys talk to Graceland Management and see if they'll provide a sample of Elvis's genuine DNA? There must be plenty around. They can probably get something from the bathroom. And they say all Elvis's clothes are still in the closets upstairs and haven't been cleaned since the day he died.'

Graceland, as it turned out, said it would be only too willing to co-operate. The Presley family and the management-company were getting increasingly annoyed with the activities of the Church of the Latter-Day Elvis and the wild, religious claims the Reverend Doctor was making about Elvis. With great efficiency they isolated some suitable material, had it analysed locally with all speed and emailed the results to the Californian laboratory Jones had specified.

The LA Biosciences Testing Laboratory had not been told the sources of the two samples it was being asked to compare, just that the tests had to be carried out without delay. For the staff there, DNA comparisons were a routine-procedure usually commissioned in disputed paternity-cases. The fact that the client was SKEPTICS-r-US had raised no special issues for them. The individual technician carrying-out the tests had simply been given two batch-numbers. 'We'll email you the result by ten o'clock tomorrow-morning', Jones had been told.

As he went to sleep that night, he was already writing tomorrow's story in his head. 'DNA-tests commissioned by SKEPTICS-r-US have unmasked the new Elvis-claimant as a fraud. A top LA laboratory has compared the analysis of DNA samples of the genuine Elvis Presley, retrieved from the Graceland bathroom where he died, with samples taken from the recent Elvis-claimant at the Cathedral of The Latter-Day

Elvis in Memphis. "There is no match of any kind", was the official, scientific conclusion. A spokesperson for the Presley family said, "We hope this puts an end to a cruel hoax which has upset the family and raised absurd, false hopes amongst his genuine fans".'

The next day, Jones arrived at his office and began to start writing the story for the website. By three minutes past ten, the copy was almost ready to be put online. All Jones was waiting for was official confirmation from Graceland that they were happy with the quote he had written on their behalf. Then there was a 'ping' on his computer announcing the arrival of a new email.

It wasn't from Graceland but from the Laboratory.

'For attention of client SKEPTICS-r-US. Order EL/17877. Markers in DNA samples and data supplied are fully consistent. Match confirmed.'

Jones read the email twice, then called a colleague over.

'Can't understand this', he said sounding puzzled. 'Must be some mistake somewhere. As I read it, it says the two samples match. We'll have to hold the story 'til we got things sorted.'

This was an unexpected delay.

'They must have muddled the samples somewhere along the line', Jones reassured himself. 'I'll 'phone them to check. Get them to do the test again if necessary.'

The Laboratory was reluctant to double-check its results.

'Our procedures don't permit sample confusion', he was told. He was assured that all the required protocols had been followed. But he insisted that this was a very special case and eventually they agreed to run the tests again. Ring-back in the afternoon they said to him.

When he called-back, he was fully-expecting the lab to admit there had been a minor mix-up. Instead, he was given a lengthy lesson in DNA-testing by a senior-scientist.

'We're looking here for a random probability-match', he was informed in weary tones which sounded a trifle impatient at having to explain technical matters to a layman. 'Usually, if we are helping the police, we get given a speck of blood from a crime-scene and are asked if it matches a DNA sample taken from a suspect. It all comes down to comparing sets of bands or spots on autorads. Do they match? Usually that's enough to convict or eliminate.

'But it isn't always that simple. We all have forty-six chromosomes in our DNA, each one containing about five-hundred-and fifty genes, and each gene contains as many as thirty-five alleles. It's the alleles that decide things like blood-group or hair-colour.

'In very, very rare cases, it is possible for a match to be found between samples taken from two different people. Then, we have to ask ourselves further questions about the suspect and population-substructure.

'Let's say we are looking at a sample found at the scene of a crime in an African tribal-village from which there has been little movement of population for generations. The chances of the DNA from someone in that locality matching someone-else from the same locality might be thousands-to-one. On the other hand, the chances of a match between two randomly-selected samples taken in New York say, where there has been a large, international mix of people for generations, are millions and millions-to-one.

'So... what do you know about the person or persons who supplied the samples we've been checking? It suggests to me quite a mix of genetic-input amounting to a pretty-rare combination. I'd say, professionally-speaking, we are into many millions-to-one against this being two different people.'

Jones had no idea what to say next. He had given his own name and that of SKEPTICS-r-US when he 'phoned originally. Should he now admit he was talking about Elvis? The decision was made for him.

'I was watching the news last night and saw about the happenings in Memphis. You said you were from SKEPTICS-r-US. Are you the guy who took the DNA sample at the press conference?'

Jones owned-up.

'So what was Elvis's background?'

'Well I think he had some Scottish ancestors. Some said he was part Cherokee. Even some Jewish blood perhaps.'

'As I suspected, quite unusual. I've no idea how it's happened. But unless you muddled the samples yourself, or somebody's playing a trick on you, that young man is Elvis Presley - or his clone.'

Since his final meeting with Mr Carioli, Barker had had a busy twenty-four hours. Arranging for the cathedral's bank accounts to be emptied and their contents assigned to one of Mr Carioli's companies was easy. Arranging for a commercial, real-estate agent to value the building and site for immediate-sale had not been a problem either. It was when Barker went into the cathedral to start removing works-of-art and any objects made of precious metal or containing gemstones that he encountered difficulties. Those vergers who were dedicated Elvis-believers could not understand why, just as Elvis had returned, Barker appeared to be attempting to close down the cathedral.

'Elvis don't like our decorations', Barker had tried to explain. 'He wants all the valuables sold and the money given away. Remember what Jesus said, sell everything and give to the poor.'

This reply appeared to satisfy the vergers but then they wanted to know where Elvis had gone and when they would be able to see him again. Barker had no satisfactory reply to give.

'He'll be here soon, I expect.'

'Where did he sleep last night?'

'In the Elvis suite in the Reverend Doc's apartment.'

'But I went round there after he died to see if he had left instructions for his funeral', said one of the vergers. 'Elvis wasn't there.'

'Must have just gone out', Barker retorted.

'But he still wasn't there when I went back over an hour later.'

Barker's temper frayed. 'Just back-off with all these damned questions', he exploded.

But the questions did not stop coming. One persistent verger kept asking if Barker himself believed that Elvis had returned? If it was Elvis, wasn't this supposed to be judgement day and if so, why did everything in Memphis appear to be going on as normal? Was there some doubt that this was the true Elvis? Was Barker keeping some secret from his followers?

Barker grasped this opportunity to stall. 'Yes. Even though Elvis was affirmed by the Reverend Doctor, there is some doubt in my mind. Sadly, the Reverend Doctor is no longer with us to ask. I don't want the Church made to look foolish. Fortunately, we now have a DNA-test being done. We agreed to give SKEPTICS-r-US some DNA-samples at the press conference.'

'So we'll know he's Elvis for sure?'

'Of course.'

'When will the results be known?'

'Sometime today I'd guess.'

'Have you looked at the SKEPTICS-r-US website to check if they're published already?' the head-verger wanted to know.

'Not yet', said Barker, who had no intention of doing so until he was well clear of Memphis.

'Isn't it about time we did? We should go through to your office now and look it up.' All the vergers agreed and Barker had little option but to stop asset-stripping the cathedral, sign-on to his computer and google.

Randy Jones was utterly mystified. He had been scrupulously careful in labelling and handling the samples. He wondered if Graceland might have made a mistake. Might they have known the true identity of the Elvis look-a-like at the cathedral and deliberately given SKEPTICS-r-US samples of his DNA? Was all this a trick being played on SKEPTICS-r-US to undermine the credibility of its other work exposing phoney bleeding-statues, crop-circle makers, trick-psychics and the like?

Jones telephoned his Graceland contact to tell him the laboratory's findings. There was a gasp of horror at the other-end of the telephone. The Presley Estate needed a returned-Elvis like it needed a hole-in-the-head. The legal and public-relations implications would be a nightmare. The financial-implications would be horrendous.

'What do I do next?' Jones asked.

'You've got to publish the results', his contact advised. 'You promised you would and we're already getting calls from the media wanting to know how the tests went. But write a piece saying you think you've been tricked and are doing everything you can to get to the truth.'

Jones agreed and at three-thirty, posted the following announcement.

'SKEPTICS-r-US is investigating a plot to distort the results of the DNA-tests taken to expose the fraudulent claims by The Church of The Latter-Day Elvis that Elvis has returned. The investigation was launched following the discovery by LA Biosciences Laboratory that the two DNA samples submitted to them for analysis were identical. SKEPTICS-r-US had believed, in good faith, that the first sample was that taken from the Elvis-claimant at yesterday's press conference in Memphis and that the other, provided by The Graceland Estate, was of DNA material from the late Elvis Presley. It is now believed that the samples may have been tampered with.'

At thirty-one minutes past three, Barker logged-on to the SKEPTICS-r-US website. The vergers crowded round the screen as the head-verger read aloud. It took a few seconds for the full meaning of the announcement to hit home.

The vergers let out whoops of joy. 'It's true. He is Elvis.'

Barker just held his head in his hands.

The telephone rang. One of the vergers answered it. It was Sky News from London, England. 'Did the Church of The Latter-Day Elvis have anything to say about the DNA results?'

'This is the greatest day the world has ever known', said the verger.

The telephone rang again and again and again and again...

Barker crept out of the office to clear his head and think. Instead of being miles away from Memphis a rich and free man, he was at the centre of a major, international news-story which to him was both highly embarrassing and ridiculously improbable.

CHAPTER ELEVEN

After leaving Memphis Elvis, Roger, Kirsty and Fiona did not stop travelling for over three hours. They by-passed Little Rock to the north of the city and took Interstate 40 westwards.

'Look, we're back in England', said Roger, breaking a long silence. 'There's a sign there for Dover and we're heading for London.' They were at a point where the Arkansas river widened to form an impressive and beautiful lake.

'Why don't we stop here', suggested Fiona. 'We've driven far-enough.' It was agreed. They drove around looking for a cheap motel but they were in an up-market vacation-area and so decided to book one, large room in the least-expensive hotel they could find. It was on the water's edge with a view west into the red sky of a setting sun.

Having been out of contact for longer than any other time on the trip, Elvis sat on the edge of a king-sized bed to text home.

'Lft Memphis gne wst', he started.

'Do I say anything about the cathedral-business?' he said to whoever might have been listening. 'Explain it was only a joke that went wrong?'

'No, it'll only worry your Mum', replied Roger from the bathroom.

'Maybe say something vague', suggested Kirsty, who was sitting on the other bed filing a broken finger-nail.

'What about something jokey?' tried Roger. 'Like... ' But before he could finish, Elvis had interrupted him. 'I can't joke about the real Elvis. They take it all very seriously. I'll just leave it at that.

'Lft memphis gne wst all well love elvis.'

Priscilla and Aaron picked up the message when Aaron switched on his mobile-phone at breakfast before leaving for work. 'Got a text from Elvis. He's heading west from Memphis.

Better not ring him now, it'll be the middle of the night. I'll text him back.'

After fifteen-minutes of activity on the keypad of his 'phone, accompanied by much mild cursing, he pressed the 'send' button. 'Good to hear from you did you see the elvis at the cathedral what was that all about speak to you soon love mum and dad.'

Seven-hours later, Elvis switched on his 'phone and read the message from his parents.

'What do I say? Do I own up?'

'No', said Roger. 'It'll be old news by now in England. You're best to let things be. You can tell them when you get home.'

Elvis, Roger, Kirsty and Fiona decided to spend the day and a second-night by the lake in Arkansas and put the events in Memphis behind them. The weather was warm, the scenery up-lifting and they hired rods to do some fishing.

At sunset, Elvis and Fiona took a walk by the side of the lake.

'Isn't it just beautiful', marvelled Elvis aloud.

Fiona agreed and took his arm as they walked. Little did either realise that they were enjoying the briefest of lulls before the fiercest of storms.

The first any of the friends knew that they were at the centre of an on-going, international media-sensation was in the early-evening back at the hotel when Roger was idly watching television and channel-surfing.

'Hey Elvis', he suddenly shouted. 'You're on the news! Cool - listen to this.'

Elvis sat on the bed next to Roger and watched as a young female-reporter stood in front of the gates of Graceland to voice her report.

'Scientists say the DNA sample taken from a mystery Elvis-lookalike yesterday is an exact match of The King himself.

SKEPTICS-r-US, the hoax-busting organisation that took the sample at a press conference and arranged for the DNA-tests to be carried out, admits it is baffled. As yet, there's no word from The Church of The Latter-Day Elvis. It was at their cathedral in Memphis yesterday morning that the Elvis-claimant was first announced to the world as The King-returned. The whereabouts of this mystery-Elvis are now allegedly unknown. SKEPTICS-r-US says it cannot accept the result of the DNA report until it has had samples retested.'

'Must have been some mistake', said Elvis after a moment's thought. 'But should I go back and offer to do another test?'

'Don't be daft. What good would that do? Keep well out of it, I'd say', Roger replied.

In Memphis, crowds were beginning to gather at the cathedral. Many of the thousands of fans who had been in the city for Elvis Week had stayed-on. Rumours were rife and the television reports of the DNA match were fuelling them. Barker sat in his office alone, with the blinds drawn, watching the news-channels. As the TV-crews arrived and parked their satellite-trucks outside the cathedral, so the story crept-up the running-order. Barker was seeing the same shots over-and-over again, particularly those showing the Elvis-pretender giving his DNA sample at the press conference. Each time he saw it, Barker groaned. How had it all got so out of hand?

The telephone rang. Barker dreaded each call. But he had to answer in case it was the one he dreaded most but dared not miss, the call from Mr Carioli.

'Hello', said Barker cautiously.

'What is happening?' It took just three words for Barker to recognise the voice, imagine the menace behind it and fear the worst.

'We seem to have hit a problem, Mr Carioli. I can't explain it but I suspect some samples have got muddled. It will all be fine I'm sure.'

There was a pause and what Mr Carioli said next Barker could never have anticipated.

'Check the DNA results and make sure the match is confirmed. Prove he is the real Elvis. Meanwhile my attorney will call. Do what he says.'

Mr Carioli rang-off. Barker was dumbfounded. Instead of being reprimanded for screwing-up his boss's plans, he was being told to confirm the mistaken-DNA match. And what would the attorney have to say? From a state of acute anxiety, Barker had been lifted to one of confusion, only to be plunged back into a deeper despair when he realised an awful truth he had briefly forgotten. How could he carry out Mr Carioli's plans, whatever they might be, if he no longer knew where the mystery-Elvis was? He had allowed him to escape and he could be mid-Atlantic by now, on his way back to England.

The telephone rang again. It was Mr Carioli's attorney.

'Hi there Tim, how y'doing? Madson Perryburger, attorney. Looks like an interesting case we got here.'

'Hi... I'm doing fine... and well, yes I suppose it is interesting... but it's all nonsense. How could he have Elvis's DNA?'

'Don't say that Tim. We've got to prove he has. There's a lot riding on it. But first you've got to sign this boy up. I'll do you a contract and get over to you with it as fast as I can. All we need do is get him to sign. You will be his exclusive-manager and look after all his money.'

'But as far as I know he doesn't have any.'

'He soon will. Now, when can I come over and meet the boy? We've got to get him to do a DNA-test for the courts.'

'Well that's the problem. He's not here. Yesterday Mr Carioli told me to send him away.'

'But didn't you get an address? A cellphone?'

'Er... no... he actually escaped before I could ask him.'

'Escaped? Mr Carioli's not going to like this.'

Madson Perryburger rang-off leaving Barker shaken and confused. The attorney's last words went round and round in his head, mocking and goading him. 'Mr Carioli's not going to like this... Mr Carioli's not going to like this... Mr Carioli's not going to like this... ' But why this sudden change of mind? What was Mr Carioli planning to do?

The 'phone rang again.

'Hi Tim. How ya doing?' It was the attorney again. 'I was just thinking. Maybe not such a smart idea to talk to Mr Carioli just now. How about we first try and find the boy ourselves?'

A relieved Barker immediately agreed. 'But why is it so important?' he asked. 'What's Mr Carioli got to gain from having the real Elvis?'

'Money, stupid.'

'Still don't get it.'

'Money. Millions-and-millions of dollars.'

'But how?'

'When we have Elvis signed-up, we start a lawsuit. We prove that Elvis is still alive and able to take control of The Graceland Estate... and all the assets... and the future income... and the new record deals... Do I have to spell it out?'

Elvis and Fiona had been shopping. They were cutting sandwiches and increasingly enjoying each other's company. 'When we make them ourselves, they're less than half the cost of a Subway,' she'd pointed-out. Earlier that morning, she had realised that her plastic was approaching its credit-limit and a régime of thrift was called-for until she got a text back from her parents agreeing to her request for a top-up loan.

'Do you think it's because I look like Elvis that my DNA might look like his too?' Elvis wondered aloud.

'It's the other way round isn't it? You look like someone because you've got their DNA first. Like identical-twins.'

'So it must be a mistake I suppose.'

'Or someone's pulling a fast one.'

'Got to be either a trick or a mistake unless you're a clone, which is very unlikely.'

Elvis laughed at the absurdity. 'Perhaps I was made in a test-tube by some mad professor using one of Elvis's pubic hairs which they found in the bathroom after he died. Then the cloned embryo was kept frozen in liquid-nitrogen in a secret-vault under the Nevada desert until the time came to grow it into a human-being and I was given for adoption to two, dedicated Elvis-fans who never knew my real identity.'

'I think you've got it in one. It's all part of a great conspiracy. There's a John Lennon-clone somewhere out there and a James Dean and a Dusty Springfield... '

'And one day we'll all meet up and form a band called *The Heavenly Choir*.'

'Or *The Grateful Dead*.'

Barker and Perryburger hatched a plan. With so few clues to work on, if they were going to find Elvis, they would need to involve the cops. Barker began to look through the video-footage recorded by the security-camera at the back-entrance to the cathedral. It took him half-an-hour to find the important frames. Elvis and another young-man were seen getting into a silver-grey car.

'It's a small Hyundai - look at the badge on the back', said Barker.

'It's an Accent 1.4', said the attorney.

'You're good on cars.'

'Had one of them damned midget-Hyundais run into me the other day.'

'What's the number?'

'Difficult to read - but looks to me like a New Jersey plate.'

'Can't be too many of them around in this part of the country. So assuming they've not flown back to England - which is a real possibility - they should still be in Tennessee or one of the neighbouring-states. I'll get the cops to pick the boy up on a charge of fraud, ID theft and impersonation.'

'But you can't do that', Perryburger protested. 'We're saying he's the real Elvis. He can't be charged with impersonating himself.'

'Sure. But all we want is for the cops to find him. When they bring him back to Memphis, we just drop the charges. Simple.'

A few hours later but several time-zones ahead, Aaron and Priscilla were preparing for a new day. *Jail House Rock* was playing in the background as Priscilla fussed-around in the kitchen. Aaron was in the bedroom, getting-dressed, listening to BBC Radio's *Today* programme for anything further about the events in Memphis. He heard presenter James Naughtie introduce a new item.

'And there's a new twist to that strange story of Elvis Presley making an appearance just up the road from his old home of Graceland in Memphis, Tennessee. You may remember, yesterday we carried the story of how a young man looking remarkably like the late-King of rock'n'roll was hailed as the returned Messiah by the leader of a religious group dedicated to Elvis. For the latest, we have on the line local, Memphis-journalist Dwight Reddy. So what's happening Dwight?'

'Well, it gets curiouser and curiouser. I was at the press conference held by The Church of The Latter-Day Elvis yesterday in their cathedral. The Elvis-claimant was there and I have to say he does look amazingly like the photos of the young Presley. He was asked by a reporter from the internet magazine, SKEPTICS-r-US, to give a DNA sample for testing - which he did. SKEPTICS-r-US is well-known as an organisation that likes to unmask what they call supernatural-hogwash and irrational-claims. Anyway, SKEPTICS-r-US has released the results of the DNA-test, after some delay I should add, and, amazingly, they have admitted that the DNA sample from the new Elvis matches that taken from Elvis Presley. The Graceland

Estate had cooperated fully, providing samples from the bathroom where Presley had died. SKEPTICS-r-US say there must be some sort of mistake and are having it all rechecked but in the meantime, crowds of Elvis-fans have gathered outside the cathedral demanding to see the new Elvis. It's almost midnight here in Memphis but the crowds are still hundreds-strong. They are quiet and orderly but occasionally start chanting, "We want to see The King".'

'And is there any statement from the Elvis Church?'

'Nothing as yet, although there are unconfirmed rumours that the reason they won't let Elvis be seen by the fans is not that he might cause a riot - but because they've lost him.'

'Lost him?'

'Absolutely. Supposedly, shortly-after appearing at the press conference, the Church's Archdeacon left him in the vestry but when he returned, Elvis had vanished.'

'Thank you for that. Strange happenings indeed. That was Dwight Reddy in Memphis... '

As *Today* switched to the weather-forecast, Aaron sat weakly on the bed. 'Oh my God', he muttered several times over.

'Are you coming down for breakfast?' Priscilla called-out.

'Yes. Just a minute.' Aaron had only a few seconds to decide what to do. Should he tell Priscilla what he had heard and the inevitable conclusion he had drawn from it? Or just see if, in time, the news-story passed without her being aware of it? After all, why alarm her? On the other hand, what if the story didn't simply go away and Elvis was in some kind of trouble? Priscilla would have to know then and she would be very angry with him if she realised he had been keeping information back from her.

Aaron went downstairs.

Priscilla had been awake most of the night thinking about the previous evening's news-story and wondering if their Elvis might have had something to do with it. She hadn't wanted to worry Aaron if it was just some silly idea but Elvis had been in Memphis at the time hadn't he?

When Aaron came into the kitchen, she was holding a teapot rather precariously.

'I think you'd better put that down', said Aaron, 'and have a seat. You know that news-story about the Elvis Cathedral in Memphis that we heard? I think it may have been our Elvis. The *Today* programme says DNA-tests have been done'.

Priscilla sat staring at her Elvis poster on the kitchen wall. It was a late, large, sweaty Elvis but nevertheless a picture that displayed his old charisma.

'They're a match, they say.'

Priscilla remained silent.

'So it must be our Elvis involved. What do you think we should do?' Aaron continued.

A tear formed in Priscilla's left eye and trickled down her cheek.

'I suppose we should have told Elvis before he went', Aaron went on. 'We knew we had to tell him sometime. But how were we to know he would go to Memphis? And why would he go to the cathedral? This whole business is our fault. We should never have done what we did.'

A tear appeared in Priscilla's right eye.

'It was a daft and irresponsible experiment', Aaron continued, as much to himself as to his wife. 'We should have had children the normal way. Let nature take its course. We never asked ourselves why we wanted to create a new Elvis, let-alone what we would do when we were middle-aged and he had grown-up. Somebody was bound to notice and ask questions.

'It's chickens coming home to roost-time. How could we have been so stupid?' He'd stopped sounding reproachful and now banged his fist on the breakfast-bar.

Priscilla held out her hand to touch Aaron and calm him down. 'Do you remember', she said quietly, 'when Elvis was little and we took him to the new cathedral?'

'And got conned out of three hundred dollars? Yes, I remember. Bloody sharks. The thing was a money-making scam.'

'No, not that. What the preacher said. How Elvis might have returned and be somewhere at that very moment, a little baby in his mother's arms, unaware of his great calling. I never told you before but I was holding Elvis and I looked down at him as he said that and he looked back at me. I'm sure he smiled as if to say, "I am aware. I know". It was as if he had spoken to me for the very first time. I could almost hear the words.

'And then all those years later, when we lost Elvis to the karaoke in the next-door hotel and that lady said, didn't I know he had to be about Elvis's business? That's what happened to Jesus, at just that age, when Mary lost him in the Temple.'

'But you're not the sodding Virgin Mary and I'm not bloody Joseph', shouted Aaron angrily, more angry with himself than Priscilla but impatient with her nonsense nonetheless. 'There was no Angel Gabriel, no shepherds, no wise men. You weren't a virgin and it wasn't a miraculous birth. We had an old wart and a petri-dish.'

'But maybe it was a miracle though', she persisted. 'What were the chances of Elvis being conceived? Hundreds-to-one against. We were hopeless amateurs playing at being scientists - and yet it worked.'

'Don't be ridiculous', Aaron retorted. 'What's important now is that we call Elvis, tell him not to get into any more trouble and fly-over to America to tell him the truth. Then tell him to keep quiet about it. The last thing we want is to find ourselves in all the papers. What would we say to our friends? How would we explain what we did?

'What time is it in America? I'll try and get back from work early this afternoon and ring him. I'll also book some leave and get two tickets.'

Priscilla said nothing and Aaron assumed she had assented to his plan. But in fact she had barely registered what he had said to her. She was remembering a verse from the Christmas-story she had heard at Sunday School. 'Mary pondered all these things in her heart.'

Aaron left for work but Priscilla, who had only-recently taken early-retirement from her position as Head of Section at the hospital, stayed at home. She went upstairs as soon as she heard Aaron's car leave the driveway and sat in front of her Elvis-shrine. She lit a scented-candle and while Elvis sang *Amazing Grace* in the background, she broke-down in tears.

She knew she could pour out her heart to her Elvis and Jesus. For eighteen-years she had been a mother, just an ordinary, working mother, juggling a responsible job and keeping a home. She had seen her son grow from babe-in-arms, through his difficult, adolescent years, to early-manhood. She had organised birthday-parties, washed shirts, cuddled, comforted and done everything expected of her. She had been loyal to her husband and him to her. They had rowed and made-up but had so much shared-history that nothing but death would break them apart. Throughout the ups-and-downs of her life she had remained devoted to her Elvis. She knew that to him she was special. She was not simply a fan but his mother too.

It had been her secret and one even Aaron was unaware of. For him, being the father of Elvis had been the culmination of the bizarre challenge he had set himself. After Elvis was born, the challenge was over and he was as proud of Elvis as he would have been of his own son, indeed, for all that it mattered Elvis was his flesh-and-blood. The birth certificate confirmed it. His relationship with Elvis was that of father-and-son. There was pride, love, gentle rivalry and fun.

But Priscilla's relationship with Elvis was different. There was the same love and pride and fun felt by Aaron, added to which there was that special, maternal bond. But there was more, a spiritual dimension, almost a mystical dimension. In her private moments she thought of herself as the vessel of God. There were times in the stillness of the night when felt she glowed with joy at having-been the one chosen one to be the mother of Elvis. She would recall from the religious classes at school *The Magnificat*, the song of Mary, together with the half-remembered words of the *Hail Mary*, and had composed her own prayer which she often recited to herself. 'My soul magnifies Elvis and rejoices in Elvis my saviour. From henceforth all generations shall call me blessed. Blessed am I amongst women and blessed is the fruit of my womb, Elvis.'

But there was a dark-side to being the mother-of-Elvis. Had not Mary been at the foot of the cross and had to watch her son die? Would sorrow and suffering be her destiny too? Would she have to watch Elvis suffer? Priscilla wondered if this was now her time to be tested.

Aaron knew nothing of his wife's religious-fantasy. There had been many days, weeks and months even, during the previous eighteen-years when he had not given a single thought to the strange circumstances of his son's conception. Yet Priscilla, as the years went by, began thinking more-and-more about what her son's special purpose and vocation might be.

While as distrustful of the motives of the Church of The Latter-Day Elvis as she was of those of the leaders of all other organised religions, she found its message attractive. As the world grew a darker and more dangerous place, she became increasingly certain in her own mind that Elvis would return in glory. With every news-report she heard of war, famine, global-warming, earthquake and natural-disaster, she became increasingly convinced that the-end times were approaching. She had read widely of Elvis-fans who were convinced that Elvis was the true Messiah, a Jesus-figure. She had read the psychic-messages published on the internet which, it was claimed, came from Elvis. These messages warned the faithful to be prepared.

'Dear Elvis', she now prayed. 'Help me know what to do.'

When Aaron returned home from work, shortly after lunch, Priscilla was taken by surprise.

'You're early', she said.

'I said I would be. I've arranged leave and looked up flights. We need to book tickets and 'phone our Elvis.'

'Yes, of course.'

'I'll ring him first to say we are coming over, just to check where he is.'

'Fine.'

'Shall I say why we want to see him? About the DNA-tests and things, or leave that until we are face-to-face?'

'I am sure he will know already but don't mention anything just yet. I want to keep that for when we're all together.'

'I'll dial the number now, OK?'

'Fine.'

CHAPTER TWELVE

Elvis and Fiona had been the first to wake-up. It promised to be another, sunny day and before it got too hot, and while Roger and Kirsty were still sleeping, they drove the four-hundred yards to the-nearest gas-station to fill-up with petrol. The plan, agreed the night before, was that after breakfast they would continue driving further west.

They paid for $30 worth of gas and had just filled the tank when Elvis became aware of something strange. A police-car had blocked the exit to the gas-station and another had blocked the entrance. Four cops got out of the two cars and, as if directed by a choreographer who had seen too many western movies, they all began to walk in their direction. With their hands poised over their gun-holsters, they were moving step-by-inexorable-step towards Elvis and Fiona.

Suddenly Elvis's cellphone rang and he put his hand into his inside-pocket to answer. Immediately the four cops drew their guns.

'Don't move or we shoot', they shouted in unison.

Elvis moved his head cautiously to see who they were shouting at.

'Freeze, I said', the lead-cop shouted again. 'Take your hand slowly out of your pocket and lift your arms up.'

Not sure who they were talking to but just to be safe, Elvis left his 'phone ringing and put his arms above his head. The next he knew, he had been jumped-on and pinned to the car. He was briskly and efficiently frisked for weapons. Satisfied he was unarmed, the police relaxed.

'Are you Elvis?'

'Yes. That's me.' He saw no reason to deny the fact.

'You gotta come with us. They want you back in Memphis to ask you a few questions - 'personation, identity-theft and fraud.'

'You darned-do look like Elvis too', another of the cops chuckled. 'Into the car.'

He motioned Elvis towards the police-car in the gas-station entrance.

The other drivers at the gas-station were astounded at what was happening. One had taken a picture on his mobile. That picture's going to make me a thousand-bucks, he thought to himself.

'But I can't leave Fiona', Elvis protested. He turned to look at her. She had been watching with alarm everything that had been happening.

'They don't want no dame back in Memphis, just you', said one of the cops.

'I'll be OK', Fiona said, as bravely as she could. She'd quickly reckoned that she and the others would be more use to Elvis if they also returned to Memphis. 'I'll tell the others and we'll follow you back and try... we'll try and get some help.' But she had no real idea what they could do.

As Elvis was being pushed into the back-seat, his 'phone was still ringing.

'Can I answer it?' asked Elvis but without waiting for a reply he took it from his pocket and put it to his ear.

He heard his father's voice.

'Hi son.'

'Hi Dad, can't talk just now, something's happening.'

'Turn that off', ordered one of the cops. A police-siren started to wail in the background.

'Call you later - tell Mum I'll always love her.'

'That's settled', said Aaron. 'We get the first 'plane to Memphis. Don't know what's up but Elvis is in trouble. I heard someone tell him to turn the 'phone off. It could have been the police from the background noise.'

He turned on his laptop to look-up flights. Priscilla went to pack. 'How long will we be away for?' she asked.

'I've no idea', replied Aaron. 'I've taken three weeks' holiday.' After a few minutes on-line, he announced that he had found two bargain-tickets leaving from London-Gatwick airport the next day. 'I'm booking them.'

'Can we afford all this?'

'We'll do it all on credit-cards and cash-in one of our savings-bonds later.'

They had money set-aside for a rainy-day. The current news from America qualified as a downpour.

The next day, as they started their journey to the airport, Priscilla began to read. She had kept the Reverend Doctor's book for eighteen-years and had looked at it from time-to-time. Now she felt was the occasion to study it carefully. It was hard-going, full of words and phrases she barely understood. When Aaron saw what she was reading, he was very dismissive.

'Why have you brought that load of old nonsense with you?'

'I think I need to understand it before we see Elvis.'

And as she read, passage after passage jolted her mind. In the chapter on the incarnation, the Reverend Doctor had written these words. 'When Elvis comes again he need not necessarily be born of a virgin as Jesus was. The Bible talks of Mary's virginity and the overshadowing of The Holy Spirit to emphasise the miraculous and extraordinary nature of Jesus' conception. In the modern world, Elvis will certainly be born miraculously but possibly in some other way. Perhaps he will have been saved in the womb by amazing microsurgery? Perhaps he will be the only, miraculous survivor of a 'plane crash? Or perhaps he will be conceived by the modern miracle of cloning? Who knows?'

In another part of the book, Priscilla read, 'When Elvis returns he will not simply be a lookalike. He will not be a different person with the spirit and soul of Elvis. My belief is that he will have the very DNA of the original Memphis King, wherever and to whomsoever he may be born'.

The more she read, the more she believed she understood. Elvis was indeed special and this was the message she had to give him. He was not simply her son, he was Elvis-incarnate and she had to be prepared to give him to the world.

She pointed passages out to Aaron and underlined the most important phrases. 'Don't be so silly', was all he would say. 'It's nonsense. I read it years ago. It's hogwash. I know what we did to conceive Elvis but our Elvis is not *the* Elvis. He's a genetic copy admittedly but not the same person. He's our son and somehow he's got himself into trouble - and as his parents we're going to help him out.'

Aaron tried to amuse himself on the train to the airport while Priscilla read but nothing held his attention. He looked out of the window at the passing scenery but quickly became bored. He got up to stretch his legs and picked-up a discarded copy of one of the day's newspapers. He looked at the front page. It was dominated by a picture of Elvis in the cathedral under the headline, 'Elvis: Fact or Fiction?'

The journey back east for Elvis was as friendly as could be expected under the circumstances. His stomach was knotted with anxiety most of the way, in particular when he was made to change cars at Little Rock. He was held for half-an-hour in a holding-room which, to him, looked just like the typical, American prison-cells he had seen on television. He was given a coffee and a burger-with-fries. Soon, he was ushered out to another car. By this time he was grateful for any food and his healthy-eating régime had gone-to-pot.

He was greeted with a big smile by one of the two cops detailed as his escort. 'Hi Elvis! I sure never had a big star in my vehicle before. Not that you're a real big star - but you're pretty famous right now.'

He showed him a copy of that morning's *US Today*. 'Front page - there you are. The Elvis Mystery. There's a picture too of you at the cathedral. I went there once. Mighty impressive. But

I'm a Christian and I call it worshipping a false-God to worship Elvis. Still, you can't be doing that! If you're Elvis, you can't be worshipping yourself.'

The cop guffawed with laughter at his own joke. 'You can't worship yourself', he said again.

'So what's going to happen?' Elvis asked anxiously.

'Well, we take you to the state-boundary and hand you over to the Tennessee cops. They'll take you back to the cathedral, the scene-of-the-crime so to speak, and you'll be handed over to the investigating-officer who'll want the guys from the Church to identify you. After that, who knows? Bail if you're lucky or five years inside. Fraud's a serious business.'

'But I haven't defrauded anyone', said Elvis, getting increasingly anxious as the miles to Memphis counted down.

'Tell that to the judge. He might be one of your fans.' The laughing-policeman roared with laughter yet-again.

The handover at the state-border was quick and simple. But the new police-escort consisted of two, taciturn and uncommunicative officers. 'See ya', said the Arkansas cops touching their wide-brimmed hats in a salute of farewell. And after a brief exchange of paperwork, they left.

The last Elvis heard from the laughing-cop was his final radio-message to control. 'Elvis has left the vehicle', was all he said, apparently slapping his thighs in delight at his wit.

With no word of explanation, Elvis was handcuffed. For the entire journey across Arkansas he had been unrestrained. He was unarmed and no threat. Yet once in Tennessee, Elvis sensed a tension in the atmosphere. He was whisked through the streets of Memphis with the police-car sirens and lights blazing. After ten-miles and scarcely ten-minutes, the car was heading-along Elvis Presley Boulevard. Elvis had a fleeting glimpse of Graceland. Seconds later the car screeched to a halt outside the cathedral.

It was a scene of pandemonium, lights flashing, television-cameras, reporters shouting questions.

'Let's go', ordered the cops. They opened the door of the car and led Elvis out. Police-reinforcements arrived to clear a path. Elvis was pushed and pulled, battered and bruised, dazzled and disorientated. He could hardly see where he was going under the harsh glare of the television-lights. Cameras and reporters' questions flashed in his direction.

'Where've you been Elvis?'

'How do you explain the DNA-tests, Elvis?'

'Have you anything to say Elvis?'

He stumbled on the steps and was at his wits' end. His police-escort pulled him through the door of the cathedral. It slammed behind them. Inside, in the almost-empty building, he saw three men standing, waiting to greet him.

'Take those restraints off', ordered a voice which Elvis immediately recognised as that of the Archdeacon. 'Welcome back, Elvis', he said, coming forward, and shaking him enthusiastically by the hand. 'I'm real sorry we had to bring you back like this but it's very important we talk.'

Barker then gestured to the man on his left. 'Meet Madson Perryburger. He's our attorney and he's got everything fixed for bail.'

'Nice to meet you Elvis', smiled Mr Perryburger. 'How ya doing? Don't worry about a thing. You'll be staying here as our guest and we're not pressing any charges. Isn't that so Lieutenant?'

He had turned to the man on Barker's right who introduced himself. Elvis didn't catch the name but he was obviously from the Memphis-police and he confirmed that, unless the Church ever changed its mind, he was happy to leave the matter there.

'That's the end of it then', said Barker. 'You guys can all go.'

The police-lieutenant and the other cops left the cathedral and Elvis, Perryburger and Barker walked through the empty building in the direction of Barker's office.

'So I'm not being charged with fraud?' asked Elvis.

'Of course not', responded Barker jovially. 'Just a bit of a misunderstanding.'

'But I do have an apology to make to you Elvis,' continued Barker in his friendliest of tones. 'When I first met you, I thought you were just having a joke with us. The idea that you could possibly be Elvis-returned... well... of course, I knew it would happen one day... but like that... just... just appearing from nowhere? It was too much. I couldn't believe it. I acted kinda hasty. But when the DNA confirmed you were Elvis, then I saw things in a new light.'

He looked Elvis straight in the eye. 'I am deeply honoured to meet you.'

'And so am I', echoed the attorney. 'Of course, returning from the dead like that raises all sorts of legal-matters but I'm sure we can sort them out.'

'But... I think... ', stuttered Elvis, 'that it's really me who needs to apologise. I was just having a joke. My friends say I look like Elvis and they got me all dressed-up. And then I had cold feet. I decided to quit - but somebody recognised me as Elvis and then things got out of control.'

Perryburger looked astonished. 'Say that again.'

'What? That it was all a bit of a joke?'

'Well any of it really.'

'But why?'

'That accent', said Perryburger. 'You sound so, English... '

'I am English', said Elvis.

'What? English!' the attorney exclaimed. 'Barker, you never told me he's a Brit?'

Barker shuffled but said nothing and left it to Elvis to explain further. 'Yes, I come from England. I'm travelling around the world before going back to college. I'm not American.'

Barker intervened at last to put matters straight. 'The Reverend Doctor never said Elvis would return as an American. He's for the whole world. There's no problem with having an English Elvis is there Mr Perryburger?'

'I can't think it makes any material difference to the case', Perryburger replied.

'Then that's fine', said Barker.

'What's fine?' asked Elvis. 'And what case?'

During the conversation, the trio had been walking towards Barker's office. On arrival Perryburger took control.

'Sit down Elvis, we've got a lot to talk about.'

Perryburger had prepared a file of papers which, when the legalise was deciphered, amounted to a surrender by Elvis of the control of his life and affairs in favour of the Church. It was essential to Barker's and Perryburger's plans that Elvis sign the papers before the conversation went any further. Once Elvis realised that he was potentially a phenomenally-rich young man, they reckoned he would want to seek independent advice before signing his life away.

So Perryburger made light of the need to sign the papers. 'First we need you to sign some papers. Just to do with bail and dropping the charges for fraud. That sort of thing.'

Elvis glanced at the top sheet. 'But I'm not called Elvis Aaron Presley', he said. 'This document is all about someone else.'

'It doesn't matter what your real name is', said Perryburger firmly. 'As far as we are concerned, you are known as Elvis Presley. The members of the congregation think you are Elvis Presley. Archdeacon Barker says you are Elvis Presley, the Reverend Doctor identified you as Elvis Presley and the DNA-tests prove it. Legally, you are Elvis Aaron Presley. That's how you have to sign it.'

Elvis still hesitated.

Barker's friendly-tones began to harden. 'Do you remember our little chat earlier? Mr Carioli would be disappointed if you didn't sign. D'you know what I mean?'

Elvis knew what he meant and signed.

'Now for the good news', said Perryburger, quickly putting the papers away in his case'. He pulled a second file out and started to place documents on Barker's desk.

'Let's start with this', he said, pointing to a set of papers on which Elvis could see the words: 'Be it enacted by the General Assembly of the State of Tennessee... '

'This act was passed in 2007 and states quite specifically that DNA-tests can be used to make an identification of an individual. It was introduced as a way of keeping a record of anyone charged with a criminal offence. "Such person shall have a biological specimen, for the purpose of DNA analysis, taken to determine identification characteristics specific to the person." I'm quoting from the legislation. The act describes how the specimen of DNA has to be taken using a buccal-swab collection-kit for DNA-testing.

'The relevance of this is clear. The State of Tennessee unreservedly accepts DNA-profiling as a means by which an individual person's identity can be proven.'

'Does that mean that under Tennessee law, if I have Elvis Presley's DNA, then I must be Elvis Presley?' asked Elvis.

'Precisely.'

'But I'm not Elvis. It's some ghastly mistake. Can I have another test to clear the matter up?'

'Of course', said Barker.

'And then I can go home?'

'Of course', repeated Barker. 'But, if it turns out that the previous DNA-test is valid, and you are legally Elvis Presley you will have to stay.'

'Why?'

'Because in the papers you just signed as Elvis Presley you agreed that you would.'

'And if I don't want to?'

'Then I'm afraid we might have to reopen the case of fraud and 'personation. Jails ain't nice places and some folk you'll meet might feel they want to do Mr Carioli a favour - and that wouldn't be nice for you.'

Elvis fell silent. He had little choice but to listen to Mr Perryburger again.

'But like I said, it's all good news. If you are Elvis Presley legally, which I believe you are, then soon you will become the rightful-owner of Graceland and The Elvis Estate. You will be a very-rich young man.'

Perryburger started to explain.

'The Elvis Presley brand is worth well over fifty-million dollars each year. Revenues include receipts at Graceland, royalties and licensing of merchandising. There is enormous growth-potential. There is a Vegas-attraction being planned, and now that Elvis has returned, income at the Church is expected to grow substantially.

'Some financial experts value the Elvis-business currently at a figure approaching one-billion dollars. A major entertainment-rights company called CKX holds 85% of the Estate, with Lisa Marie controlling the remaining 15%. CKX is very powerful and will contest our claim. It's very rich too and its business, as it says itself, is to buy and control "globally-recognized entertainment-content and related-assets, including the rights to the name, image and likeness of Elvis Presley". But you see, if you have the DNA and are therefore Elvis, it can't any longer control your name, image and likeness. It might even have to sign Graceland over to you.'

Elvis was astonished but not convinced of his apparent good-fortune. Despite being excited by the idea of incredible wealth, he still wished he could turn the clock back to a time when life was so much simpler.

'I need to think about this', he said cautiously. 'I need to sleep on it. But where am I going to stay? I don't even have a tooth-brush with me?'

'You will be staying right here', answered Barker. 'For eighteen-years, the Reverend Doctor had kept a place ready and waiting for your return in his apartment. It has everything you will need, including a complete collection of clothes. We'll talk further in the morning.'

Barker rose to his feet and beckoned to Elvis to follow him. He took him to a room in the apartment-block adjoining the cathedral. It was furnished rather like the Graceland Jungle Room with fake-zebra skin carpets and faux-leopard skin covers on the furniture. On the walls were replica, African shields and spears.

'Sleep well', said Barker. And, while Elvis stood still and looked around, Barker left, closing and locking the door behind him.

As promised, the room had everything. In fact it was more than a room. It was a suite with bathroom, sitting-room, bedroom and numerous closets. Elvis started to wander around and open the closets. The clothes he found covered every style the original-Elvis had ever worn and were in various sizes from slender to obese. By the bed, he noticed a room-service menu which explained that he could call up peanut-butter, banana or steak sandwiches at any time of day-or-night.

The bathroom was the only part of the suite not designed in the idiosyncratic jungle-style. It was very large, with a round sunken-bath in the centre and taps and plumbing in seventies-chrome. On the wall, by the lavatory, there was an emergency call-button should Elvis feel unwell. There were comics on the table in the sitting-room and a shelf of popular, spiritual books.

Elvis took one at random, *The Prophet* by Kahlil Gibran. He sat on the emperor-sized bed and flicked casually through the pages before returning it. Then he thought that he would try the television to find a news-bulletin. The first channel he found was showing the Elvis western, *Flaming Star*. So he pointed the remote-control at the set to change channels and Elvis in the American wild-west was replaced by Elvis in Hawaii. Another channel-hop gave him Elvis in the army. The channel was showing *G.I. Blues*. The set obviously showed nothing but old Elvis-movies so he switched it off.

The only sound left in the room now was the gentle background-hum of Elvis crooning which pervaded every corner of the cathedral office-and-apartment building. As he sat contemplating his situation and wondering what he was to do next, he thought anxiously, sadly and fondly of his parents and friends, especially Fiona. The background-track changed and he listened to the real Elvis Presley singing, *Are you lonesome tonight?*

'Yes I am', Elvis replied to no-one but the sounds in the air.

CHAPTER THIRTEEN

Aaron and Priscilla's flight across the Atlantic was scheduled to take ten-hours. After touching down at Dallas/Fort Worth they had three hours to clear customs and immigration before taking the much-shorter flight to Memphis.

After an early start and a wakeful night, Aaron fell asleep almost as soon as he was settled in his seat for the long first-leg. Priscilla, however, remained engrossed in her thoughts and study of the Reverend Doctor's book. The more she read and pondered, the more the neural-paths in her brain lined-up to present her with a picture of herself, her son and their situation which made a bizarre sense to her. She had underlined sentences, dog-eared important pages and written notes in the margins.

She began to see her past life with intense clarity. Questions which had bothered her for years, suddenly answered themselves. She came to understand why, when her friends mocked and derided her, she had been so obsessed with Elvis Presley. It was Elvis calling her to give her life to him! She realised not simply how but why her own son had been born as the re-embodiment of her idol. He was destined to fulfil a Messianic calling! As she travelled at six hundred miles-per-hour towards Graceland, Priscilla believed she was experiencing a profound spiritual-awakening.

When Aaron eventually woke from a deep and snuffling sleep, she started to talk. She felt she could no longer contain herself. With the manic enthusiasm of someone who has just seen the light, her words poured out in a torrent.

'I am the chosen-one, the chosen vessel of God. I am the Virgin Mary of the New Age. Don't you see, God needed someone to give birth to Elvis reincarnated and he chose us? You are the Joseph. I am Mary. He was born a second time, like the first, in Tupelo. That's the name of our house. It's another sign. Elvis is the Messiah. He must be.

'It makes so much sense of his life, the beautiful baby and lovely, little boy. Then he had the years of temptation in his wilderness years of adolescence. He had to find out who he was, to discover his vocation. Then God took him by the hand and led him back to Graceland. He didn't ask to go. He didn't expect to go but he couldn't stop God. It's not coincidence. It was divinely ordained. He has come back to complete his mission. The world is in such an awful state that the time is ripe. It is now he must come back. And God is here in the form of our Elvis... Oh Aaron, isn't it exciting and awe-inspiring!'

Aaron became alarmed. He wondered if his wife was having some kind of breakdown. She was sounding obsessive. What if she needed treatment? Doctors were so expensive in America. Would the travel-insurance cover the costs of psychiatric-care?

As he listened whilst Priscilla babbled-on, his concern for her mental-stability grew. While she spoke, she furiously thumbed backwards and forwards through the Reverend Doctor's book, finding highlights and reading them aloud. Aaron noticed other passengers glancing in their direction. When a flight-attendant paused at their seats to collect Priscilla's untouched lunch-tray, she asked kindly if Priscilla was alright.

'Oh yes,' responded Priscilla excitedly, 'everything is absolutely wonderful'. Aaron took her arm to distract her from embarrassing him further by explaining why. The last thing he wanted was to have his wife tell everyone-else on the 'plane that she believed she was the reincarnation of the Virgin Mary and the mother of Elvis Presley, the true Messiah.

Elvis lay awake much of his first night in his purpose-built suite. He was a prisoner in an opulent cell. His only connection with the outside world, he realised, was his mobile-phone. Foolishly, he had left it turned-on during his journey back to Memphis and he realised now, with some alarm, that it was running short on battery-power. He had, perhaps, only one or two calls left before it would lose all life. One of them would have to be to his parents and so, at two o'clock in the morning, just as he thought his parents would be getting ready for work in England, he dialled their number. It rang and rang until the answer-machine cut in. Elvis left a hurried message, never thinking that Aaron and Priscilla had left early for the airport and were on their way to find him.

'Hi, Elvis here', he said. 'We need to speak. I am at the cathedral in Graceland. Things have gone sort-of pear-shaped. Can't take 'phone calls, no battery but ring Roger for background. Lots of love.'

When he rang-off, Elvis realised he had power for just one more call. It would have to be to Roger, Fiona or Kirsty. He decided to wait until morning.

Despite his anxieties, and the stuffy heat of his room, Elvis eventually managed to fall asleep. He was woken at half-past seven when the suite was unlocked and a young man in a white jumpsuit entered carrying a tray of breakfast.

'Good morning, Elvis, Sir', he said cheerfully. 'Coffee, orange-juice, eggs, hash-browns and toast.'

He placed the tray on a table and left without further word, locking the door behind him.

Elvis looked at his watch. He sleepily climbed out of bed and went to the bathroom. A few minutes later he sat at the table and sipped at a coffee, with his elbows on the table, holding the cup in both hands. After a few minutes, he picked at his breakfast and drank the orange-juice, killing time before he could decently call his friends. It was his last lifeline and one he could not afford to waste by ringing too early and discovering Fiona's 'phone switched-off.

He watched the digital clock by his bed and as soon as 07.59.59 switched to 08.00.00, he called. Fiona answered after two rings.

'Elvis? Is that you? We're so worried. Where are you?'

'I'm at the cathedral in Memphis. I think I'm being kept prisoner. They say they... ' But Fiona heard nothing more. Elvis's 'phone went dead, its battery exhausted. She never heard him say '... think I really am Elvis and say they can make lots of money by... Hello Fiona... Are you still there? Damn'.

The 'phone in the suite rang. Elvis answered.

'Good morning Elvis. I hope you have slept well?' said Barker. 'We have a busy day ahead. You need to be ready in half-an-hour.'

'Why? What are we doing?' Elvis asked.

'I'll answer all your questions later', Barker replied. 'See you soon. Wear what you want... anything in the closet. I hope the selection is to your liking. Have a nice day.' And he hung up before Elvis could say any more.

'I've drawn up a schedule', announced Barker, precisely thirty-minutes later after he'd knocked on the door, turned the key and let himself into Elvis's quarters. He gave Elvis a sheet of papers embossed with the Church Crest, a lightening-bolt superimposed on a cross. It was the day's schedule.

'We have a meeting with the attorneys for an hour. Mr Perryburger and his guys. More papers to sign. Then a photo-shoot for publicity pictures. At noon, the rehearsal for the Healing Service with the orchestra and choir. You will be singing of course. Then it's lunch with the cathedral-vergers so that we can introduce you properly to the staff. At two o'clock the Healing Service is scheduled to start. We have one every week but this time, as you will be there, it'll be bigger than ever with TV and press. You'll probably have to bless a few handicapped kids and give teddy bears to the ones with cancer. I'll show you which ones they are - but no interviews. At three-thirty, we have a series of back-to-back, brief meetings to introduce you to our key Church members and leaders of the affiliated fan-clubs. At five-thirty, after a fifteen-minute bathroom and drinks break, you will be meeting with the robemakers. At six-thirty, you will be signing five-hundred copies of the Reverend Doctor's books. These will be sold after the Service on Sunday at $250 each. At seven, you will dress for dinner and at seven-fifteen, we take you to The Peabody Hotel for the "Welcome-back to Memphis" Banquet. Everybody who is anybody will be there and they're paying $2,000 each for a ticket. At ten o'clock you will be back here. After a video-link with the fan-club in Hawaii, your time will be your own.'

'But I can't do all that.'

'No choice. It's all arranged. Unless you want to spend the next five-years inside a Tennessee penitentiary? And don't forget, when you're talking to people, you are Elvis-returned. None of this nonsense about being from England. Sound American.'

'But what do I tell people when they ask where I've been or what my plans are?'

'Just say it'll all be revealed in due course. Don't try and be clever.'

'When do I get to do the test to prove I'm not Elvis?'

'Oh, didn't I say? After the photos with the crips. The local police-department will take swabs with the press watching.'

'Can I have a sample to test privately?' asked Elvis. He was suspicious that Barker might have the police-scientists under his control too. In fact, by this time, Barker had no need to call-on any favours to get the DNA confirmed. He had taken the back-up DNA-sample given by Elvis at the first press conference, checked it with a sample taken from the wart and knew for certain that the police-test would confirm the match.

'I want my own sample to test', Elvis repeated.

'Sure thing', said Barker. 'I'll get your personal-manager to arrange it.'

'My personal-manager? Who's that?'

'Me, of course. Now get your butt moving, you're keeping people waiting.'

As they walked from his suite back to the offices, Elvis noticed they were being followed by two, muscular vergers. Every time Elvis and Barker took a left, the vergers took a left, just three paces behind. When they took a right, the vergers took a right.

'Why are we being followed?' Elvis asked.

'Security', said Barker and then added, as if remembering something he had forgotten, 'do you have a cellphone with you?'

'Er, no', lied Elvis.

'Check him out', said Barker nodding at one of the vergers.

Elvis was held against the wall and frisked. The verger felt a tell-tale lump in an inside-pocket. He held out his hand for Elvis to hand the 'phone over.

'You be straight with us and we'll be straight with you', said Barker. 'No more messing, or the cops get involved.'

The verger held the cellphone in his hand for a moment and then dropped it on the ground. Without saying a word he crushed it under his foot and pushed the remnants to the side of the corridor with his shoe.

Barker walked-on and Elvis followed.

After Elvis's arrest, Roger, Kirsty and Fiona had driven back to Memphis. They booked into the same hostel they had stayed at before. Roger was keen that they try 'phoning Elvis but Fiona vetoed the idea. 'No, please don't do that', she implored. 'They might shoot him.' She described how the four cops had drawn their guns when Elvis had reached into his pocket to answer his 'phone at the gas-station. 'Wait for him to call us. He will, as soon as he can.'

That night Fiona kept her cellphone by the bed. She barely slept for anxiety. What would she do if Elvis did not call? Roger had suggested they go to the police-headquarters in the morning. 'If we haven't heard by eight in the morning', Kirsty agreed, 'let's go to the police'.

At seven-fifty-nine Fiona was watching her digital-watch. At eight o'clock, prompt, they would leave for the police-headquarters she told the others. But then, just three-seconds after eight, her 'phone rang.

'Elvis, is that you? We're so worried. Where are you?'

'I'm at the cathedral in Memphis. I think I'm being kept prisoner. They say they... ' The line went dead.

'He's been cut-off', said Fiona. 'But he's at the cathedral being kept prisoner. Come on. Let's get round there. Now.'

'Hang-on', said Roger and Kirsty together.

'Once we get there', Roger continued, 'what will we do?'

'What can we do?' Kirsty added.

'I don't know', said Fiona, 'but we've got to do something and once we are there we might see him. Or we can ask where he is'.

'But if the police picked him up, why would he be a prisoner at the cathedral?' asked Kirsty.

'I don't know', said Fiona, 'but that's what he said. "Being kept prisoner at the cathedral"'.

'I don't understand what's going on', said Roger. 'He's clearly in some sort of trouble. My God, I wish I'd never thought of the stupid joke in the first place. Pear-shaped or what. But those DNA-tests. What on earth is that all about? Elvis can't possibly have Elvis Presley's DNA. How did they swing that?'

With no plan in mind and not quite knowing what to expect, the three friends set-off for the cathedral. They arrived to find a large crowd of fans milling around outside. The gossip was that Elvis Presley had spent the night there and would be making a public appearance sometime during the day. The cathedral itself was closed and from time-to-time a verger emerged to make a short announcement.

As Roger, Kirsty and Fiona arrived, an announcement was being-made to the effect that Elvis had had a comfortable night and was looking forward to starting his new ministry. 'He asked me personally', the verger lied, 'to send his love to every one of his loyal friends here today'.

'We want Elvis! We want Elvis! We want Elvis!' the fans began to chant.

'When will we see him?' someone shouted.

'Later, I promise you', said the verger and he walked up the cathedral steps and into the building again. Two cops immediately came-forward to stop the fans from following him.

Roger said that he would have a look around the back of the cathedral and see what was going-on. He returned only a minute later. 'Everything is cordoned-off', he reported.

'So that's what Elvis meant by being kept a prisoner', said Fiona. 'We can't get in and he can't get out.'

'We need to try and find out what's really going-on', said Kirsty. 'Why don't we split-up and go and talk to people? Roger talk to the fans and Fiona and I will chat up the security-guys and the police. Meet back here in half-an-hour.'

For Elvis's first engagement of the day, attorney Perryburger was accompanied by several associates. There were accountants, financial-advisers and several other legal and commercial-specialists so far as Elvis could make-out from the introductions. They were planning a major legal-case to wrest control of The Graceland Estate away from CKX and Lisa Marie.

'We have no problem in proving you are Elvis', Perryburger said. 'We do have some difficulty in explaining where you've been since you died and how it is you've returned as a young man.

'While the courts will accept the word of the scientists that you have the matching DNA, the court won't accept that you are the Messiah, miraculously returned-to-earth by the will of God.'

'Well I haven't', began Elvis. Then he quickly assumed his best, British accent and continued. 'I am English. Born and bred in England. My parents are UK citizens. I am in The States as part of a round-the-world trip before continuing with my education. And how you think I am Elvis-reincarnated is a mystery to me. My friends dressed me up as Elvis as a joke and the whole business in the cathedral was a ghastly mistake.'

'I don't doubt that for a minute,' said Barker, 'but we, I mean you of course, stand to make billions of dollars by maintaining the story that you are Elvis. We've got to find a story that will convince a court'.

'So it's all just a money making-sham!' retorted Elvis. 'Well I don't want anything to do with it.'

He stood up, pushing his chair back.

'Fair enough', said Barker calmly. 'I'll 'phone the cops then. I hope you enjoy the next five-years as a guest in one of our state's prisons meeting Mr Carioli's friends.'

Elvis sat down again.

'So we understand each other now, do we Elvis?' enquired Barker.

Elvis just nodded.

'And don't let me hear you talk British again.'

'Now let's just get back to business', said Mr Perryburger. 'We've just got to get the story straight and Presley's Estate is there for the asking.'

Roger, Kirsty and Fiona spent a useful thirty-minutes gathering intelligence. Kirsty persuaded one of the security-guards to point-out the room where Elvis had slept the night before. 'Will he be there again tonight?' she asked innocently. 'I guess so', the guard replied. 'This is his home now.'

Several of the fans told Roger that they hoped to see Elvis later that day at the Healing Service. 'One of the vergers promised Elvis would be there. I expect there'll be a big turnout and some amazing miracles.' One fan introduced herself as Joleene. She was in Memphis on vacation with her daughter Holly. 'I'm a real big Elvis-fan', she said, 'and I sure want Elvis to give Holly a blessing. He can't cure her or nothing but to have his blessing... wow!' Holly, who was standing beside her mother, gave a big toothy grin. She was a lively-looking, eight-year-old but her limbs were a bit shaky and when she spoke her speech was slow and slurred.

She held out her hand for Roger to shake. 'Hi, I'm Holly', she said. 'What's your name and where are you from. We're from Chicago, Illinois.'

'I'm Roger and I'm from England.'

'Wow', said Holly, impressed. 'Have you met The Queen?'

'No', answered Roger, 'but I did see her once. I was in London and she drove past in a black car with a police-escort. At least, I think it was The Queen. It might have been Prince Charles.'

'Holly's got cerebral-palsy', said her mother protectively. 'She's a bright girl and walks and talks great considering, but she's just a bit wobbly.'

'I'm fine', said Holly. 'You fuss too much. It was my idea to come to Memphis. I am the hugest Elvis-fan in the world and I want to meet him.'

'So what happens at the Healing Service?' Roger asked. 'Can anyone go?'

'Oh yes', explained Holly. 'We were here last week and there was plenty of room, though I expect today it'll be packed out with everyone wanting to get a glimpse of Elvis. It's amazing isn't it? I always knew I'd see him one day.'

Fiona gathered from one of the vergers that the Healing Service would also be open to the media. 'It'll be like a turkey-race on Thanksgiving -'cept they'll all be wanting a slice of the action', he said.

Kirsty was accosted by one fan to be told that if there was someone inside the cathedral claiming to be Elvis, then he was an impostor. The fan was brandishing that morning's paper with its headline, 'Elvis arrested at gas-station'.

'He gotta be fake. Look, the photo shows he's a young man. And I saw him on TV too. He can't be twenty. Elvis is an old man now. He never died, you know. He faked his own death to get away from the shallow world of being a celebrity and his deceitful and parasitic friends. I expect he found himself some nice, quiet place to live. He'd be an old man now of course, not like that young fella they've got in there.'

Kirsty nodded but didn't feel she wanted to be drawn into this particular argument. She mumbled something about having to find her friends and left the fan talking to anyone who'd listen to him. 'He's a fake. I tell you, he's a fake.'

With the rest of the morning and some of the afternoon to get through before the Healing Service began, the three decided they needed some provisions. Fiona volunteered to stay behind to keep their place in-line while Roger and Kirsty went to go and buy bottles of water, burgers and chips and some cookies. By the time they returned, the crowd outside the cathedral had doubled in size. Each one of the hundreds of fans converging on the cathedral had had the same idea. The best chance of seeing Elvis, they all reckoned, was to be at the Healing Service at two o'clock.

The long, hot wait was livened by the cheery mood of the fans. They swapped Elvis stories and memories. Strangers soon became old friends. Around noon however, a great hush descended on the crowd as everyone listened to the celestial sounds of a choir and orchestra inside the cathedral accompanying the unmistakable voice of Elvis. It was the rehearsal and sound-check for the service.

It was around two o'clock, local-time, that Aaron and Priscilla were expecting to land in America. Their flight was on time and it was at precisely twelve-minutes past two that the flight-attendant invited them to deplane at Dallas/Fort Worth and follow the signs to customs and immigration. Aaron tried several times to telephone Elvis as they walked through the airport but each time an impersonal voice told him the telephone was switched-off and to try his call later. After waiting in-line for almost an hour they found themselves at the head of the queue, ready to go through the formalities of entry which included providing a thumbprint as unique identification. When asked by the official behind the glass screen for the purpose of her visit to the USA, Priscilla's answer sounded so ludicrous that Aaron feared she might be refused entry.

'I am the mother of Elvis', announced Priscilla. 'I have come to see my son return in glory to save the world.'

But the official seemed unconcerned. 'Have a nice vacation', he simply replied.

Once successfully welcomed into the USA, they had to collect their luggage and clear customs before checking-in for the domestic-flight to Memphis. After several more attempts to rouse Elvis on his mobile, Aaron gave up. 'Have you got Roger's number?'

Shortly before two o'clock, almost a thousand people were waiting on Elvis Presley Boulevard outside the cathedral. When the doors opened there was a rush for the best seats. Roger temporarily lost the girls in the crush but eventually they found themselves together with seats near the front, well-placed to see the action. Vergers were ushering anyone in a wheelchair, or with a carer, to the front row. Roger spotted Joleene and Holly walking down the aisle and being personally escorted to the front row by Archdeacon Barker in his robes.

'We'll find you somewhere to sit', Barker was saying to them reassuringly. 'Look, here's a place.' There was an ordinary seat with a spare wheelchair placed next to it. He suggested Holly sit in the wheelchair. 'You don't mind do you?' he said. 'It'll save us having to fetch another chair and no-one seems to need it just now. It's one of the cathedral's spares.'

Holly beamed with pleasure at having found a seat so near the stage.

The entry of the choir indicated that the service was starting. They filed-in, humming to the sound of the Gospel music on the organ and swaying in time to the beat. After a brief introduction by Barker, in which he said that Elvis himself would today be blessing those in need of his prayers, he invited *The Elvis Rainbow Gospel Choir* to praise the Lord and welcome Elvis home.

They sang several numbers and Barker read from *The Good News of Elvis*. He recounted how Elvis Presley used to arrive, unannounced, at local hospitals with presents for children and how he once, anonymously, paid for a life-saving operation for a child whose parents were on-welfare. As the minutes ticked by the congregation began to get restless. They had come to see Elvis but Elvis had not materialised.

Elvis was in the building but still in his suite. Two vergers had been detailed to keep him company and were under strict instructions not to let him on-stage until they were given the signal.

The signal came as a knock on the door just as the choir was standing to sing Elvis's most famous Gospel number. He was escorted back-stage.

The first-verse was entrusted to a soloist, a small girl with a pure, soft voice that filled the cathedral with a warm spine-tingling sound.

O Lord my God, When I in awesome wonder,
Consider all the worlds Thy Hands have made;
I see the stars, I hear the rolling thunder,
Thy power throughout the universe displayed.

At which point the whole choir exploded with sound.

Then sings my soul, My Saviour God, to Thee,
How great Thou art, How great Thou art.
Then sings my soul, My Saviour God, to Thee,
How great Thou art, How great Thou art!

Elvis stood just out-of-sight of the congregation, waiting for the entrance he had rehearsed earlier. The second-verse was sung *pianissimo* by the sopranos.

When through the woods, and forest glades I wander,
And hear the birds sing sweetly in the trees.
When I look down, from lofty mountain grandeur
And see the brook, and feel the gentle breeze.

For the refrain, the choir and organ again thundered.

Then sings my soul, My Saviour God, to Thee,
How great Thou art, How great Thou art.
Then sings my soul, My Saviour God, to Thee,
How great Thou art, How great Thou art!

As the third-verse started, a technician thrust the microphone into Elvis's hands. 'After this verse', he whispered, 'you're on'. Elvis waited, listening to the basses with their deep, velvety voices.

And when I think, that God, His Son not sparing;
Sent Him to die, I scarce can take it in.
That on the Cross, my burden gladly bearing,
He bled and died to take away my sin.

Again the whole choir responded with a waterfall of music.

Then sings my soul, My Saviour God, to Thee,
How great Thou art, How great Thou art.
Then sings my soul, My Saviour God, to Thee,
How great Thou art, How great Thou art!

As the final verse began, sung by a lone, male voice, the congregation strained to see who was singing. Was it Elvis?

Could it be Elvis? Then, unobtrusively emerging from behind the choir, Elvis was on-stage.

When Christ shall come, with shout of acclamation,
And take me home, what joy shall fill my heart.
Then I shall bow, in humble adoration,
And then proclaim, My God, how great Thou art!

The cheering, the applause, the tears, the hysteria that followed caught Roger, Kirsty and Fiona entirely by surprise. Their friend, Elvis, was up on-stage and everyone in the building except for them seemed to be standing and screaming, giving him an ecstatic, amazing welcome. They didn't want to be conspicuous, so stood-up and joined in the applause. The choir sang again, the organ played *fortissimo*, the press-cameras flashed. The television-cameramen pushed and elbowed everyone aside for the best shots. And no-one noticed Barker checking that everything was in place for his coup-de théâtre.

Then sings my soul, My Saviour God, to Thee,
How great Thou art, How great Thou art.
Then sings my soul, My Saviour God, to Thee,
How great Thou art, How great Thou art!

The cheering continued for several minutes and Elvis looked stunned. He had never imagined anything like this reception. Barker indicated he should go to the far side of the stage and the vergers began to push the wheelchairs of disabled and sick children up the ramp, across the stage and past him as he stood there. As each wheelchair passed by, he was given a scarf to hand-out. By the time the cheering had died-down, some twenty-youngsters with their carers had received scarves and a blessing from Elvis. Just one wheelchair was left. It was Holly. She had been wheeled up the ramp by Barker himself, and while she was protesting that she would prefer to walk and didn't need the chair, all the congregation could see were her jerking limbs and grimacing face.

Once on stage, Barker stopped pushing and whispered in Holly's ear, 'Sorry, I forgot you could walk. I won't wheel you any further. You just walk to Elvis yourself'.

Holly pulled herself out of the chair and ran towards Elvis in her excitement to meet him. Quite taken by surprise, Elvis held out his arms to catch-her and spontaneously lifted her into the air with a whirl.

The TV-pictures were stunning - and of course the camera never lies. Without waiting for anything further to happen, the TV-crews knew they had the shots they had promised their editors. They all dashed-out of the cathedral lugging their equipment in which the amazing footage had been electronically-captured. Within minutes it had been sent by satellite all-around the world.

Aaron and Priscilla were in the domestic-departures area at Dallas/Fort Worth, trying to ring Roger, when Aaron glanced at a TV-screen showing the latest world-news.

'Look Priscilla, it's the Elvis Cathedral', he said pointing, and they both started to watch a news-flash.

'I saw it with my own eyes', said the reporter. 'A young girl, disabled from birth and in a wheelchair - yes, in a wheelchair - rose out of her chair and not just walked but ran across the stage to the man they say is Elvis-reincarnated.'

'Oh my God', exclaimed Aaron. 'It can't be. What is Elvis playing at?'

'Oh my God', said Priscilla. 'It's all true. I knew it, I knew it. Elvis has performed his first miracle!'

CHAPTER FOURTEEN

Barker brought the service to a close shortly after the apparent-miracle had occurred, just as the congregation started to look dangerously enthusiastic. People in the front rows were starting to move forward, pushing chairs aside. Fans, weeping hysterically, pressed towards the front with their arms outstretched, determined to make direct contact with Elvis in the flesh. Elvis became increasingly alarmed and beckoned to Barker to get him off the stage.

Roger was in the crowd surging towards Elvis, thinking this would be his best chance to make contact with his friend. He caught Elvis's eye, and had a desperate look of recognition in return, before Barker bundled Elvis backstage. They went through a side-door into the office reception-area and Barker shut and locked the door behind them. Then he motioned to Elvis to help him drag a heavy desk against the door in case the fans tried to break it down.

Roger watched Elvis and Barker disappear from view and then pushed his way back to Fiona and Kirsty against the flow of the determined, human-tide. 'Let's get out of here', was all he said. 'It's getting scary.'

'I can't be certain', he said once they were out on the street, 'but I think Elvis spotted me and knows we're here. I can't imagine they'll try and get him out of the building now, far too risky. They'll bunker-down in the back and hope that things quieten-down. Let's go and get a coffee and work-out what to do next'.

They were sitting in the fast-food restaurant opposite the cathedral, watching fans being shepherded away. Roger switched his mobile-phone on and immediately it rang.

'Roger? It's Aaron, Elvis's Dad. We're in America and on our way to Memphis and can't get hold of Elvis on his mobile. What's going on?'

'It's Elvis's Dad', Roger mouthed to Kirsty and Fiona, 'He's in America.'

'Yes, it's Roger. No, Elvis isn't with us. We're not quite sure what's happened. But I'll tell you what I know.'

He told him the whole story, from meeting Fiona and Kirsty, through to hatching the practical joke which had gone so badly wrong, and ending with Elvis's arrest and the amazing scenes in the cathedral they'd just witnessed.

'Yes, we've just seen some of it on the airport television. We're changing 'planes in Dallas and coming to see what we can do. We knew something awful had happened. We should arrive in Memphis in about two-and-a-half hours time.'

'Shall we meet you at the airport?' Roger offered. Fiona and Kirsty nodded.

'That would be kind, if it's no bother.'

'No bother at all, especially in that I think it's really all my fault for dressing him up as Elvis in the first place', apologised Roger.

'We'll 'phone you when we land and fix where to meet. I wouldn't blame yourself', said Aaron, 'I blame myself far more'.

Roger repeated Aaron's words back to the girls. 'What on earth do you think he means?'

'That was stupid. I shouldn't have said that', said Aaron as he finished the call. 'I shouldn't have even hinted. Elvis has to be the first to know the truth.'

'He will know already', replied Priscilla confidently. 'He is God's chosen-one. He'll know everything.'

'Priscilla,' Aaron turned towards her with notes of both determination and steel in his voice. 'I know what you've been reading but don't jump to any conclusions until we have spoken to Elvis ourselves. He's probably worried sick about what's going-on. And who knows what the Church's motive is in all this? There's something very odd going on.'

'But we've seen the miracle ourselves', said Priscilla.

'We've seen a girl on television run across a stage. We don't know any of the details or what the story behind it might be. So promise, not a word about Elvis the Messiah or how he came to be conceived until we talk to Elvis ourselves. Promise me.'

'I promise.'

Aaron and Priscilla landed on time and 'phoned Roger. He and the girls were already at the airport. They fixed a rendezvous and fifteen-minutes later he was introducing them to Kirsty and Fiona.

'We've got to see Elvis urgently', said Priscilla. 'We have something very important to tell him.'

'Just a moment darling', said Aaron, emphasising the word 'darling', as he did when he wished to emphasise he was taking control of the situation himself. 'More important is finding-out if he really is a prisoner and why.'

'We were thinking of going back to the cathedral', said Fiona, 'and trying to get a message to him. We know which is his room. Perhaps we can attract his attention or throw him a note.'

'Why don't we just walk up to the door and say who we are?' Priscilla suggested.

'Because they wouldn't let you in. There are hundreds of fans there, trying every possible story to get to see him. They simply wouldn't believe you.'

Barker came to see Elvis bringing a pile of books for him to sign.

'Just write "Elvis"', he instructed. 'I've got a sample autograph here for you to copy. We don't want any clever-fans saying it ain't the real thing.'

'We never had that DNA-test you promised', Elvis reminded him as he started writing.

'Well it was kinda difficult after the Healing Service', responded Barker. 'We'll find another time. Sensational pictures though.'

'What pictures?'

'On the television. They're all talking about the miracle. That little girl who leapt out of her wheelchair and ran to see you. They say you have healing-powers.'

'But I didn't do anything', Elvis protested vehemently.

'Well, something amazing sure happened there. Now hurry-up with those books and don't forget it's the big banquet, downtown this evening.'

Aaron, Priscilla, Roger, Fiona and Kirsty crammed into the small hire-car and drove to the cathedral. Even though the crowds had largely dispersed, they nevertheless had to park several blocks away. Aaron had written a note to Elvis which he planned to hand-in to one of the vergers. It simply told him that he and his mother were in Memphis and hoped to see him. On arrival at the cathedral, a security-guard took the envelope and shoved it in a box with several-hundred other letters and cards from fans. 'Sure he'll read it', he said with a note of indifferent weariness in his voice. 'I'll give it to Elvis myself.'

No-one was being allowed into the cathedral so Kirsty took the others round the side of the building to show them where Elvis's window had been pointed out to her earlier. It was around seven-fifteen and there was a light on. Priscilla said she thought she could see Elvis's silhouette. There was certainly someone in the room.

'Let's all shout together, as loud as we can and see if he hears us', said Fiona. 'One, two, three... ELVIS!'

A security-guard noticed them but shrugged his shoulders. More crazy fans, he thought.

'ELVIS! ELVIS! ELVIS!'

Elvis was in his room. He had been given fifteen-minutes precisely to change for the dinner. A white tuxedo had been prepared along with perfectly-creased, black trousers, or pants as he now had to call them, an embroidered-shirt and highly-polished shoes. He'd had a quick-shower, changed, and as he walked back into the sitting-room heard voices outside shouting his name. Just more fans, he thought but then wondered if there was something in the timbre of the voices which was familiar. English accents? He peeked around the drawn-blind to see what was going on. To his amazement, he saw his parents and his three friends jumping up-and-down in the street below and shouting out his name. He pulled back the blind and waved. They waved-back frantically.

'He's seen us', cried Priscilla. The others fixed their eyes on the window. Elvis put his finger to his mouth miming the 'ssh' of 'silence'. Then he retreated behind the blind and began to write with his finger on the fabric in mirror-writing.

'What's he doing?' whispered Roger.

'He's spelling something out for us', said Aaron. 'P, E, A, B, O, D, Y.'

'Peabody?' said Kirsty. 'Have we got that right? What does he mean?'

'It's the big hotel downtown', said Aaron.

Elvis disappeared from view abruptly. He had thought he heard someone coming into his suite and did not want to be caught signalling a message. The group outside stayed looking up at the window for several more minutes until the light was switched-off.

'Out the way', the security-guard said to them curtly. 'We've got to open the gates.'

They were hustled aside as a black stretch-limo swept-in. Two minutes later it swept-out again.

'I bet Elvis is in it', said Fiona.

'Then it'll be going to The Peabody Hotel for sure', said Roger. 'That's what he was trying to tell us. Let's go.'

The $2,000 tickets for the banquet to welcome Elvis back to Memphis had all been snapped up within minutes of appearing for sale on the Church website. Within hours, they were selling second-hand for twice-the-price via on-line auction-sites. A number of well-known celebrities had changed their busy schedules at short-notice to fly their private-jets to the city. The Mayor would be in attendance and all the leading, Memphis business-people and billionaire-residents. The State Governor, two senators and five congressmen all had tickets. The cream of Tennessee-society was planning to be there, the great, the good and the rich. Despite having barely thirty-six hours to make arrangements, the hotel-management had pulled out all the stops. At the Reverend Doctor's insistence, the Church had had contingency-plans in place for just such an event for years. Barker had had nothing to do but make it happen. Everything had been set-out in detail in a specially-prepared folio of instructions in his personal-safe. Barker had telephoned Mr Carioli to invite him but he declined. 'I don't do public', he said. 'I'll watch on TV.'

As eager as every guest was to see Elvis in person, there was another question on everybody's lips. Would his daughter, Lisa Marie, be there to greet him as her father? And if she decided to attend, how would she greet him? Would she endorse his claim to be the reincarnation of Elvis Presley?

The stretch-limo arrived at the hotel on the dot of seven-thirty. Crowds of fans and photographers were waiting outside. A posse of large vergers cleared a space for Elvis. Somehow a woman evaded the cordon and fell at Elvis's feet.

'Heal me, heal me', she pleaded, grasping at his clothes. Elvis looked shocked as she was brusquely shoved aside. Once inside the hotel he was taken straight to an elevator. 'I've booked the Presidential Suite', said Barker. 'You stay there till everybody's ready for dinner and come down when I tell you to.'

Elvis was escorted upstairs by four vergers while Barker went to the Ballroom. The Grand Ballroom was immense, forty or fifty yards square he'd reckoned. Well over one-thousand tickets had been sold and the room was full but not crowded. Comfortable and exclusive was what the atmosphere had to be according to the very-specific instructions given by the Reverend Doctor. On a stage, at one end of the room, was a string-quartet. 'The guests will be entertained by a classical-quartet playing Elvis-hits', he had written. As Barker walked down the central-aisle, the musicians were playing an incongruous arrangement of *Jailhouse Rock*. Dozens of round tables seating twelve-apiece were dispersed through the glittering room. There were substantial floral-decorations in the centre of each table and exotic flower-arrangements set against the walls. A life-size ice-sculpture of Elvis stood in the centre of the room adjacent to the table where Barker, Perryburger and Elvis would sit with a hand-picked party of celebrities and Lisa Marie, if she turned up.

With Roger as navigator, Fiona still got lost several times on the way to downtown-Memphis. Kirsty sat with Priscilla and Aaron in the back, holding Priscilla's hand and plying-her with tissues as she gently wept to herself. It proved very difficult to find space to park the car near the hotel since so many fans had come to see Elvis. The parking lot opposite was full and every space on the streets seemed taken. Rounding the block for the second-time, Roger realised the hotel had its own subterranean car-park. 'Turn here', he commanded suddenly when he spotted it, grabbing and turning the steering wheel himself. Fiona screamed at him but within seconds, and accompanied by an impressive squeal of tyres, they were going down a ramp into a concrete cavern of a garage.

As most of the guests had been driven by chauffeurs who were due to collect them again at the end of the evening, it was surprisingly empty, as Roger had hoped. Fiona found a space easily.

With the car safely parked, they began searching for a way into the hotel. They found a concrete walkway leading to a carpeted lobby and Priscilla asked a young man in hotel-uniform if Elvis was in the building.

'He sure ain't left yet, Ma'am', he replied.

'Where is he now?'

'The banquet's in the Grand Ballroom or he might still be in the Presidential Suite.'

They found their way to an opulent foyer crowded with photographers and television-crews milling all-around the elevator.

'We're expecting him to come through here sometime soon', one of the reporters told Fiona. 'Just like the ducks.'

'Let's wait here', said Roger. 'He's bound to see us.'

A few late-arrivals for the banquet were making their way past and Roger noted the direction they were being sent.

A frisson of activity went through the press-corps when Barker was spotted, approaching the elevator-doors. His timing was perfect, for the moment he arrived the doors opened and Elvis, escorted by four, large vergers, stepped-out. Cameras started flashing everywhere and two TV-reporters rushed forward with microphones.

It was his mother Elvis noticed first. Taking his escort by surprise, he pushed past the media-scrum and threw his arms around her. Then he saw Aaron and embraced his parents together. Instantly Barker was alongside him, flushed and angry. 'What are you doing?' he demanded.

'Hey, these are my parents', exclaimed Elvis delightedly, quite-forgetting to use his American-voice. 'From England. And these are my friends, Roger, Fiona and Kirsty.'

'I don't care who they are', exploded Barker, in fury. 'You can't talk to them now.'

'Just five minutes?'

'No way! You've got a thousand people waiting to see you. And talk properly. American-like. Just remember what I told you...'

'Don't you talk to my son like that', broke-in Aaron, surprised at his own audacity. 'We've travelled thousands of miles to see him. We want to check he's OK and not in any kind of trouble. His mother's very worried.'

'OK... afterwards...', snapped Barker with no intention of keeping his promise. 'Meet-up in the Presidential Suite when the banquet's finished.'

Elvis had been looking at his mother and thought he had detected a strange look in her face. It seemed an odd mix of anxiety and adoration which he could not quite understand.

'We have something very important to tell you', she said, taking his arm.

'Important? What about?' Elvis asked.

'We need to talk to you somewhere in private.'

Elvis looked at Barker. 'We need five minutes together now.'

'Later.'

'Now', said Elvis emphatically.

Barker suddenly realised that every word was being recorded by two television-crews. If this middle-aged, English couple were indeed Elvis's parents, it might be best if what they had to say to their son was not made available for public consumption.

'OK then. Back in the elevator. I'll stall them at the banquet. But five minutes and no more.'

When Elvis, his parents and his friends were in the elevator and the doors had closed, Elvis tried to explain what had happened to him.

'It just started as a joke', he said. 'Fiona dressed me as Elvis Presley and we went to the Cathedral Service. They were expecting the real-Elvis to return to earth or something daft. I chickened-out when it looked kind-of serious but some kid in the congregation saw me and before I knew what had happened, I'd been propelled up the front and an old man, who later died said I was Elvis Presley. The whole place went mad. I managed to escape but got picked-up by the police and brought back to the cathedral where I'm being made to pretend to be Elvis Presley. If not, they say the police will re-arrest me for fraud and I could go to jail for five-years. The whole thing is crazy.

Aren't I glad you've found me. And the craziest thing of all is that they say I stand to inherit Elvis's fortune because they can prove with DNA-tests that I really am Presley. How utterly ridiculous is that?'

By this time Elvis, Aaron and Priscilla were standing in the sumptuous principal-room of the Presidential Suite. But Priscilla did not notice the surroundings. She had taken Elvis by the arm again. Her face was pallid and tear-stained. She knew she had no option but to tell him the truth.

'Elvis', she said, quietly but with a voice full of emotion. 'Elvis, my darling Elvis. You are Elvis Presley.'

'I am Elvis Presley', Elvis repeated, not understanding what his mother was talking-about at all.

'Yes. You have returned to earth to be the redeemer.' She sank to her knees and kissed his hands. 'My son and my God.'

Elvis was stunned and turned to his father. 'What's happening?'

'I don't know about all this religious-stuff', Aaron said, 'but I can confirm that genetically you are Elvis Presley. We've brought you up and loved you as our son but in fact you are his clone.'

'I don't believe I'm hearing this', Elvis retorted in amazement. He looked to Fiona for support and then to Roger and Kirsty. He turned back to his parents. 'What's going on? Has Barker been threatening you? Did he tell you to say all this about me being a clone? How could I be? All my memories are of living as your son at our home?'

'This isn't easy and we should have told you much earlier', Aaron said shamefacedly. 'You weren't conceived in the normal way. We cloned you from Elvis's DNA. Genetically we are not your parents. You are not our flesh and blood even though we love you and brought you up as our own... ' His explanation trailed-off...

'So where did you get the DNA?'

'From a wart in a travelling Elvis Exhibition... '

'And how did you clone me from that?'

'Well, you know I was working on animal-cloning at the laboratory and your mother was working at the hospital in the IVF unit. We had the means. She retrieved a human egg, I extracted the DNA from the wart and we made you with a pipette and a petri-dish at home. Your mother then carried you for nine-months and gave birth to you.'

'Oh my God!' shouted Elvis. 'Why? Why?'

'I so desperately wanted my child to be like Elvis', broke-in Priscilla.

'But you've just told me I'm not your child', Elvis screamed back angrily. 'I am the product of some bizarre scientific experiment and you've lied to me all my life!'

'But don't you understand', pleaded Priscilla, 'it was all ordained. I realise now what we were really doing. We thought we did what we did because we wanted a child like Elvis but we were really part of a great cosmic-plan to bring Elvis back'.

'But I'm not Elvis Presley. I might look like him and sing like him but I feel like me. I am me.'

'No you have a special-mission', Priscilla insisted.

'Have you been listening to all that claptrap at the cathedral?' Elvis demanded in exasperation, having abandoned all semblance of caution.

He had listened to Barker in the cathedral and read passages from the copies of the Reverend Doctor's books left in his room. He had thought hard about the supposed-miracle and was quite sure it was nothing of the kind. The out-and-out greed of Barker and Perryburger had convinced him that the Church of The Latter-Day Elvis existed to worship mammon not God. The shadowy-influence of Mr Carioli and the mob was behind it all. The suckers who gave their money to Barker were sad and deluded fans who had left their common-sense at the door. These thoughts had churned around in his mind all day and at last he gave them expression. He felt a pang of sympathy for his mother, who had been duped like the many-other thousands of

Elvis-fans into thinking they had joined a genuine church but his guiding emotion remained one of confusion and anger. He let his thoughts tumble out in a tirade. Roger, Fiona and Kirsty listened speechless. Elvis concluded with his summary of the whole set-up. 'Garon Love was a nutter and Barker is a conman.' Priscilla collapsed into a chair and began wailing loudly.

Barker, who was now outside the Presidential Suite pacing-up and down the corridor, looked at his watch. Elvis had had his five minutes he decided and he would go and get him. His cellphone rang. It was Perryburger in the Ballroom.

'How much longer will you be?' he asked. 'Things are getting restless down here. They want to know where Elvis is.'

'I'm going to get him right now', replied Barker. He opened the door to the suite just as Elvis had reached his angry conclusion. 'Garon Love was a nutter and Barker is a conman', he heard. Barker stopped in his tracks.

'What are you saying?' he demanded.

'The truth', responded Elvis fiercely.

'These are my parents', he continued, 'or at least I thought they were. But I'm not their son. My father's a wart and my mother's a petri-dish. They cloned me from Elvis's DNA in their weird devotion for this obese, dead, American entertainer they and so-many-others are obsessed with. Elvis-f***ing-Presley. And you', Elvis was jabbing his finger right in Barker's face, 'are exploiting them. You're not an archdeacon, you're an asshole. A nasty, manipulating shit. Call the police if you like', he threatened. 'Have me arrested and I'll have my day in court.'

'Wait a bit', said Barker, desperate to calm things down and trying to make sense of the extraordinary story he'd just heard.

He had shut the door behind him and had indicated to the vergers with him to wait outside.

'Look, I think we all need to talk. Downstairs, I have a thousand of the most-important people in this and the neighbouring-states, each of whom has paid thousands-of-dollars to see you. If this evening goes well, we will have the backing of everyone who counts when we make the legal claim for Elvis's estate. With the same DNA, legally you are Elvis. Even if you're a clone, who needs to know? We all stand to make millions and you will be very rich.'

Priscilla had stopped crying, dried her eyes and adopted the sheepish look of someone who has just realised how foolish she might have been. Now her look changed to one of expectation and hope as she realised that all might be well in the end. She looked at her husband. Aaron had the gleam in his eye of someone who has just glimpsed a pile of gold.

'Rich?' asked Aaron tentatively.

'Very, very rich', assured Barker. 'Your Elvis will own The Graceland Estate and all rights to Elvis-merchandising from now on. Millions-and-millions of dollars a year. All you have to do is say nothing. I don't want to know how Elvis was cloned. I will even forget I heard it said that he was cloned. Leave it to me and say nothing to no-one.

'So now, Elvis,' Barker began again, 'come-on down and don't forget your American accent'.

But Elvis didn't move. 'This whole thing is sick. I don't want to pretend to be a dead-singer even if I do become mega-rich. I would be living a lie. I'd be a complete fraud.'

He looked at his friends for support. 'What do you think Roger?'

Roger shrugged his shoulders. 'It's a no-brainer. Take the money. You got a lucky break.'

'And you Kirsty?'

'I'm with Rog', she said quickly. 'Go for the money and think about quitting later, if you still want to.'

'I think they're right', said Aaron. 'You will be secure for life. And think what good you can do with all that money - helping charities and people-in-need.'

'And maybe blessings will come from it', added Priscilla. 'Something of what the Reverend Doctor was saying might even be true. You may have a great destiny ahead of you, even if you're not the real-Elvis returned.'

'Fiona', asked Elvis. 'What do you think?'

'Do what you think is right', she said firmly. 'Go downstairs with Barker, meet the Memphis rich and sign your life away. Or walk out of here now.'

Looking Elvis straight in the eye, she continued, quietly, 'if you do quit now, you needn't be alone. I'll come too if that's what you want?'

'Let's go', said Elvis after a short pause. He walked to the door and opened it and headed for the elevator.

Barker was relieved. So the lad has seen sense after all, he thought. He's going to the banquet. 'Yup, let's go', he repeated and followed behind Elvis, as did Fiona, Roger, Kirsty, Aaron, Priscilla and the vergers.

Nothing was said by anyone as the elevator descended. When the doors opened, the scrummage of reporters, photographers and TV-crews all converged together. Barker and the vergers were first out of the lift and knew exactly where they were going. They struggled through, heading purposefully for the Ballroom. Everyone followed them. Roger, Kirsty, Aaron and Priscilla were all jostled around as they tried to keep-up. Elvis grabbed Fiona by the hand and, in the confusion, Barker never noticed when they turned and headed in the opposite direction.

'Where's the car?' Elvis demanded as their determined-walk accelerated to a run.

Fiona quickly dragged him out-of-sight down a side-corridor. 'I think we can go this way', she said. 'The car's in the basement. We might just get away before they realise you're missing.'

CHAPTER FIFTEEN

On their way back to the hostel Fiona and Elvis swiftly made their plans. They were assuming the worst and that Barker would soon be hot on their trail.

'We can't take the car, the police might be looking for me again and they'd have the plate-number', said Elvis.

'And Barker could have his men at the airport', said Fiona, 'so we can't fly out of Memphis'.

'We could hitch?'

'Far too conspicuous.'

'Greyhound bus?'

'Good-thinking, Batman. There's a city-plan somewhere in the room. Let's see where the bus-station is.'

They had little time. They were acutely conscious of the possibility that Roger, Kirsty and Elvis's parents might burst in at any moment, followed by Barker and a contingent of his hefty, cathedral-vergers. Elvis found his passport and clothes. They had been packed by Fiona and brought back from Arkansas after his arrest. He had already changed from the tuxedo into his own, more-familiar gear when Fiona grabbed a pair of scissors and an electric razor and told him to sit-still on the edge of the bed.

With speed and no finesse, she started hacking at his hair, desperately trying to restyle it. Her mistake the first time they had left Memphis, was to change Elvis's clothes but do nothing about his hair. After a couple of minutes she looked at her handiwork with horror and decided on the ultimate solution. All of the hair would have to come off. Elvis himself was not consulted. His brain was so full of the anxieties of the moment, of escaping with all speed from Barker, Memphis and the USA that he gave no thought whatever to what Fiona was doing.

'That'll do', she muttered to herself, when she'd finished. 'No-one will ever think of looking for a bald Elvis.'

It was only when he inadvertently caught a glimpse of himself in the bathroom-mirror that Elvis realised how drastic his haircut had been.

'Oh my God!' he exclaimed. 'What have you done?'

'It'll grow', said Fiona unsympathetically. 'The main thing now is that you look like anyone but Elvis.'

Having packed the bare-essentials for the journey, they left the room, the hostel and the car behind them and, with just one rucksack each, started running for the Greyhound bus-station. They zig-zagged past pedestrians, crossed roads with reckless disregard for the traffic and didn't stop until they stood, breathless, before the long-distance bus-timetable.

They didn't care in the least in which direction they went from Memphis. All they wanted was a bus that departed as soon as possible and would take them overnight to a big city. The plan, to the extent that there was one, was to get as far away from Memphis as possible and then catch a 'plane to Britain. Fiona had calculated that having already asked her parents to top-up her credit-card account, she had enough credit to fly them both home.

They had both realised it was to their advantage to have a choice of buses and destinations since that would keep Barker guessing, should he ever think of looking for them on the Greyhound-network. After reviewing their options, they decided to take a bus heading north for Chicago. They didn't have long to wait before it left and it was scheduled to arrive in Chicago in time for breakfast. They were sure there would be direct flights to Britain from the city's international-airport.

Fiona bought the tickets while Elvis sat with the rucksacks. He had pulled his collar up to hide his face and then, thinking he might look too much like The King in a jumpsuit, had second thoughts and pulled his cap forward to hide his face. After a few minutes, Fiona came back to report that there were seats available on the Chicago bus and they could board soon.

Shortly-afterwards they were settled on the back-seat for the long journey through the night.

They huddled close to each other and slept fitfully. Around three o'clock in the morning, as the bus raced through Illinois, they were both awake and talking in a low whisper so as not to disturb the other passengers. As Elvis rested his head on Fiona's shoulder, he felt that she was the only person left in his life he could rely-on. There seemed nobody and nothing else on which he could depend. His friend Roger had let him down and his parents had shocked him to the core with their confessions. No longer could he even trust in his own identity. Who was he?

'I can't understand', Elvis whispered to her. 'If I'm his clone, why don't I feel more like Elvis? I don't really go for any of the things he liked, not even peanut-butter. Surely, if I am Elvis genetically I would be more like him in how I behave.'

'Well perhaps it's not all in the genes', Fiona replied softly. 'What about all the other influences in life? Upbringing for instance? You had Aaron and Priscilla as parents not Vernon and Gladys. You lived a comfortable life in England but Elvis lived in poverty in America. Your dad never went to prison.'

'He's never even had a parking-ticket as far as I know, though presumably stealing the DNA from the wart was hardly legal...

'But I remember how they used to dress-me like Elvis, take me to Elvis-concerts and play Elvis-music in the house all the time. Looking back, it was weird. As if they were trying to indoctrinate me into being Elvis.'

'They probably were', said Fiona. 'But Elvis himself had to discover who he was. He had to invent himself. However we're brought-up and whatever our parents want for us, we all have to decide for ourselves who we are.'

Fiona gave his hand a comforting squeeze and pondered for a while the things her Elvis had been saying. It was not long before something else occurred to her. 'Twins. Twins have the same DNA.'

'Yes, at least, identical twins do', said Elvis, wondering where Fiona's thoughts were taking her.

'At my school, there were identical twin-sisters. No-one could tell them apart. They spoke the same and, since they had to wear the same uniform, the teachers mixed them up all-the-time. Yet curiously, one loved sports and the other hated them. One played the piano and was very musical, the other was good at art. One was right-handed, the other left-handed. They had different circles of friends and, out-of-school, they always dressed in totally-different styles as if they were deliberately saying to everyone, "we might be twins but we are also two, different people".'

'Elvis had a twin.'

'Really? I never knew that. What was he like? What happened to him?'

'Nothing. He died at birth. It was very sad. He was called Jesse.'

'So perhaps you're not another Elvis at all but another Jesse.'

'Yes', said Elvis, feeling surprisingly cheered by the suggestion. 'Another Jesse. Free to be different.'

'Of course.'

'Who knows, Jesse might have grown up to hate music, become a baseball-player or organic-farmer. Or a writer or something totally different.'

'You'd make a great research-project for some professor', Fiona said with a light chuckle. 'One of those geeks who studies twins separated at birth.'

'God, no, I want to forget Elvis and anything to do with him or his twin as soon as possible. I think I might even change my name.'

'We could get one of those 'Choose-a-name' baby-books and go through it 'til you find a new name you like. We'll skip A for Aaron but what about Brian or Charles or Derek or Eric or Gordon or Hamish... ?'

'Ian.'

'Or John.'
'Ken.'
'Len.'
'Or Martin.'
'Nigel.'
'Oswald.'
'Or Pete... Quentin... Ray... '
'Or Sam.'
'Timothy.'

The free flow of names stopped abruptly at U and they both began to giggle.

'There isn't a boy's name beginning with U - at least I can't think of one.'

'There must be.'

'No, there isn't.'

'If you were a girl you could be Ursula.'

'I can think of surnames - like Unwin and Urquhart.'

'But you can't have a surname as a first name.'

'You can in America. What about Harrison Ford?'

'But some Americans have crazy first-names. Do you want to be Forest as in Forest Gump?'

'How about Ulysses', they said together triumphantly and rather too loudly. 'Like Ulysses Grant.'

'Sshh... We'll wake-up the others.'

'V's next.'

'Vernon.'

'No way will I be called after Elvis's father.'

'Victor... or William... or Xerxes or Yves or Zac', said Fiona finishing-off the list of possibilities with a flourish. 'I've got an even-better idea. We could just look-out of the window and take the first name we see on a sign.'

She started looking-out of the window and soon burst out laughing.

'Sshh... ' whispered Elvis.

'I've just seen a sign for a store.'

'What's so funny?'

'It's called Piggly Wiggly.'

Elvis and Fiona snuggled together even more closely. Fiona kissed him gently. 'I love you Piggly Wiggly', she murmured.

Amazingly, it took Barker several minutes to notice Elvis was missing. During that time, he had compounded his predicament by going on-stage in the Ballroom, taking the microphone and starting to make a flamboyant announcement.

'Ladies and Gentleman. Tonight, history is made. The greatest son this proud city of Memphis has ever-produced is returned. I give you the one-and-only, the incomparable, The King of rock'n'roll, Mr Elvis Presley.'

The string-quartet attempted its rather thin version of Strauss's famous fanfare as Barker looked across the room to the distant entrance where a crowd of people including Roger, Kirsty, Aaron, Priscilla and the cathedral-vergers were gathered. He couldn't immediately see Elvis in the group but confidently expected him to step forward.

Nothing happened.

Barker stepped forward to the microphone again. 'Let's give a great Memphis welcome to Mr Elvis Presley!'

For a second time nothing happened.

The applause which had originally followed his announcement petered-out and instead, a groundswell of muttering crept through the Ballroom, followed by some isolated boos. Then, a slow-handclap and the stamping of discontented feet began. Barker started to perspire.

The photographers looked expectantly around, the television-camera-lights blinked red. One station was already beaming the action, or lack of it, back with a live-broadcast. But of Elvis, there was no sign.

Barker rushed off the stage and dashed across the Ballroom growling to himself, 'where's that son of a bitch?'

'Where's he gone?' he demanded as soon as he reached Aaron and Priscilla.

'I've no idea. I thought he was with you', said Aaron.

Only Kirsty had noticed Elvis and Fiona making their exit and guessed what they were doing. Should she tell? Or should she stall so as to give them more time to make their getaway?

'Well?' asked Barker, looking fiercely. 'Does anyone know where they are?' The vergers looked menacing.

'I think he said he had to go to the bathroom', Kirsty lied hesitantly. 'I think he was feeling sick. Nerves got the better of him I expect.'

'Check it out', Barker ordered the vergers and went back onto the stage. He took the microphone again and gestured for calm. 'I'm real sorry for that delay folks. Elvis, I'm told, will be with us very soon. He is in the building. A slight delay. Just a minute or two longer. He's kinda nervous. It's a real big-night for him.'

But the minute or two stretched to five... and then to ten. The vergers reported that there was no sign of him in any of the bathrooms. For Elvis and Fiona this was bonus-time but for Barker it was a disaster.

More-and-more guests crowded around the harassed Archdeacon demanding to know what was going on. The cream of Memphis society was turning into a terrifying and angry mob.

'I've paid $10,000 for my family to see Elvis', one irate diner complained loudly. 'I want my money back. Now.'

'I'm cancelling my membership of your church', shouted another angry Elvis-fan. 'I've given a million-dollars over the years and you'll not get a dime more.'

Barker could do nothing but splutter apologies. Amidst the chaos his cellphone rang. It was Mr Carioli.

'I'm watching TV. What's happening?'

'I don't know. I can't find Elvis.'

'I am disappointed', said Mr Carioli. 'Very disappointed.'

He rang-off.

'So that's it', said the irate diner. 'All these excuses but the truth is, you've promised what you can't deliver. That's fraud. We'll have you in court.'

At that very moment, Barker's eye was caught by the sight of the Elvis ice-sculpture dripping water. In the heat of the room, it was starting to melt. He took it as a sign, an omen. And that moment he made a crucial, life-changing, skin-saving decision, just as the string-quartet, struggling to make itself heard above the noise, began to play an arrangement of *It's now or never*.

'Excuse me', he said and pushed his way through the crowds. He headed for the nearest exit, determined to get out of Memphis as fast as he possibly could.

Elvis and Fiona's bus took them to downtown-Chicago. They immediately caught another bus to O'Hare international-airport. They found themselves in a vast terminal, teaming with people. It was all very confusing. Following signs to the British Airways section, they walked and walked until at last they found the sales-desk. There was a direct flight to London that afternoon they were told, and seats were available. But when the price of the tickets was quoted, Fiona realised it was unaffordable. They tried several of the other airlines and discovered much-the-same picture. The cheapest quote, by a few critical dollars, was the Irish airline, Aer Lingus, so they bought two tickets to travel to Edinburgh via Dublin.

'You're coming back to Scotland with me', Fiona declared. 'We can stay with my Gran until we decide what to do.'

The screens in the airport waiting-areas were showing the news, including clips of the absurd events of the night before. The fiasco was third in the CNN running-order.

'Near-riots broke out at the world-famous Peabody Hotel in Memphis when Elvis Presley went missing. A thousand diners had paid over $2000 a-head to attend a banquet in his honour and the Memphis-based Church of The Latter-Day Elvis promised the reincarnated-Elvis would attend. But when

Archdeacon Barker, the self-proclaimed leader of the cult, personally announced Elvis, The King failed to show-up. Angry diners demanded their money back and by the time police restored order, Barker had disappeared. Police are now looking for him and have issued this picture. As for Elvis, he has disappeared once before after showing-up at a cathedral service. When he was sighted a second-time at a healing service there, he appeared to perform a miracle but the girl in the wheel-chair has since given an interview to CNN saying that she was tricked. So the return of The King has ended in farce. But one intriguing mystery remains. How did Barker manage to fool America's leading hoax-busting organisation, SKEPTICS-r-US, that DNA from his Elvis matched that of The King?'

Fiona and Elvis watched in guilty astonishment that what had started-out as a harmless prank had got so absurdly out of control and was now making the world-news.

'I suppose if Barker is on the run, at least he won't be looking for us now', said Fiona.

But Elvis still felt very conspicuous. What if he was spotted? Would he be accused of being an accomplice in fraud? They had over three hours to wait for the flight and he became increasingly anxious not to be seen by anyone who might recognise him. He spent long periods in the bathroom until he thought that too might look suspicious.

'I'd feel happier if we went through security and passport-control as soon as possible', he confided. 'I'll feel safer once I think there's no-one official looking for me.'

Fiona agreed and they gathered up their rucksacks. They didn't have to be checked-in the hold as they were small enough to be classed as hand-luggage.

The officer at passport-control looked at Elvis very closely. 'So you're called Elvis are you?' she said, looking down at his documents and seeing his name on the passport.

'Yes.'

'Anything to do with that guy in Memphis?'

Elvis began to feel nervous. Perhaps it hadn't been such a good idea to check-through early? Perhaps they would have been better waiting for the rush?

'What guy's that?' he asked, feeling his top-lip tremble very slightly.

'The one who's been impersonating Elvis.'

'Do I look like him?' panicked Elvis, not knowing what else to say.

'Kinda. You certainly don't look like your picture in the passport. Where's all your hair gone?'

'That was my idea', said Fiona butting-in.

'Just a moment', the official said and looked-down at her screen before looking at Elvis again. 'Where are you heading for?' she asked.

'The UK.'

'That Memphis-Elvis, they say was a Brit... '

She looked at her screen again and called-over a colleague. Elvis's hands went clammy and his lip-tremble stepped-up a gear. The colleague looked Elvis up-and-down and then looked at the screen again. Finally, the first-official spoke. 'Nothing here. Even if you are that Elvis from Memphis, we've no reason to detain you. The FBI ain't looking for you. Have a nice day.'

Elvis was enormously relieved to have got over what he hoped was the last hurdle on his way home. What he did not realise, however, was that he had actually been recognised.

As soon as the passport-control officer had her next break, she was on the 'phone to her boyfriend, a local journalist. They had an arrangement.

'Let me know if any celebs go through', he had told her. 'It could make us a few bucks.'

Little was she to know that the next day, the relationship would end in tears. 'You stupid bitch, you've ruined my reputation. Why didn't you check his ticket properly?' her boyfriend had shouted.

209

'How was I to know they weren't heading for London? Their flight wasn't due to board for three-hours', she wailed back.

So, while the international media-pack stormed both London-Heathrow and Gatwick international-arrivals, Elvis and Fiona slipped quietly into Dublin. From Dublin they flew to Edinburgh before taking a bus to Aberdeen and the overnight-ferry to Fiona's original family-home.

As soon as they arrived in Scotland, Fiona had phoned her grandmother.

'What did she say?' Elvis asked when Fiona was finished.

'She says she would love to meet you and we can stay with her. I didn't exactly tell her what had happened but we can be sure no-one will think of looking for you on an island in Shetland. Oh, and I said you were called Mike. Is that OK?'

Elvis had never been to Shetland before. In fact, he couldn't remember being further north than Liverpool. He had no recollection of visiting Scotland as a baby and he was astounded to learn from Fiona that Shetland was nowhere near mainland-Scotland but halfway to Norway. The sea-crossing was calm and they slept well, stretched-out on padded benches in the bar with their rucksacks as pillows. When they woke in the morning, Fiona was eager to show Elvis the islands she called home. They went up on-deck. Elvis had never breathed such fresh air.

'We've passed Fair Isle', Fiona told him, 'and we've come by Sumburgh. That island's Mousa over there and that island ahead is Bressay. And, you'll never believe it! On Bressay, there's a real place called Elvis Bay! The boat will dock in Lerwick, the capital. When we arrive, you'll be a soothmother.'

'A what?'

'A soothmother! It's a Shetland word for someone who arrives from the south. You'll pick up the local words before long.'

Fiona kept up a running-commentary about the landscape and culture of the Shetlands for the next hour as the boat sailed up the east coast of Mainland, Shetland's largest island, on its way to dock in Lerwick. She told Elvis about her Shetland friends and relations and the places she knew and her memories from her early childhood. Elvis just listened and enjoyed the sound of her voice as it gradually lost its Edinburgh accent and took on a Nordic lilt. Everything that had been 'wee' became 'peerie'. Even the birds had different names. 'Skuas' became 'bonxies'. 'Puffins' turned into 'tammy nories'.

'We get a bus as soon as we leave the boat', Fiona explained, 'and then there's two more small ferries before we get to Gran'.

Aaron, Priscilla, Roger and Kirsty had been left standing in the hotel feeling foolish. As the angry scenes escalated, they crept away, taking a cab together to the hostel. They soon realised that essential items belonging to both Fiona and Elvis had disappeared and noticed Elvis's hair, scattered across the floor and over the bed.

The next day they all flew back to the UK, a sad party with little to say to each other. Roger felt guilty for his part in the fiasco and mean that he hadn't supported his friend when he could have done. Kirsty was hoping that Fiona had made a successful getaway with Elvis and that she would hear from her when everything had died down.

Aaron and Priscilla felt utterly dejected, having lost both a dream and a son. It was to be several months before Elvis felt sufficiently healed of his hurt to write to them and suggest a meeting. But they would have to come to him, he insisted, and promise to say nothing about Elvis. They would also have to call him Mike.

By the time they heard from Elvis, Aaron had also changed his name - back to Keith - and Priscilla had let her friends and former work-colleagues know that she would prefer to be known as Kellie. The Elvis-shrine had been dismantled. The Elvis compilation-albums had been replaced by collections of Lloyd Webber hits. The house was renamed, *Dundreamin*.

On arrival in Shetland, Elvis was introduced to everyone by his new name. Only Fiona knew his secret and waited until they were alone together before calling him Piggly Wiggly!

After staying with Fiona's Gran for a while, they found a place of their own, a small, warm house with beautiful views out to sea. Fiona had to go south to mainland-Scotland for university term-times but Elvis, or Mike as he was now known, grew so entirely contented with the pace of life on the island that he never ventured further away than Lerwick.

He took on a part-time job at a fish-farm, volunteered as both fireman and coastguard, helped behind the bar at the hotel on Wednesdays and Saturdays, and grew a full-beard for the island's annual fire-festival of Up Helly-Aa. As he marched with his squad, dressed as a Viking-warrior and carrying a flaming torch, he never gave a thought to his former life.

After she had completed her studies, they were delighted when Fiona was offered a job as a teacher on the island. Life was good. Living as part of a small island community suited them both, the work, the weather, the social life, even attending the kirk on Sundays. There, Elvis found the simple services in a plain building more meaningful than the razzmatazz of the worship in the ornate Elvis Cathedral, the only other religion he had ever known.

It was sometime later, when he was asked to help-out with some odd jobs at the local care-centre, that Elvis met American-Jo. He was an old man who had come to live on the island more than thirty-years before. He had drifted-in as a tourist, stayed on the island for a summer, survived a winter and then never left Shetland.

For a while he rented a furnished-place. Then, after a year or two, he bought some essential items of furniture and a small, single-storey house to put them in and settled-in by himself. He was friendly to his neighbours but no-one knew him well. He had a good garden that he kept protected from the wind by a stone-dyke on two sides and fencing on the others. He became so experienced at coping with the local climate that over the years he won several prizes for his vegetables at the annual-show.

The few people who were invited inside Jo's home found it clean, neat and sparse. The main room was white-walled and almost empty except for a couple of modern, black-leather chairs and a small table. There were no pictures, no plants and no decorations.

He gave his surname as Smith, and that was the name on his driver's-licence and credit-card. Some wondered if he was a famous artist in retreat from the world but no-one ever saw any paintings or drawings. Others proposed he was on-the-run from the FBI. Yet others suggested he was recovering from a tragedy, was a traumatised Vietnam veteran or simply someone fleeing a failed-marriage. He never spoke about his past or of his family. As the years went by and he became a fixture on the island, folk had stopped speculating.

He drove an old mini, dressed in jeans and Fair Isle sweaters and lived modestly but he never appeared to be short of cash and gave both his time and money generously. He was well-respected and liked. He attended the local church and played the guitar in the island dance-band but never sang. He always supported local-businesses and bought everything he needed from the island-shops. He was completely self-reliant until the day he was found slumped on the floor of his bathroom. He had had a stroke and after a few weeks in hospital in Lerwick, was taken to the island's care-home to be looked-after.

He had been in the home for several years before Elvis, or Mike as he introduced himself, met him. He had been asked to fix a door-handle in American-Jo's room. They fell into conversation, or rather, Elvis chatted away inconsequentially. It had to be a rather one-sided conversation as Jo found it very difficult to talk. The left-side of his face still drooped from the stroke.

Elvis prattled about this and that, island gossip and news, before asking Jo, casually, which part of America he was from.

'Mississippi', answered Jo slowly. Elvis didn't realise but this was the first time Jo had revealed to anyone in Shetland his home state. He'd always just said 'here and there,' when asked the question before.

'Tupelo's in Mississippi, isn't it?' continued Elvis.

Jo nodded.

'That was where Elvis was born wasn't it?'

Jo nodded again.

'Did you know Elvis? You weren't at school with him or anything, were you? He'd have been about your age? Did you ever hear him sing? Go to one of his concerts?'

The old man made no response but a tear formed in his eye. Elvis was suddenly worried that he might have touched-on something personal or brought back a painful memory. He quickly carried-on talking to change the subject.

'You'll never believe this', he said. 'I haven't told this to anyone in Shetland before, so promise you won't tell.'

Jo nodded and slowly raised a finger to his lips to show he would keep-mum.

'Do you remember a while-back, all those news-reports about Elvis returning to Memphis?'

Elvis had sat on the edge of Jo's bed, feeling unexpectedly relieved to be talking to him about the events he had been trying to put behind him. He knew what he said would never go further. Jo was well-known as a man of his word and anyway, could now scarcely talk at all.

'That was me', he confessed to Jo. He told him all about the cathedral and what had happened to him when he had dressed-up as Elvis Presley. How the stupid joke had gone so-embarrassingly wrong. He felt the tears in his eyes as he recalled how his parents had flown to Memphis to tell him that he had been created out of a piece of Elvis's DNA.

'How sick is that! But I'm not Elvis', he declared firmly at the end. 'Fiona thinks I'm more like an identical-twin.'

American-Jo had taken hold of Elvis's hand while he was speaking. And when Elvis cried, Jo had cried too.

Then Jo indicated he wanted to say something. He was very weak and managed just one word. Elvis had to bend forward and get close to him to hear him.

'Jesse', whispered Jo, then closed his eyes.

American-Jo was buried on the island where he had found contentment in life and in death. 'I wonder who he really was', said the minister conversationally to Elvis as they walked back from the kirkyard together after the funeral. 'Did he ever have a family do you suppose? What might he have been escaping from? I suppose we'll never know.'

As Jo had no known-relations, Elvis had volunteered to sort and clear his house. In his will, Jo had stipulated that all his personal papers were to be burned and the house and any contents to be sold. The money raised was to be put in-trust for the community. In one drawer in the bedroom, Elvis found a small filing-cabinet of papers. It contained receipts, bills and bank-statements, all kept neatly and systematically. But there was no birth-certificate or passport. Nothing that went back further than 1977. He lit a fire in the grate and watched the smoke curl-up the chimney.